MORAY DALTON
THE MYSTERY OF THE KNEELING WOMAN

KATHERINE DALTON RENOIR ('Moray Dalton') was born in Hammersmith, London in 1881, the only child of a Canadian father and English mother.

The author wrote two well-received early novels, *Olive in Italy* (1909), and *The Sword of Love* (1920). However, her career in crime fiction did not begin until 1924, after which Moray Dalton published twenty-nine mysteries, the last in 1951. The majority of these feature her recurring sleuths, Scotland Yard inspector Hugh Collier and private inquiry agent Hermann Glide.

Moray Dalton married Louis Jean Renoir in 1921, and the couple had a son a year later. The author lived on the south coast of England for the majority of her life following the marriage. She died in Worthing, West Sussex, in 1963.

D1447256

MORAY DALTON

THE MYSTERY OF THE KNEELING WOMAN

With an introduction by Curtis Evans

DEAN STREET PRESS

Published by Dean Street Press 2023

Copyright © 1936 Moray Dalton

Introduction Copyright © 2023 Curtis Evans

All Rights Reserved

Published by licence, issued under the UK Orphan Works
Licensing Scheme.

First published in 1936 by Sampson Low

Cover by DSP

ISBN 978 1 915393 82 1

www.deanstreetpress.co.uk

"Peace for our time"

Moray Dalton's *The Mystery of the Kneeling Woman* (1936)

At Brighton, England sometime in January 1921 Katherine Mary Deville Dalton, aka British crime novelist Moray Dalton, wed Jean Louis Renoir, a presumed native Frenchman about whom I currently know nothing beyond his name. Around fourteen months later, in the spring of 1922, Moray Dalton at the age of forty gave birth to a son, grandly named Louis Anthony Laurence Dalton Renoir. Evidently not long afterward Dalton and her husband parted ways, leaving the author to raise her son Anthony essentially as a single mother, although she and Renoir apparently never actually divorced. In October 1936 Dalton published *The Mystery of the Kneeling Woman*, her sixth Inspector Hugh Collier detective novel (after *One by One They Disappeared*, 1929, *The Night of Fear*, 1931, *The Belfry Murder*, 1933, *The Belgrave Manor Crime*, 1935 and *The Strange Case of Harriet Hall*, 1936) and the novel in the series which most directly drew on her own experiences raising a son singly, as well as her fears for her progeny in world hurtling toward another war.

Dalton published her fifth Hugh Collier mystery, *The Strange Case of Harriet Hall*, in February 1936 and presumably was even then writing *The Mystery of the Kneeling Woman*. On September 15 of the previous year, the German Reichstag had passed the Nuremberg Laws, stripping Jews of legal rights and German citizenship and prohibiting marriage and sexual relationships between Jews and those of "German blood." The next month the Fascist government of Italy launched an unprovoked invasion of Ethiopia, in defiance of the League of Nations, beginning the Second Italo-Abyssinian War. In March 1936, Nazi Germany remilitarized the Rhineland, in defiance of the Treaty of Versailles. A few months later, in July, the Spanish Civil War between Fascist-supported Nationalists and Communist-supported Republicans broke out, while in October Soviet Union dictator Josef Stalin commenced his Great Purge. Rarely had events in Europe seemed darker.

In the United Kingdom there was much resistance among the war-weary British public, particularly among the Labour and Liberal constituencies, to commencing a program of military rearmament, even after the rise of belligerent German ruler Adolf Hitler. According to the so-called Peace Ballot, the results of which were announced on June 27, 1935 at a huge rally at the Royal Albert Hall, the public strongly supported reduction of armaments by international agreement. In the General Election of 1935, held on November 14, the National Government led by Conservative Stanley Baldwin, won 52% of the popular vote and a strong governing majority of seats in parliament, with Baldwin promising, in deference to the pacifist sentiments of a great swathe of the British public, that while the government in response to global menaces would modernize the country's defenses and remedy deficiencies, "there will be no great armaments." Yet the government in 1936 committed to a policy of rearmament, expanding the Royal Air Force, and Royal Navy and reequipping (although not expanding) the British Army, albeit at an insufficient pace to satisfy M.P.'s like Winston Churchill, who during a House of Commons debate about rearmament in November, memorably attacked the government's policy as "decided only to be undecided, resolved to be irresolute, adamant for drift, solid for fluidity, all-powerful to be impotent."

Most unusually among British Golden Age mysteries, the preponderance of which tend to repeat unreflectively the patriotic mantra of God and country, Moray Dalton's *The Mystery of the Kneeling Woman*, which was published just a few weeks before the November parliamentary debate, reflects pacifist sentiments that still held sway with much of the British public, Winston Churchill's warnings notwithstanding. The novel opens with kindly Reverend John Clare paying a social call upon glum Simon Killick at his forbidding home, The Grange. Both individuals are lonely single men "verging on sixty," Clare having lost both his wife and his only child, his son Dick (the latter a casualty of the Great War), and Killick being a staunch misanthrope who relies on three dogs and a parrot for company. "The most destructive, the most wantonly cruel of all living things," pronounces Killick of human beings; and he cuttingly tells Clare: "I always enjoy a chat with you. It amuses me to hear all the old clichés. I believe you'd even quote *dulce et decorum* with perfect sincerity." (Here Killick is ironically referencing Wilfrid Owen's famed antiwar poem "Dulce et Decorum est," which in turn ironically references the ancient Roman credo "It is sweet and fitting to die for one's country.")

It is on this occasion that Killick, a retired chemist and partner in a cosmetics and perfumery company, maliciously divulges to Clare that he has invented a new awesomely destructive poison gas which he is planning to sell to certain agents of a foreign power. Killick soon is found murdered in his cottage, however, while in a nearby wood a local schoolboy, twelve-year-old Christopher "Toby" Fleming, discovers a dying man, this one locally unknown, whose last words cryptically concern a "kneeling woman." Could this man have been one of Killick's agents of a foreign power, perhaps? It is a complicated case for the local police, headed by stolid Chief Constable Lowther and irascible, bullying Inspector Brett, and it is not long before Scotland Yard, in the personal forms of Inspector Collier and Sergeant Duffield, is called to the scene to take over the case (much to Brett's irritation). There seems to be a resolution, but then more murders follow (by poisoned chocolates, no less). Are all the murders connected? Who is the kneeling woman? What does Sir Henry Webber, retired manufacturer and the new owner of Brock Hall, know about the case, or, for that matter, his snobbish wife Beryl, Lady Webber and their two ghastly hooligan sons, Godfrey and Keith? Or odd jobs man Tommy Yates, who is "not exactly," and his village "daily" mother, or Florrie Soper, cook at the Hall, who adores Edgar Wallace thrillers and is intent on marrying Tommy.

All in all, it is a most vexing matter for Inspector Collier, although it has its compensations in Toby, a winning young chap, and his appealing widowed mother Sandra. Has love finally entered the life of Inspector Collier, as it did around this same time for Lord Peter Wimsey, Albert Campion, Roderick Alleyn,

Jimmy Waghorn and Bobby Owen, to name some other appealing vintage British mystery sleuths from the period? Let me just divulge that Sandra and especially Toby will reappear in the next Inspector Collier case, *Death in the Dark* (1938).

Clearly Moray Dalton, like other British detective writers, was influenced by Dorothy L. Sayers in introducing love interest into the life of her series investigator, but just as obviously she was drawing to some extent on her own life in making that love interest a single mother. Sandra Fleming hardly pines for her late husband: "When she thought of him, which was not very often, it was without regret." Yet she also thinks regretfully of her sensitive, bookish son, badly bullied at public school: "If only Toby had a father."

As for Collier, when he hears Brett disdainfully refer to the "sensitive and highly strung" sufferer of a terrible shell shock case from the Great War as a "coward," he turns "rather white" and angrily rejoins: "If you care to use that word about boys who, through no fault of their own, were thrust into that pit of hell, I'd rather keep it for the people who make the wars." With his sergeant, Duffield, Collier has this exchange, which in sentiment is a long way off from the author's own patriotic Great War poetry:

"Are you a pacifist, Inspector? I've sometimes wondered from the things you say."

"I've a right to be, haven't I, after three years of hell? You were in it too. What do you say?"

"Nothing. What's the good? Once I started I might not be able to stop."

Moray Dalton died in 1963 when she was eighty-one and her son Anthony was forty-one. Anthony himself would pass away a half-century later in 2013, at the age of ninety-one. Little about the son of Moray Dalton is definitely known beyond the facts that he was a schoolmaster and an avid book collector—his entry in the 1985 *International Directory of Book Collectors* lists his bookish interests as art and architecture, along with histories of public and grammar schools and works by or about the noted gay writer and eccentric Frederick William Rolfe, better known as

Baron Corvo (aka Corviana), who died, appropriately, in Venice in 1913 and two decades later, when Anthony Renoir was a child, was the subject of book collector and Julian Symons sibling A. J. A. Symons' famous biography, *The Quest for Corvo*. During his long life Anthony Renoir evidently never married or produced issue and he never strayed for long from his mother's home turf in southern England, finally passing away at 100 Sea Place, Goring-by-Sea. I do not even know whether he served, like so many of his countrymen, in the Second World War—he would have been just seventeen when the Germans invaded Poland—but happily he lived, unlike so many others in that era of twin man-made global catastrophes, to a ripe old age.

Curtis Evans

CHAPTER I
A GAME OF CHESS

"AH, HERE you are," said Simon Killick. "Come in." He stood aside to allow the vicar to pass.

The latter hesitated. "I am not disturbing you?" he said doubtfully. He was a lonely man and though he never felt quite at his ease with Killick he looked forward to the evenings he spent at the Grange. There was nobody else in the parish who played chess or who cared to talk about books. He had grown shy of women since his wife's death, but there were none at the Grange. Killick did not even have a housekeeper living in. There would be no one to notice the frayed sleeves of the vicar's old coat or the stains of earth on his knees if he did not trouble to change after an afternoon spent in his garden. Killick was never expansive. He could not be described as a genial host. He never went to church and he had resolutely declined to enter the vicarage, but he had made it clear that he looked forward to the vicar's visits. "And he is even more alone than I am," thought John Clare pityingly, "because he's shut God out."

The two men belonged to the same generation; both were verging on sixty. Clare was over six feet and broad in proportion. He had a florid, good-humoured face, child-like blue eyes, and a thatch of silvery white hair. Killick was tall, but he was lean to the point of emaciation and harsh featured, and there was something ruthless in the fixed and frowning gaze of his deep set eyes. Yet his dogs, of whom he had three, loved him, and his parrot, a bird of great antiquity and no charm, would spend hours perched on his shoulder. There was a hedgehog, too, who had come out of the overgrown and neglected garden and established himself in the house, and who ran up confidently to his master when Killick whistled, to drink milk from a saucer.

"He's fond of animals," the vicar would remind himself as he made his way home through the churchyard after some more than usually disconcerting revelation of the divergency of their points of view. "There can't be any real harm in a man who's fond of animals. And he's got a queer warped sense of humour. That's what it is. Pulling my leg " And he would try, not very successfully, to laugh at the recollection of some biting phrase that had shocked him at the time of utterance.

"I should have been disappointed if you hadn't come," said Killick. "I'm making coffee, as you see. Fill your pipe. Your favourite tobacco's in the bowl."

"Thanks."

Clare sank into the chair he usually occupied, with a sigh of satisfaction, and produced his briar. Killick stirred the logs on the hearth and the firelight flickered over the book lined walls. Heavy curtains were drawn over the windows.

The Cairn climbed out of his basket and came over to sniff enquiringly at the visitor's boots. Clare leaned forward to stroke the little dog's shaggy head. "It's good churchyard mould, laddie. But I should have wiped my feet," he added apologetically, observing the lump of earth that had dropped from his heel on the hearth rug.

"It doesn't matter," said Killick indifferently. "But I thought the path was asphalted."

"It is, but I stepped aside to take some chrysanthemums to Dick. There's a dear old soul down the village who always brings a bunch from her garden for him. He was a great favourite in the parish. They haven't forgotten him."

Killick made no comment. He was busy with the coffee machine. But the vicar needed no encouragement to talk of his only son, who had won the V.C. on Vimy Ridge, and had died a few weeks after the Armistice. "I keep a big jar in his bedroom filled with those I grow in the vicarage garden. They last on into December in sheltered corners. By the way, talking of boys, that's a nice little chap of Mrs. Fleming's."

"Who is Mrs. Fleming?"

"A newcomer. She has rented what used to be the blacksmith's cottage across the green. She's a widow, left badly off, I fear, and she hopes to serve teas and perhaps take lodgers during the summer. We're off the main road, but I hope she succeeds."

"Here's your coffee."

"Thank you." The vicar helped himself to sugar. "Toby, the boy's called. He happens to be at home just now, on account of an outbreak of measles at his school. I gather that she's straining every nerve to give him a sound education. He seems a bright, intelligent, well-mannered chap."

"Young things are usually attractive," said Killick grimly. "Personally, I except the young of the human species. One knows too well what they'll grow into. Fools or knaves."

"You don't mean that, Killick."

"Don't I?" snarled the other. The parrot was clawing his way up his master's sleeve to his perch on his shoulder. Killick lifted a lean, long-fingered hand to stroke the rumpled grey feathers. "The most destructive, the most wantonly cruel of all living things, except, perhaps, the cat. Cats kill for sport as men do. No, Vicar, you can keep your Toby. If you've been planning to bring the brat to my notice to soften my hard heart, forget it. The ossification of that organ is more complete than you imagine."

The vicar's hand shook slightly as he stirred his coffee. He was beginning to wish he had not come. Killick was evidently in one of his most difficult moods.

"Well," he said pacifically, "have it your own way, Killick. The loss is yours. What about our game?"

"Presently," said his host. "You mustn't take offence, Clare. I always enjoy a chat with you. It amuses me to hear all the old clichés. I believe you'd even quote *dulce et decorum* with perfect sincerity."

The vicar reddened. This was going a little too far. "I hope so," he said.

Killick looked at him for a moment with a cold smile. Then he said, "Very well. I won't argue the point. I daresay you'll be interested to hear that I am expecting visitors very shortly."

"I am delighted," said Clare heartily. "The hermit life you have led since you came here is not good for any man. Friends to stay with you. Excellent. I have no doubt Mrs. Yates will rise to the occasion—"

"I did not say friends," interrupted Killick, "and Mrs. Yates won't be called upon to cook any meals for them. I've half a mind to tell you more about it, Vicar. Your face is so expressive."

"You talk in riddles," said Clare rather stiffly.

"If I confide in you I must first exact a promise that you will neither repeat nor act upon any information I give you."

"Dear me," said Clare. "That sounds quite alarming. But I give you my word, of course."

"Your word of honour."

"Certainly. That is—I don't want to intrude on your private affairs, Killick, unless you feel I can help you."

"I want to tell you," said Killick. "I am sure to enjoy your reactions. You run so true to type, Vicar."

"Is that a compliment or an insult?" asked Clare good-humouredly. "Perhaps I had better not ask."

"You're one of those incurable sentimentalists whose acceptance of the established order—" he broke off. "What's the use?"

"Killick," said the other earnestly, "if you could tell me why you're so terribly embittered. I realise that somehow, at some time, you were deeply wronged. I'm no psycho-analyst—but if you could get it out of your system."

"Thanks. I know you mean well. I'm going to show you something." He rose and left the room, stopping on his way out to replace the parrot in his cage. The two terriers sat up in their basket and watched the door. Kim, the yellow mongrel, had followed his master out.

"Your dogs are devoted to you," said Clare when Killick returned.

"I dare say you find that reassuring," said the other, "but little children don't cluster around my knees, thank God. So don't rely too much on my one redeeming point, will you."

He was removing the brown paper wrappings from a glass jar which he set down on his writing-table. He tilted the shade of his reading-lamp so that the light fell on it. "What do you think of that?"

The vicar stared at the distorted pink mass to which some fragments of grey cobwebby material adhered in patches. He swallowed hard and his hands shook slightly as he adjusted his glasses.

"It suggests one word—agony—to my mind," he said very gravely.

"A good guess," said Killick. "It was a rabbit. Nobody touched it, but it turned to what you see in about nine seconds. Agony, no doubt, but not unduly prolonged. Won't you sit down, Vicar? You look rather white. I'll put it over here where it won't offend your eyes."

He resumed his seat and took the mongrel Kim on his knee.

"I am fond of animals, Clare, but a few had to be sacrificed in the course of my researches. A regrettable necessity. I've been a chemist and the business I was in—the manufacture of synthetic perfumes, involved a good deal of experimental work. I sold the business as a running concern after the Armistice and carried on with a certain line of enquiry in a small laboratory of my own. I wanted to find a poison gas more destructive than anything that had been yet tried out. You know something of what science has given to humanity in that direction? Dichloro diethyl sulphide will eat into your flesh. Chlorvyl dichlorarsine burns and paralyses. Chlorine and phosgene merely destroy the lungs. You'll admit I had set myself a hard task." He glanced at the vicar's horrified face with a gleam of amusement. "Don't you feel well, padre?"

"I'm all right," said Clare hoarsely. "Please go on. I want to hear."

"Very well. I won't trouble you with an account of the years I spent over my experiments. As you have often remarked I am fond of animals and as far as possible, I used rats when testing my compounds. I found what I had dreamed of at last by accident, by the addition of an ingredient which would certainly never have occurred to any sane chemist. It was an accident, but the results were remarkable. It is so highly concentrated and so easily portable that two planes could easily carry—in containers that would break on touching the ground—a sufficient quantity to wipe out an army or devastate a whole countryside. You think

I'm exaggerating. I have had no opportunity to make any test on a large scale, but I am sure—"

"Gas is not an admissible weapon in civilised warfare," said Clare. "Dick was gassed."

"You think a bayonet thrust in the stomach is kinder?" said Killick with his mirthless smile. "Civilised warfare is just the sort of phrase I expected from you. But I see I'm distressing you and I'll cut my story short. I have given the matter due consideration and I have decided that the time is ripe to market my discovery. I have been in communication with agents of two countries and they are both coming to investigate my claim and probably to make offers for the formula. I shall close with the one that seems most likely to make full use of any opportunity to wipe out God's worst failure, homo sapiens, and that will be that."

"You'd do that?" stammered the vicar. "But—is one of these countries England?"

"No."

"But—you are an Englishman?"

"I am."

"And you would sell this—this fiendish stuff to be used against us if war broke out? Killick, for God's sake, think! Isn't there suffering enough in the world? I know you've been hurt. I know you are terribly unhappy. I've seen that. I'm not eloquent. I'm just a rather stupid old fellow—but I do implore you to listen to me for your own sake."

"I am listening, padre," said Killick blandly. "And I'm not surprised. I knew you wouldn't surprise me. What do you want me to do?"

"I want you to forgive those who injured you in the past—and to destroy this formula."

Killick laughed. It was not a pleasant sound. "No."

There was a silence after that. Clare broke it. "Your idea of a joke, perhaps," he suggested.

Killick shook his head. "No."

Clare sighed. "I'll pray for you," he said gently. He sounded very tired.

"That's kind of you," said Killick, "but, I fear, a waste of time."

"When are these men coming to you?"

"On Thursday."

"And this is Monday. There is still time for you to change your mind, Killick," said the vicar, still with that same strange gentleness. "I have overlooked a great deal that was purposely offensive in your manner to me to-night. I try to make allowances. I am sure that you are not—not yourself. I want you to reconsider this and talk it over again with me before it is too late. Will you do that?"

"My dear padre, by all means. Come in again Wednesday evening and we'll thrash the whole thing out if it pleases you, but I must warn you that you are not likely to get your own way. I am not acting on impulse. Ever since—I tell you, Clare, the human race isn't worth preserving. You saw the contents of that jar. That was the result of the vaporization—I'll try not to be technical—I placed a healthy live rabbit in a glass case and introduced one drop of the diluted liquid. It turned to what you have seen in—as I told you just now—nine seconds."

"Good God!"

"In the open air it might not act quite so quickly, but I believe it would be no less sure."

"The nation that secures this formula will be master of the world."

"Not necessarily. My invention isn't so epoch making as all that. Every country manufactures poison gas in some form or other. The United States uses tear gas to put down strikes. Mine is more highly concentrated. That's all. And now—what about that game?"

He drew forward the chess table and set out the men. Clare sat with his elbows on his knees and his face in his hands.

"You'll take the white as usual, Clare?"

The vicar roused himself with an evident effort. For the next half hour there was silence in the room, broken only by the occasional whimper from Kim, hunting in his dreams, and the crackling of the burning logs on the hearth. Killick was the first to speak.

"Checkmate. You're not playing up to your usual form, vicar."

Clare passed his hand across his forehead. "I know. I can't concentrate. You—you have shocked me, Killick. I—it's no use.

I can't play to-night. I think I had better go home. I must ask for help."

Killick's saturnine face hardened. "You gave me your word of honour that anything I told you would go no further. I hold you to that."

"Yes, yes. I shall not repeat our conversation to a living soul. I shall ask for help—on my knees, Killick."

"Oh, I see. I'll come with you to the door. Have you got your torch? It's a dark night."

Both men had risen. The vicar half held out his hand and then drew it back again. The look of hurt bewilderment in his child-like eyes deepened as he met Killick's iron smile.

"Killick," he exclaimed. "I don't want to begin imagining things. There's no reason, is there, why you should hate me?"

Killick had preceded him down the passage to the garden door. He unlatched it and held it open.

"My dear padre, how—I can't find a word—shall I say fantastic? Good night."

"Good night."

The vicar's big and bulky figure was swallowed up immediately, for a fine rain was falling and the darkness was profound. But the dim ray of light from his torch wandered rather uncertainly along the path that crossed the churchyard, pausing, once at his son's grave and again at the war memorial, and Killick watched it until it vanished behind the laurel shrubberies of the vicarage garden.

CHAPTER II
DEATH IN THE WOODS

THE harsh whispering ceased, choked by dreadful bubbling sounds in the dying man's throat.

His stiffening fingers clutched at the fronds of dead bracken as he made a last effort to ruse himself and slid down again into the dank undergrowth.

A voice that Toby hardly recognised as his own said: "I'll get help—"

There was no answer. Birds do not sing much in the November woods but even so the silence seemed unnatural. Trees had always seemed friendly to Toby, but to his fancy they loomed up threateningly now between him and the path. He was too flurried to pick his way and he fell twice, heavily, before he reached the stile where he had left his bicycle. It took him some time to mount it, for his heart was thumping against his ribs and his knees seemed to be made of jelly, but he succeeded at last, wobbling a good deal at first, and then regaining control until his riding became not much more erratic than that of any other small boy on a machine several sizes too large for him.

He was on a little used by-road with woods on either side and there was nobody in sight; the beech mast was thick on the ground and the last leaves on the trees were drifting down gently in twos and threes, through the gathering dusk. Five miles to Durchester—and all the time he was going farther away from Brock Green and home, and his mother would be making the toast for their tea. He was just turning into the main road when a big car travelling much too fast, missed his front wheel by a couple of inches. Toby swerved frantically and a hedge seemed to be rushing to meet him. He sat up, after an interval of confusion. An A.A. man who was bending over him helped him to his feet.

"You all right, sonny? No bones broken, eh? No thanks to that blighter. I thought you were for it—this is a high road, not a speed track, and if I'd got his number—but I was in the call box and he was practically out of sight before I got out. The dirty swine."

"What about my bike?"

"You can't ride it. The front wheel's buckled."

"Bother," said Toby. "I say—could I telephone from this box?"

The scout hesitated. "It's for the A.A. members only."

"It's frightfully important," said Toby. "I want to ring up the police at Durchester."

The man looked curiously at the chubby freckled face raised to his. He had never met a small boy who wanted the police before. It was usually the other way about. "Why, sonny? What's wrong?"

"You know the path through the woods at Hammerpot? I'd gone in to look for conkers. There's several chestnut trees just before you come to the little old church. I—I saw a man lying in the undergrowth. He had a hole in his chest. I thought I'd better ride into Durchester to get the police. But it's a long way—"

"No need," said the scout. "I'll phone for you. You wait here. A dead man. Shot himself, I suppose. Why they have to go into woods to do themselves in this time of year—" he went into the box and closed the door.

Toby sat on the bank under the hedge. He was feeling rather sick. The scout came back to him presently. He was a middle-aged man with a good-natured red face. He produced a spare mackintosh which came down to the boy's heels, and a Thermos flask.

"What's your name, sonny?"

"Christopher Fleming. But I'm called Toby."

"All right, Toby. You and me'll have a good hot cup of tea while we're waiting for the cops, to keep out the cold and the damp." The tea was poured into a cracked mug, but it was really hot as well as sweet and strong, and Toby felt better when he had drunk it.

"I suppose I couldn't go home now?" he said. "Mother'll think I'm lost—"

"'Fraid not. The police said I was to keep you until they came. They'll want you to show them the place. But I daresay they'll give you a lift home. Here they are—"

Toby, feeling rather shy, stood up as the dark blue saloon car slid to a standstill and a big man in a lounge suit got out, followed by two constables in uniform. A third, who had driven the car, remained at the wheel.

The A.A. scout spoke to the first man deferentially.

"This is the boy, sir."

"It's getting so dark I can't see him properly. Switch on those headlights, Hale. That's better. Now, my boy, what's your name and where do you come from?"

"Christopher Fleming," said Toby again. "I live at the Forge, Brock Green."

"And you found a dead man in the wood?"

"Yes."

The plain clothes man, who seemed to be the leader, pointed to the wreck of the bicycle lying in the ditch. "What does that mean?"

The A.A. scout explained. "He was riding to fetch the police, Inspector Brett, and he came a cropper just here—"

"I see. All right. Now tell me exactly where you saw this man."

"At the foot of a pine tree about a hundred yards from the footpath in Hammerpot woods."

"Why did you leave the path? You're not supposed to. They put up enough notices."

"I—I was looking for conkers," said Toby.

"I see. Well, hop in."

"What about the bike!" asked Toby anxiously. "It isn't mine—"

"You'll get it back. We'll attend to that. Get a move on now."

The A.A. scout, whose day's work was over, had already departed. Toby got into the car and sat on one of the tip up seats facing the Inspector. In less than five minutes they were all getting out again at the stile. It had turned much colder since the sun had set. Their feet sank into the moist earth and the drifts of fallen leaves. There was a penetrating smell of fungi. Brett, leading the way with Toby, nearly slipped on a crushed mass of yellow agaric.

"This wood's full of toadstools," volunteered Toby. "I expect that's the one I trod on when I was running away—"

"Running away?" said the Inspector sharply, "what did you run away from?"

"Him. I—I got the wind up—"

The Inspector stopped and flashed the light of his torch in a circle. The grey trunk of a beech, the reddish brown trunk of a pine were silhouetted for an instant against the dark background of dank undergrowth. The light was lowered until it rested on a huddled figure half buried in the bracken at the foot of the pine tree.

"Ah, there he is—"

Brett moved forward quickly.

"He's dead right enough," he said after a minute. "I say, Ward, look here—"

The elder of the two constables who had accompanied him and who, so far, had remained discreetly silent, now stepped forward.

Brett turned the light of his torch on the soles of the dead man's feet. "No shoes. Black silk socks. Quite dry, and not a stain on them."

"Must have taken off his shoes before he shot himself," opined Ward, "to make himself more comfortable like, same as they put cushions in the gas oven."

"Where are they then? Look at his pockets, man, turned inside out. And the lining of his coat's slit. He was searched for something as he lay here. Whatever it was the searchers didn't find it in his pockets or they wouldn't have taken his shoes. Come here, boy—"

Toby approached with evident reluctance.

"Had he his shoes on when you found him?"

Toby glanced, very unwillingly, at the motionless figure and shut his eyes tightly.

"I—I don't know."

"What do you mean by that? You've got eyes in your head," said Brett brusquely. The two constables standing behind him exchanged glances. Brett was an able officer, but he had an unenviable reputation in the force. He got results, but his methods with witnesses sometimes failed to inspire the necessary confidence. A more persuasive manner would have served him better in this case.

Toby swallowed hard. "I—I only saw his face—and the blood—" he muttered. "Please—can't I go home now—"

"Not yet," said Brett curtly.

Ward ventured a suggestion. "A tramp might have taken the shoes."

"And risk getting mixed up in a job like this? Not likely."

"You think it's a—"

"Murder. I do. If he shot himself where's the weapon? Besides, see this mark on the bark of the tree? He was fired at twice, and the first shot missed him. We'll have to go through this undergrowth with a fine tooth-comb to-morrow. It's murder right enough," said Brett complacently. "I suppose neither of you chaps can identify him? No. What about you, boy?"

"I never saw him before," said Toby in a flat voice.

Brett grunted. "Dark skinned, black-haired. Stoutish build. Getting on for forty. Looks like some kind of foreigner to me.

Dunning, you and Hale run back to the station in the car and report to the superintendent. We'll need the ambulance, but I want the doctor to see him before he's moved; and I'd like some photographs, so bring the doings."

Dunning hesitated. "What about the boy, sir? He won't want to walk home in the dark, and it's a good three miles to Brock Green."

"All right. Run him home in the car. It isn't much out of your way. And see here, young 'un, not a syllable about all this even to your mother. We'll have to ask you some further questions but that'll be to-morrow. Meanwhile keep your mouth shut."

"Yes, sir."

Mrs. Fleming was standing at her gate peering anxiously into the surrounding darkness when Toby ran up. When he saw her, Toby was glad he had persuaded the good-natured constable to put him down at the end of the lane instead of bringing him up to the house. It would not have been easy to explain his return in a car driven by a policeman without telling Mrs. Fleming the whole story.

"Darling, how late you are," she said. "I don't like you to be out alone after dark. I began to be afraid you'd met with an accident."

"Well, I did buckle the front wheel, and an A.A. man helped me, and after a bit I got a lift in a car."

That was true, thought Toby, though it was not all the truth. They went in arm in arm. The fire was burning brightly, the lamp was lit and the curtains were drawn. Tea was laid ready and the kettle was singing on the hob.

Toby wriggled uneasily as he underwent the usual maternal inspection. His mother had sharp eyes and he did not feel that he could stand any further questioning. It would not be so easy to lie to her as to that plain clothes policeman, for he loved his mother while he had taken a great dislike to Inspector Brett.

But, after one quick glance at his small set face, Mrs. Fleming only said, "You're wet and muddy. Run up and change while I make the toast. And don't forget to wash your hands."

She gave him his candle and he went up to his tiny bedroom under the eaves. He was gone rather a long time and Mrs. Fleming called up the stairs twice before he came down. During tea they talked about what they would do on his birthday.

"It's such luck that it comes just before half term when you have to go back to school," said Mrs. Fleming. "Of course it isn't a nice time of year for picnics, and I'm afraid it would cost too much money to go up to Town for a matinée. I think we'll have to be satisfied with Durchester and the Pictures. And you shall have the book on brass rubbings for your present. By the way, was there a brass in that church?"

"I didn't get as far as that. Mummie, do you mind if I go to bed now? My head aches rather."

"I was going to suggest it. You look awfully tired."

"You'll come up and say good night?"

"Of course. Shout when you're ready."

Sandra Fleming usually hummed a tune as she stood at her little scullery sink washing up, but tonight she was silent. It was obvious that Toby had received some kind of shock. "I mustn't force his confidence," she thought anxiously, "but I do wish I knew what really happened. Perhaps there was a horrible car smash and people hurt and he saw it. He's such a soft-hearted old thing. And if he bottles it all up it may give him a complex or something. Oh dear—" For Sandra Fleming, being a modern young woman, had read books on the psychology of the child which alarmed her very much whenever she remembered them. If only Toby had a father. And yet Mr. Fleming had never said anything but "Bosh!" when she had tried to discuss inhibitions and repressions with him. James Fleming had been years older than his wife. He had been kind to her when she was very lonely and miserable. She had been too young to understand what she was doing when she married him. He had been a good but uninspiring husband. When she thought of him, which was not very often, it was without regret. He had been satisfied, apparently, with the tepid affection which was all she had to give.

"Mummie—"

Toby was in bed, with the clothes drawn up to his chin. Sandra bent to kiss him and he hugged her convulsively.

"Mummie, mummie—"

Sandra was deeply moved. "What's the matter, darling?"

"Nothing."

His eyes followed her as she moved about the room folding and putting away the clothing he had scattered over the floor.

"Didn't you wash your hands, Toby?"

"Yes, I did."

"What did you do with the water in the basin?"

He gulped. He had hoped she would not have noticed that. "I—I threw it out of the window."

"Why?"

"I—I thought it would save you trouble," he mumbled. He could not tell her that the water had turned red after he washed out a dark smear on his coat sleeve.

She seemed to accept that explanation. "That was very kind and thoughtful of you, darling, but I'd rather you didn't another time. This window's just over the front door. Suppose the vicar had been coming to call and got a shower bath—"

She had wanted to make him laugh and she succeeded. She dropped the subject. "Is the window open at the top? There's a light just gone up in the vicar's study. I expect Tommy Yates has gone to see him about having his banns called."

Tommy was their charwoman's son and sometimes helped in the garden. He was, in the village idiom, "not exactly," and the fact that he was soon to be led to the altar by the cook at the Hall had aroused a good deal of interest.

"She's that fat woman in purple who sits with the Sunday school children, isn't she?" asked Toby.

"Yes."

"I suppose she'll cook him lovely dinners."

"I expect so. Have you said your prayers?"

"Yes."

"Good night then. God bless you—"

"Mummie—" he clung to her. With the dark would come pictures of the silent wood with the undergrowth and the tree trunks behind which might be hidden not the pirates and highwaymen of his childhood but real murderers, or the livid distorted face of the victim.

"Mummie—may I have a nightlight?"

Sandra held the small, shaking figure very close. "How would you like it if I made a bed for you tonight on the sofa in my room? Just for a treat—"

"Oh, Mummie—yes—"

CHAPTER III
AT THE GRANGE

THERE was a beech tree overshadowing the old forge that filled the front garden of the cottage with a golden carpet of leaves every autumn, and Mrs. Fleming and Toby had agreed to devote the following morning to clearing them up. It was an unending task, for while they worked the leaves were still coming down, drifting gently through the still windless air.

Mrs. Yates, who was Mr. Killick's daily woman, but who sometimes came to the forge cottage to help with the cleaning, stopped at the gate for a chat.

"They leaves is a dratted nuisance," she remarked.

"Yes, but I love them," said Sandra. "Isn't it nice to see the sun again? Has Tommy seen the vicar about the banns?"

Tommy's mother snorted. "She has. And she made him go along with her. Well, I must be getting on. Mr. Killick, he likes me to come round about eleven. Suits me all right—" Mrs. Yates broke off to stare with unconcealed curiosity at the saloon car that had been driven up and stopped at the gate. There were three men in it, and two of the three were policemen. Toby was aware of a very unpleasant sinking sensation in the pit of his stomach. He glanced apprehensively at his mother and saw that she had turned pale. Inspector Brett opened the gate and came in, followed by one of the constables.

"You are Mrs. Fleming?"

His manner was brusque but not actually uncivil.

Sandra answered rather faintly. "Yes." If only Mrs. Yates had not been standing there open-mouthed. She was a great gossip. It would be all over the village.

"Can we come inside?"

She nodded and led the way into the living-room. "Please sit down," she said formally. "Toby, come here by me."

"You don't know what we've come about?"

"No."

"I told your boy to keep his mouth shut, but I wasn't sure that he would."

"If you've come to tell me he's done anything wrong," said Sandra defiantly, "I shan't believe it."

"That is our usual experience with the parents of youthful misdemeanants, madam. But we've nothing against your son. He found a dead man in the woods yesterday and was coming to tell us about it when he fell off his bicycle. An A.A. scout rang us up—"

Sandra drew a long breath. "Oh Toby, why didn't you tell me?"

"He said not to——"

He slipped his hand into hers. She held the grimy little paw tightly. Brett produced his note book. "The inquest will be opened to-morrow, but it will be adjourned almost at once. Your son's evidence will not be required at this stage. The medical evidence will be the main thing."

"Was it—suicide?"

The inspector shook his head. "No, madam. We have definitely ruled out that possibility. Two shots were fired, and from some distance." He checked himself. "I'm not here to answer questions, Mrs. Fleming, and I shall be obliged if you'll keep that to yourself for the present. There'll be an account of the inquest in the local papers the day after tomorrow and then it'll be common property. To broadcast any details now might defeat the ends of justice."

"Was it poachers?" asked Sandra. "Of course, I won't repeat anything you say."

"The victim has not been identified as yet. Your son didn't recognise him, but I hear you haven't been very long in this neighbourhood?"

"Only since July."

"I see. You haven't a car?"

"No."

"Doesn't your boy attend any school?"

"Oh yes. But there was an outbreak of measles and it was so bad that they sent the boarders home. He's going back at half term."

"When is that?"

"The third of November."

"Is the school far off?"

"It's in Hampshire."

"You may have to keep him at home a little longer," said Brett. "I'll let you know about that later."

He got up, and as Sandra and Toby stood up too he turned rather suddenly on the boy.

"Was he quite dead when you found him?"

Toby shrank a little involuntarily. "Not-not quite."

"How do you know?"

"He-he tried to raise himself and then he fell back. I said, 'I'll get help—' I don't know if he heard me—"

"Why didn't you tell me that before? " asked Brett harshly.

Toby said nothing.

"It helps to establish," began Brett and broke off to look out of the window. "What the hell's going on—"

A small crowd consisting of two errand boys, a girl with a baby in a push cart, an old man and several small children had collected at the gate where they were passing their time staring at the policeman in the driving seat of the car, but the focus of interest had shifted from him to a more familiar figure, that of Mrs. Yates, who was running across the green towards them and crying out and waving her arms.

"Like as if a bull was after her or she were trying to catch a bus," said one errand boy to the other.

Brett hurried out of the room and Sandra would have followed, but Toby held her back.

"Let him go, mummie. I—I don't suppose it's anything—"

She glanced at him quickly. It was very unlike Toby not to want to be on the spot when anything was going on. But she only said, "Very well, dear. We can see from the window. Look, that other policeman is trying to drive those children off. I'm glad. They'll break down the palings if they hang on to them like that. What can be the matter with Mrs. Yates? Oh, they're bringing her in here. You can go into the back garden if you like, Toby, I'll call you in if you're wanted again."

He shook his head. "No, thanks. Brett's a beast, I think, but I won't run away from him. I—I haven't done anything wrong, mother."

"I know that, darling."

She got up as the inspector reappeared.

"She seems a bit upset," he explained. "Perhaps a glass of water—"

Mrs. Yates' decent black bonnet, a Victorian relic, carefully preserved, had slipped to the side of her head, her lips were white and her eyes staring. Sandra laid a firm but kindly hand on her arm. "Sit down here. Don't try to speak for a minute. I'm going to give you a drop of brandy. Toby, you'll find the flask in the cupboard. You shouldn't have run like that, you know. It isn't good for your heart. There, that's better."

When Mrs. Yates had recovered from a fit of choking she sat up and tried to straighten her bonnet.

"Well, there now, I know I didn't ought to have, but seeing the police was here handy, and I was afraid they'd drive off again before I could catch them, and it gave me such a turn finding the poor gentleman lying there and too dark in that passage to see him properly, but I did bring myself to touch his hand and it was that cold it sent a chill to my very marrow—"

Brett intervened. "Whom did you find?"

"Mr. Killick. The gentleman over at the Grange. He always leaves the front door on the latch for me, but this morning I couldn't get in. I knocked and rang and there wasn't any answer though I could hear the dogs howling upstairs. So I went round to the garden door and got in easy. But it's dark inside. There's a narrow passage, you see, sir, with hooks for coats and hats, from that little side door into the hall, and there's no way of lighting it. So—I—I very near fell over him."

"I'll go over at once," said Brett. "Keep her here until I return please, Mrs. Fleming."

Dunning had not succeeded in dispersing the children. They had re-formed in a semi-circle a little farther off, and the two errand boys still leaned on their bicycles at a safe distance. Brett ignored them. "You come with me, Dunning. Hale, make these people move on. We don't want a crowd collecting here."

Brock Green, as its name implied, was one of those hamlets that have grown up around a central patch of common land. The villagers had retained their ancient rights to pasture cows and goats on the green and to keep ducks on the pond. The old forge and the blacksmith's cottage were directly opposite the Grange, but the common at this part was a quarter of a mile wide, and little could be seen of the house but a chimney stack and one end of the roof. The place was screened from the road that went past the gate by a high stone wall and a dense growth of trees and shrubs. It stood somewhat isolated, as Brett noticed, for there was a field on the right between it and a row of cottages, and on the left the ancient parish church, standing in an unusually spacious churchyard, divided it from the long low two-storied house which Brett knew to be the vicarage.

"Did you say this was your native place, Dunning?"

"No sir. But my wife comes from here. We're often over to see her family."

"What about this Mr. Killick? Do you know him?"

"No, sir. The Grange was to let. He came only about a year ago. Lives alone, they say, with only a woman to come in for an hour or two—that'd be Mrs. Yates. Keeps himself to himself like."

They had reached the gate and were going up the short drive. As they came up to the house they could hear the pitiful whining of more than one dog and a rhythmic, thudding noise.

"They're jumping up against a door," said Dunning. "Poor brutes. An uncle of mine died like that. Heart failure. They found him the next morning. It don't do to live alone."

Brett made no reply. They were making their way through the dank shrubberies to the rear of the house. They had no difficulty in finding the garden door for Mrs. Yates had left it open. The two men entered the passage, Brett leading the way. An old tweed cape and a broad brimmed felt hat hung from a hook on the right hand wall with some dogs' leads. Brett switched on his torch and directed its light downwards. He uttered a sharp exclamation. The body of Simon Killick lay face downward, with his head towards the garden door. There was a large dark stain just there on the coconut matting that covered the stone floor of the passage.

"Not another murder!" gasped Dunning. His ruddy face lost some of its colour.

"You've said it." Brett stooped to touch one of the hands. "She was right. Stone cold. He's been dead some hours. Plenty of time to make a get away. We'll just go through the house, and then I'll have to ring up the superintendent."

Brett had his faults but a lack of thoroughness was not one of them. He began with the basement. The kitchen was in perfect order and there were no signs of any preparations for a meal, but a large bowl filled with mashed dog biscuits moistened with gravy was standing on the floor in the scullery untouched. There was some food on the pantry shelves. The inspector eyed the stewed prunes and rice pudding, flanked by cheese and a dish of cold potatoes, without enthusiasm. "Seems to have been a vegetarian," he remarked. "You wouldn't think a meek and mild sort of chap like that'd get done in, would you."

On the ground floor the only room that showed traces of occupation was one at the back of the house. The others were furnished but a glance was enough to show they were seldom or never used. In the living-room Brett threw open the shutters and drew back the heavy curtains, letting in the pale autumn sunshine. There were ashes on the hearth but the bricks were cold. A book was lying on the seat of one of the two arm-chairs drawn up on either side of the fireplace. Brett read the title but was careful not to touch it. "That binding will be good for finger-prints. *Hassan.* Seems to be a play or something."

"Never heard of it," said Dunning. "Look at that, sir." He pointed to a parrot's cage standing on a side table. It was supplied with food and water but the bird was gone.

Brett was opening and shutting the drawers of the writing table. They were all empty.

"Everything as neat as a new pin. Darn it. There's nothing to help us so far. But it happened last night. Must have done. Plenty of time for the killer to put everything straight. Let's go up. That row is getting on my nerves."

Since the dogs had heard them moving about a perfect pandemonium had broken out upstairs. Dunning followed his chief with some reluctance.

"They may fly at us."

"We've got to risk it," said Brett curtly. "Did you shut the passage door? I don't want them to find the body."

"Yes."

"All right." He turned the handle of the front bedroom door, pushed it open and stood back.

Two rough-haired Scotch terriers and a small yellow mongrel rushed out and tore down the stairs. Dunning, looking over the banisters, saw them trotting from door to door and stopping at each one to scratch at the panels and whimper for admittance.

"They'll be back here when they don't find him," said Brett grimly. "Meanwhile we'll have a look round his bedroom."

It was a large, light room and almost as bare as a monk's cell. The walls were colour washed and there were no pictures. There was a dark blue quilt on the narrow camp bed and a dent at the foot where one of the dogs had lain.

"They're coming back," said Dunning hastily.

The Aberdeen had returned alone. He stopped on the threshold and gazed at them enquiringly.

"Good old fellow," said Dunning in his most ingratiating tones. "Nice doggie."

The terrier growled and the hackles rose along his back.

"Don't move," said Brett sharply.

Both men remained perfectly still. The terrier's head was on one side. Obviously he was listening. After a moment he turned and after sniffing anxiously at the doors of the other rooms on the landing, went pattering down the stairs again.

What are the other two doing?" asked Brett.

Dunning went to look over the banisters. "Waiting at the door into the passage. Dogs know a lot more than you'd think. Pity they can't speak."

Brett grunted.

"I should say they were shut up in this room when it happened. Have you noticed how hoarse they all are? I'll bet they've been barking all night," said Dunning.

"I'm no use with dogs," said Brett, "but you're fond of them, aren't you, Dunning?"

The constable, foreseeing what was coming, answered cautiously. "Well, it depends."

"We can't leave them there in the hall. You go down and open the kitchen door and try to persuade them to go down. Their food's there and they ought to be hungry. Shut them in there for the present. I'm going to leave you here while I ring up the station. You'd better stay in the hall, and don't touch anything."

"Very good, Inspector."

Dunning was still trying to induce the dogs to come down to the kitchen for their food when Brett left the house. They did not snarl or attempt to bite him, they simply ignored him. They were all three sitting as close as they could get to the passage door. It was evident that they knew that their master was on the other side and their quivering eagerness to get to him was painful to witness. Dunning, who was soft-hearted about animals, felt a lump in his throat as he watched them.

"It's no use. You come along and have your grub."

They were listening, but not to his voice. The mongrel suddenly threw up his head and uttered a prolonged and despairing howl. It was a hair-raising sound in that house of death.

Dunning looked at his wrist watch. Brett had been gone twenty minutes. If he came back and found that nothing had been done he—Dunning—would get in trouble. "Well, if you won't come you'll have to be carried," he said. He picked up the Aberdeen. Much to his relief, though the dog struggled in his arms it made no use of its teeth. He shut it in the kitchen and came back to fetch the others. He was in the hall tying his handkerchief round his wrist when somebody knocked at the front door. He unlocked and unbolted it and admitted Brett.

"So the curs set on you? Not badly bitten, I hope. You must ask the doctor to look at it when he comes. He'll be here in a few minutes."

"It was the little yellow chap," said Dunning. "I'm not blaming him."

"Well, that's all—" began the Inspector. The sentence was never finished. He started back, giving vent to a sound that Dunning, relating the scene later to his wife, described as a sort of yelp. "Ouch! What the hell—"

The parrot, who all this while had been roosting on the upper rim of the hanging hall lamp, and watching their comings and goings with a beady eye, had spread his wings and, flitting grey and ghostly in the half darkness, had landed on Brett's shoulder with a suddenness that had a shattering effect on his nerves.

Dunning, who had hoped for some commendation of his conduct during his chief's absence and had been disappointed, had some difficulty in suppressing a smile.

"Fancy him being up there all the time. Seems to have taken a fancy to you, Inspector."

Brett gritted his teeth. "Take the thing off me, can't you, and put him back in his cage." He hated to feel a fool.

Dunning hesitated. "I've heard parrots can bite."

"Well, I hear the cars stopping at the gate. The doctor'll be here to bandage you in less than two minutes. I've given you an order, haven't I? If you don't carry it out I'll report you."

Inspector Brett had very definitely lost his temper, and when that happened his subordinates had learned to walk as delicately as Agag.

"Yes, sir," said Dunning meekly, and offered his undamaged wrist to the bird. To his great relief the parrot showed a positive alacrity in leaving Brett and allowed himself to be replaced in his cage. Dunning left him sitting on his perch and smoothing his rumpled feathers, and hurried back to the hall.

Chapter IV
TOBY GETS A LIFT

"Not the right time of year for the country, unless you're fond of a bit of rough shooting," remarked Superintendent Cardew, "but life's like that, Collier, one damn thing after another as the saying is."

"Yes, sir," said Collier dutifully. His eyes, which had wandered when he first entered the superintendent's room to the gulls circling over the river and the brown sail of a passing barge, were now fixed on the elder man's face.

"The Durchester people have called the Yard in and the A.C. asked me if I could spare you. I can't, but I suppose you'll have to go."

"Very good, sir."

"It's a queer business. A man was found shot in a wood last Wednesday afternoon. He seems to have been a stranger in the district and so far all efforts to identify him have failed. The following morning another man named Killick, living in a village about three miles away from the scene of the crime, was found in his own house with a fractured skull. Probably there's some connection, but a week has gone by and the local chaps don't seem to be much forrarder. So now they're calling in the Yard—"

"When the scent is cold—"

"Exactly. Can you get off this afternoon?"

"Yes."

"Good. Is that thing you call a car functioning?"

Collier grinned. "She's O.K."

"Then I think you'd better go down by road."

"If I can charge up repairs and spare parts as required."

Cardew waved his hand. "That'll be all right. Stick it all down in your exes. What time are you likely to get there?"

"May I have a look at that railway time table? Thanks. Durchester. Distance from London 59¼ miles. I'll have to go back to my diggings and collect my suit case. I can get there about four, barring accidents."

The superintendent nodded. "Right. You're to go straight to the police station. The Chief Constable will be there to meet you and talk things over. I'll put through a trunk call and tell them when to expect you. You'll have to be tactful, Collier. Nothing definite was said but I rather gathered that the fellow who's been in charge of the enquiry so far is sore about this. He may not be easy to work with."

"I'll do my best," said Collier.

But when, an hour later, he crossed the bridge at Lambeth the outlines of the buildings along the Embankment had grown dim. He was obliged to drive very slowly and even so he had to brake hard more than once to avoid a collision. It would be clearer, he hoped, when he came to the country beyond Croydon, but when houses gave place to hedgerows he was still feeling his way through a cold clammy impalpable white curtain of mist.

He took a wrong turning after passing through Leatherhead but it was not until some time later that he had to admit that he was hopelessly lost. It was past four already and the mist was so thick that he could hardly see across the road. The last sign-post he had seen had informed him that he was two miles from Hammerpot. The name connoted the old Sussex iron country and he realised that he had become involved in the network of by-roads intersecting one of the few remaining densely wooded parts of the Weald, a last outpost of the great forest of Anderida. He had turned so often that he had lost all sense of direction, and he had forgotten to bring his compass.

"And the Chief Constable waiting. Oh darn!"

He had stopped by the roadside to study his map again. Hammerpot was not marked, unless—yes, there it was. In that case he could not be far from Durchester. He drove on slowly, sounding his horn at frequent intervals. At last he heard a motor-cycle coming towards him. He stopped and leaned out of the window to hail the driver.

"I say—" he was relieved to see the yellow coat and leggings of an A.A. man. "Where am I?"

"Within fifty yards of Hammerpot crossing. Go straight on for Brock Green."

"I want Durchester."

"That's five miles further on. You should have kept to the main road."

"I know. I missed it somehow."

Both men looked round as a loud excited barking broke out in the woods on their right.

"Nothing wrong, I hope," said the scout. "A chap was done in just over there a week ago."

"Really?" Collier extricated himself from the driver's seat and joined the other man on the road. The trunks of trees loomed ghostly through the fog. The heavy silence was broken by a rustling of dead leaves and a crackling of twigs and light running footsteps. A boy climbed the stile and two terriers, a Cairn and an Aberdeen, wriggled through and waited for him to pick up their leads.

"So it's you again, sonny," said the A.A. man. "A nice afternoon for a run in these woods, I don't think. I shouldn't have thought you'd have cared to go in there again alone. This is the boy that found the body," he added in explanation.

Collier realised that, after all, his luck was in. "That must have been pretty grim," he said sympathetically, "or didn't you mind?"

"I didn't like it much," said Toby. He was breathing hard as if he had been running, and his mother would have noticed that he was unusually pale. "I ought to be getting on now. It's a long way home."

"You came all that way on foot?" said the scout. "Haven't you had your cycle put to rights?"

"It wasn't mine. I'd borrowed it," the boy explained. "The dogs wanted exercise."

"Those were Mr. Killick's dogs, weren't they? I heard about them."

"Yes, the vicar, Mr. Clare, asked us to take care of them. I was jolly glad to. I'd always wanted a dog."

"Perhaps the gentleman'd give you a lift—"

"I was just going to make the suggestion," said Collier, "if I'm going your way?"

"I live at Brock Green."

"Straight on," said the scout, "you can't miss it."

He remounted his motor-cycle and chugged away. Collier opened the door of his car and the two terriers scrambled in without waiting for the boy.

Collier smiled, "You see. I expect they're used to motoring. Most dogs love it. It makes them feel so superior to the mere pedestrian curs. Jump in—what's your name, by the way?"

"Toby Fleming. They aren't. Mr. Killick hadn't got a car."

"Mine's Collier. I'm glad to have met you like this," he said as he let in the clutch.

"Oh—why?"

"Well—can you keep a secret?"

"Yes."

Collier glanced down at the small freckled face and noted the firm lips and resolute chin.

"I believe you could," he said thoughtfully after a while. "I like people who can. It was lucky for me meeting you because I happen to be interested in this case of the man found in the wood. What's the matter?"

Toby had turned so white now that Collier was alarmed.

"Don't you feel well? Hold on a few minutes until I get you home—"

"I'm all right," said Toby with an effort. "Please stop here. That's our gate."

"Very well," said Collier, "but I wish you'd tell me why you were so frightened when I said I was interested in the case?"

Toby looked up into his face. "I—just for a second I thought you were one of them—"

"One of—?"

Toby shuddered. "Of the—the killers."

"Thanks," said Collier dryly.

"Oh—there's my mother."

The door of the cottage had opened and Sandra came down to the gate.

"Toby—where have you been? I was getting worried." Toby had got out of the car. Collier followed him.

"I was able to give him a lift," he explained.

"How kind of you. This fog is awful, isn't it?"

"Yes. I'd missed my way because of it. I've been wandering about for hours. I wonder if you could direct me to some place where they supply teas. I'm chilled to the bone."

She looked at him and apparently was satisfied by what she saw for she said without hesitation, "if you'll come in I can give you a cup of tea."

Collier had fished for the invitation but he was careful not to jump at it. "Very good of you—but I don't want to give trouble—"

"It won't be any trouble. You were kind to Toby—where is he? Oh, he's run into the house. Please come."

They found Toby kneeling on the hearthrug in the warm, lamplit living-room with the two dogs beside him. He was making toast.

"I wondered where'd you'd got to," said his mother. "Mind you don't burn it. Sit here if you're cold, Mr.—"

"My name's Collier. I've been sent down from Scotland Yard to take charge of a case down here."

Sandra looked rather startled. "Oh—mind, Toby, the bread's on fire."

Toby blew out the flame and stuck another slice on his fork. He looked up and met Collier's eyes.

"Why didn't you tell me that before, sir?"

"Don't you remember I asked you if you could keep a secret? I am on my way to Durchester, Mrs. Fleming, where I shall hear what has been done up to now."

"Both the inquests were adjourned," said Sandra. "Toby ought to go back to his school, but they asked me to keep him at home a little longer. I can't imagine why. He happened to find the man in the wood and he cycled off at once to get the police—do you take sugar?"

"Two lumps, please." He looked up at the oak beams in the ceiling.

"What a delightful old place you have here."

"Yes, it is rather sweet, isn't it. I'm hoping to give teas and have one or two people to stay in the summer."

"Do you get many motorists passing this way?"

"Not many. We're off the main road. But I'm going to put up a notice board and advertise in the local papers. Everyone says there is money in teas," she added rather wistfully.

Collier agreed, and then felt obliged to add that a good many people were doing it. He declined a second cup and rose from the table. He had been successful in establishing friendly relations and that would have to suffice for the present. He offered to pay for his meal, but Sandra would not hear of it.

"I asked you in. You were good to Toby."

"Well, but I wanted to be your first customer. I might bring you luck."

"Toby, keep the dogs in. I'll go down to the gate with Mr. Collier."

Collier took a genial leave of the boy but met with little response.

"I think Toby is rather shy of you," said his mother as she walked with him down to the gate where the headlights of his car were a pale blur in the mist. " It's not like him to be so quiet."

"I suppose finding the body was a shock, and he hasn't got over it," suggested Collier.

"It must have been. He came home and never told me a word about it until the policeman came the next morning. It's the first time he's kept anything from me. I think he was so horrified he couldn't bear to speak of it. I knew something horrid must have happened. He asked for a light in his room. I do hope you'll be able to arrest somebody soon. I can't keep Toby shut up indoors, but it isn't very pleasant to think the—the murderer may be still about here."

"I'll do my best," said Collier for the second time that day. He set the engine running. "I go straight on from here, don't I?"

"Yes. Until you come to the main road. Turn to the left then. Good-bye—"

"Good-bye, Mrs. Fleming."

The clock of Durchester town hall was striking half past six when Collier was shown into the rather gloomy room, smelling of gas and scorched leather, in which Captain Lowther, the Chief Constable, sat at a roll top desk initialling reports.

He looked up as Collier was shown in, nodded curtly, and pointed to a chair. "Sit down, won't you. I must finish these."

He kept Collier waiting ten minutes before he laid down his pen and turned in his swivel chair to face his visitor.

"You're late," he said. "I arranged to be here at four at some personal inconvenience."

"I'm sorry, sir. It was the fog. I came down by road, and I lost my way."

Collier's tone was calm and reasonable. He was not put out by his reception. He realised that the Chief Constable had some excuse for his irritation.

The captain grunted. "It's a bad beginning. Why didn't you come down by train? We could have lent you a car."

"That's very good of you sir. But in my experience cars haven't always been available. And sometimes they are too well known locally as being used by the police."

"Are you alone?"

"No, sir. I shall have the colleague who usually works with me, Sergeant Duffield. He was held up by another case, but he's coming down by the last train."

"Well," the Chief Constable made an effort to be more cordial, with partial success. "I hope I've done right to call in the Yard. I've heard of you, Inspector Collier. I had hoped we could pull this off without assistance, but a week had passed and we've made no progress. I'll get Inspector Brett to give you an outline of the case. You must excuse him if he seems rather surly, Mr. Collier. He's worked hard, and he's sore."

He rang a bell. There were heavy footsteps in the passage and a burly man who looked to Collier like the typical sergeant-major of the comic press, came in.

"Ah, Brett. This is the officer they've sent us from the Yard, Detective Inspector Collier. He was delayed by the fog."

Collier stood up and offered his hand. Brett ignored the gesture and merely nodded.

"I've brought my notes on the case, sir," he said woodenly. "Do you want me to run through them?"

Collier sat down again with rather more colour than usual in his face. Clumsy oaf, he thought. As if this sort of investigation wasn't hard enough without petty jealousies. Brett began his exposition. When he had done the Chief Constable summed up.

"It comes to this, Collier. Two men were killed last Wednesday within five miles, and apparently within five hours of one another, but there is nothing so far to show that the crimes are connected. If they are not the coincidence is extraordinary." "Let's take the man in the wood first," said Collier. "We had his description at the Yard, and his finger-prints."

"Yes," said Brett, "and we circularised every police station in the country and got the B.B.C. to broadcast a description. No result."

"There were no identifying marks on his clothing?"

"None. He was dressed entirely in ready made stuff bought at multiple stores. His underclothing was new so there were no laundry marks. He had a silver wrist watch and fourteen and sevenpence halfpenny in silver and copper in his pockets. His pockets and the lining of his coat had been slit with a knife and his shoes had been taken off, probably after death."

"That's interesting. It gives you the motive."

"Yes. He must have had some paper on him they wanted. Or jewellery."

"Hardly jewellery. It had to be something that could be hidden in his shoes," Collier pointed out.

"There was a fellow caught by the American police the other day with diamonds in the heels of his boots."

"So there was. You're right there, Brett," said Collier. He was anxious to placate the local man if possible. "Well, he's not an old lag or we should have identified him by his finger-prints. On the other hand it's rather odd that nobody has come forward to give him a local habitation and a name. You'd think somebody would miss him if it's only his landlady."

"I don't know about that," argued Brett. "Take the case of a commercial traveller. They're often away for weeks."

"Yes, but they keep in touch with their firms, I fancy. Stoutish, swarthy. Did it strike you he might be a foreigner?"

"It did. I had enquiries made about any foreigners living here or passing through. There's an old organ grinder, and a fellow who runs an antique shop, and a chap who gives French and German lessons, and another who used to play the violin at the Palladium before they put in the organ. But there's nothing to connect any one of them with Hammerpot woods last Wednesday, though only two of the lot have got alibis. I've got their names and addresses here."

"Thanks. I'd like a copy."

"I'll have one typed for you. I haven't actually questioned them. I thought it best not to put them on their guard."

"There's another point. Was the dead man seen anywhere in the neighbourhood before his body was found?"

"I can't find anybody who remembers setting eyes on him, and people in these country places are apt to notice strangers."

"The boy who found him had gone into the wood to look for conkers, leaving his bicycle by the stile."

"Here's a sketch plan of the spot, Inspector." The two men bent over it together. "Here's the footpath through the wood. The body was lying at the foot of a tree here—"

"The poor wretch wasn't quite dead when the boy found him?"

"That's right. He was still breathing according to young Fleming."

"What does the doctor say about that? He was shot through the lungs wasn't he? How long would he be likely to live?"

"The doctor hedged a bit, but he seemed to think not more than a quarter of an hour in this particular case."

"Then the murderer can't have been very far off when the kid arrived on the scene. That's pretty grim," said Collier, thinking of Toby.

"I don't know about that," said Brett. "If he had a car waiting he might be a good ten miles away."

"Allow five minutes for searching the pockets and removing the shoes. Had the boy seen a car on the road?"

"You'll see by this plan, Inspector, that there's another road to the west of the wood. The footpath leads to it as well as to the little church of Botolphs which is sometimes visited by archeologists.

There may have been a car on that road, but I haven't been able to find anyone who saw it. We've been through the Hammerpot woods very thoroughly—"

"I'll say you have," said the Chief Constable ruefully, "we had every available man in the force on that job, and an army of chaps from the Labour Exchange—"

"And you found nothing?"

"Nothing but the usual litter left by picnic parties, and none of that within a hundred yards of the scene of the crime."

"There was nothing to suggest that the body was carried there?"

"Nothing. I think we can rule that out, Inspector. Men carrying a heavy weight would have trodden down the undergrowth, and one would expect to find drops of blood."

Collier said nothing. He was not in the habit of ruling anything out at so early a stage.

"This plan is very clear," he said, "but I'd like to see an ordnance map."

"I have one here," said Brett. He unfolded it. "Here's Hammerpot. I used to go there myself for conkers when I was a kid," he added. "It wasn't preserved in those days. The present owner is very down on trespassers. I warned young Toby Fleming he'd get into trouble if he went there again."

"I had a very stiff letter from Sir Henry the day after we carried out our search of the wood," said the Chief Constable. "Very strong language about heavy-footed bobbies scaring all his birds into his neighbours' coverts. I've done my best to smooth him down. He gave two hundred pounds towards our new motor ambulance only last month."

"A local magnate?" said Collier.

"Sir Henry Webber? Yes. He lives at Brock Hall. He's not one of the old landed gentry, a retired manufacturer. Made his pile during the War, I fancy. Here's his place, about three miles from the village of Brock Green."

Collier was looking at the map. "These roads from Brock Green diverge one on either side of the Hammerpot wood," he said thoughtfully.

"Yes. The village is built round a long narrow strip of common land. The Fleming boy lives at the old blacksmith's cottage on the east side of the green so he would naturally take the road nearest to him. The other road leads past the Grange, the scene of the second murder."

"Before we come to that I'd like to make a note of the time the boy found the man who'd been shot."

"Young Fleming says he looked at his watch before he went into the wood and it was then ten minutes past four. Herbert Missenden, the A.A. scout, rang us up at five minutes to five."

"How far is the call box from the place where the body was found?"

"About two miles."

"I see."

"You're thinking the boy took his time," said Brett. I thought the same. But he was knocked off his bicycle, or fell off, as he turned into the main road and took a little while to come round. Missenden was on the spot luckily. And in my opinion the boy's not too bright at the best of times."

Collier fancied the burly inspector might be mistaken in his estimate of Toby's intelligence. It was obvious that Brett with his parade ground voice and hectoring manners was not likely to gain a small boy's confidence. But Collier had said nothing of the chance that had enabled him to make the acquaintance of Toby and his mother, so he only said, "I daresay he was scared out of his wits. How old is he?"

"Twelve. He's not one of the village lads. His mother's a lady. Hard up, I fancy."

"Well, now, about the second murder. I gather that there's no evidence that the two crimes are related?"

"None. I was at the forge cottage Thursday morning putting a few questions to young Fleming when the woman who went to the Grange to do some cleaning and prepare the midday meal for Mr. Killick came running to fetch us. I went over at once with Dunning. The front door was locked and bolted, but a side door was on the latch and we found Mr. Killick's body just inside with the back of his skull battered in."

"More than one blow?"

"The doctor thought not. One blow from some blunt instrument delivered with great force. We went through the house. The dogs—there were three of them—were shut up in Mr. Killick's bedroom. Sergeant Gore took over. My hands were full with the other case—but the next day he went sick—he's got pleurisy—and I've carried on—"

The Chief Constable intervened. "That's really why I asked the Yard to send somebody down, Mr. Collier. The sergeant and the inspector here could have managed between them, but it's too much for one, and there was nobody else I could spare."

"I quite understand," said Collier, hoping that enough had now been said to salve Brett's wounded self-esteem. "One can't be everywhere at once. I gather there were no helpful clues in this case either?"

"None," said Brett gloomily. "Mr. Killick lived alone and the only rooms in use were his bedroom on the first floor in front and a ground floor room at the back where he had his meals and read and wrote, and the basement kitchen. It's one of those late eighteenth century houses, large and full of stairs and passages, hard to run, and not everybody's money. It stood empty a long time before Mr. Killick took it about a year ago. The daily woman didn't trouble much about dusting and we got plenty of finger-prints, but they were all hers or Mr. Killick's or the vicar's. He used to go in regularly on Monday evenings to play chess. He's terribly upset about this, poor old gentleman. It was his suggestion that I should take his finger-prints. But Bertillon's a wash out nowadays. Most criminals know enough to wear gloves."

"Did you find any marks made by gloved hands?" asked Collier quickly.

Brett nodded. "Several on the writing table. And the drawers which one would expect to find stuffed with papers, old letters, receipted bills and so forth, were empty."

"Did he write and receive many letters?"

"Very few according to the village postmistress. He seems to have been a silent, reserved sort of man, not the kind who makes friends. He was known to live alone, but the motive of the crime can hardly have been robbery. He had nearly five pounds in notes and silver on him, a valuable gold repeater and a signet ring."

"No suspicious characters seen lurking about during that day?"

"None."

Collier reflected a moment. "Could Killick have been killed by the other man? He might have been shot by a confederate while they were making their get away."

"A very nice theory," said Brett, "the only drawback to it is that the chap in the wood was found about four o'clock while Mr. Killick was seen by the vicar between half past six and seven. Mr. Clare went over to the Grange to return a book Killick had lent him. Killick asked him to stop and have a game of chess but he couldn't. He had to hurry home to interview a young couple who were coming to ask him to put up their banns."

The Chief Constable glanced at the clock. He wanted to get home to his dinner. Collier was quick to take the hint. He stood up.

"I must thank you for giving me such a clear account," he said rather formally. "I'll think it over and have a look round to-morrow."

"You can rely on us to give any help you may require," said Captain Lowther in a rather more friendly tone than he had yet employed. Inspector Brett said nothing.

Collier thanked him and said he had thought of staying at the Station Hotel.

The Chief Constable nodded. "Quite a decent little pub. Well—good night."

Chapter V
GETTING THE BACKGROUND

Sergeant Duffield got out of his third-class compartment. The fog had been thick all the way down and the train was nearly an hour late. His tired face brightened as he saw his superior officer waiting on the platform.

"Good of you to meet me, sir," he said as they went out together.

"I'm darned glad to see you," said Collier, "and that's a fact. Nobody loves me down here. I was late, just as you are, and kept them waiting, and they're peeved anyway."

"It's usual," said Duffield placidly. "They'll come round."

"I wonder. You're staying with me at the Station Hotel for the present anyway. I've engaged a private sitting-room and ordered a bit of something hot for supper."

When both men had done justice to a large dish of sausages and mashed and a jam tart, washed down by plenty of strong tea well sweetened, they drew their chairs up to the fire and filled their pipes. Collier, who had made some shorthand notes at the time, repeated the substance of Brett's narrative and ended by describing his meeting with the boy Toby.

"Brett thinks he's dull. I don't. He struck being an unusually bright boy but, as often in such cases, nervous and highly strung. Brett handled him wrong. The poor little chap was scared and he's shut up like an oyster. I believe he could tell us more but the longer he keeps it bottled up the harder it will be for him to come clean. His mother is worried about him. I could see that."

Duffield grunted. "Isn't it queer he should go into those woods again? You'd think he'd be afraid."

"He was afraid," said Collier. "You're right. Unless it was a morbid fascination. Might be, I suppose. Anyway I mean to cultivate Master Toby's acquaintance."

They both smoked in silence for a while. Then Duffield said,

"The chap in the wood couldn't have killed Killick—but it might be the other way round. What was Killick before he came down here?"

"Nothing murky about his past apparently. He was a partner in a firm trading as the May Morning Cosmetic and Perfumery Company. He retired a good many years ago to live on what the income tax people so amusingly call unearned increment. Nothing against him. Nothing to help us now. But we may get a line on something when we've been through his house. We'll do that the first thing to-morrow. And now—" He yawned. "What about a bit of shut eye?"

Sergeant Duffield went round to the police station to get the key of the Grange before they started the following morning. The house had been shut up since Brett had made his second and more intensive search the previous Saturday. So far, in spite of the publicity that had been given to the case, no relative had written or appeared to make any claim.

The fog had cleared off but the sky was overcast and a fine rain was falling. It was cold outside but colder still in the empty house. The two detectives spent some time in the living-room. Collier was especially interested in the large quantity of white ash on the hearth.

"Somebody burnt a lot of papers here. That's worth noting in connection with the empty drawers of the writing table." He looked at the books on the shelves.

"Lucky the char's not given to dusting," he remarked. "It's quite easy to see which were his favourite authors. *Gulliver's Travels*, *The Way of all Flesh*, Shaw and Aldous Huxley. Not exactly an optimist, judging by his taste in literature."

"He should have spent more of his time working in the garden," said Duffield with his usual solid good sense.

"On general principles, or as a cure for the blues—if he had them? But you're right." Collier looked out of the window at the overgrown shrubberies and borders choked with weeds. They spent some time in the passage leading from the front hall to the garden door.

"Not much use," said Collier finally, straightening his back and switching off his pocket torch. "Battalions of bobbies traipsing round, eh, Duffield, removing the body and what not. Boots, boots boots, in the words of the poem."

"You've got something, though," said Duffield, referring to the fact that the Inspector had twice scraped up some flakes of dried mud from the stone flags just beyond the large dark brown stain where the body had lain.

"Yes. Two different kinds of mould. Probably some local and the rest brought from Durchester by Brett and his minions. Now for the bedroom."

"What do you feel about this?" asked Collier after a while.

Duffield looked from the uncarpeted floor and the bare walls to the narrow camp bed. "He didn't pamper himself."

Collier nodded. "The dog baskets are the only human touch. Look at those marks on the paint of the door. Brett told me he found them shut up here. They were here while their master was being done to death downstairs. I've had enough of this house, sergeant. I think I'll go and call on the vicar. You can take a walk down the village and buy some stamps at the post office. Get the local reactions."

"Very good, sir."

They parted at the gate and Collier drove along the road past the lych gate leading into the churchyard to the adjoining vicarage. The middle-aged woman who opened the door seemed doubtful about admitting him.

"Mr. Clare's come back from the church. He always has matins and litany on Fridays, but I don't know about him seeing anyone. He's at work on his sermons for Sunday."

"I'm sorry, but my business is urgent."

At this point the study door was opened and the vicar himself appeared.

"How often have I told you, Mrs. Watkins, that I'm never too busy to see people. Come in, sir."

The study was shabby and untidy, but a bright fire burned on the hearth and the air was thick with tobacco smoke. The vicar waved his visitor to a chair and sat down himself.

A grey parrot was dozing in a steel cage on a table by the window. The vicar filled his pipe and pushed the tobacco jar across his desk. "Help yourself."

"Thank you, sir. I don't think I'll smoke."

"Just as you please. I can't do without it somehow. Soothing. Shouldn't become the slave of a habit." He fumbled short-sightedly over his matchbox. He was a big man, with a handsome florid face. Collier felt sure that normally he might be described as jolly looking. But his blue eyes had a shocked expression and he faltered when speaking and seemed to have some difficulty in finding the words he wanted.

"Well—what can I do for you?" he said, after a moment. The match he had thrown down was flaring on the hearthrug. Collier moved his foot forward to tread it out.

"I am Inspector Collier, of New Scotland Yard, sir. I've been sent down in connection with the death of Mr. Killick. I thought perhaps you would be kind enough to answer a few questions."

"Certainly," said Clare, "anything I can do. A terrible tragedy, Inspector. Poor Killick"—his lips were quivering "—he wasn't fit to die," he muttered, "he wasn't ready."

"I understand that you saw him on Wednesday evening?"

"Yes. I went across to the Grange with a book he had lent me. He asked me to stay and have a game of chess, but I couldn't. I was expecting Mrs. Yates, Tommy and Florrie Soper, and I had to be here to let them in as it was my housekeeper's evening out. I called their banns for the first time last Sunday. It's most unsuitable. She is at least twenty years his senior, but I daresay she has savings. Cooks, I believe, get very high wages."

Collier listened patiently. He felt sorry for the old man.

"Can you give the exact time?"

"Yes. The clock was striking seven as I came in here. Tommy and his intended arrived a few minutes later."

"Mr. Killick was a close friend of yours, sir?"

"Hardly that. There were many subjects on which we disagreed. He was very intellectual—very—often went altogether beyond me. I—I couldn't cope with him at all in that way—in argument, you know. I feel—and I can't put my feelings into words. No. But we were next door neighbours and both lonely men. I got into the habit of dropping in at the Grange on Mondays for a game of chess."

"When you saw him on the Wednesday evening he didn't say he was expecting a visitor?"

"No. No."

"He was just as usual?"

The vicar sighed. "Wait a minute. You must excuse me. I haven't been sleeping well since this happened. My attention wanders. You were saying?"

"I was asking if you recall anything about him that was not normal? I mean, excited—or worried, or—"

The vicar's eyes had wandered to a photograph on his writing desk, an enlarged snapshot of a young man in a second lieutenant's uniform, in a silver frame.

"He seemed in better spirits than usual," he said at last. "He was very morose at times. He was not a happy man, Inspector."

"Did he ever tell you he had enemies?"

The vicar passed his hand across his forehead. Collier noticed that all his movements were curiously slow and uncertain. He was beginning to wonder if the shock of the tragedy had not brought on a slight stroke. "I'm sorry to have to bother you," he said. Mr. Clare smiled for the first time. He had a very sweet smile.

"That's nice of you, my dear fellow. I'm getting old, and nowadays I feel it. About poor Killick—there were times when he spoke as if the whole world were against him. No—put that way it gives a wrong impression. It would be more accurate to say that there were many people and institutions that he hated—and he had it in him to be a bitter and unrelenting enemy—but I don't think he cared what they thought of him."

"Did he mention any of these people he disliked by name?"

"I gathered that he meant the Government, heads of departments, those in authority generally. He tried to restrain himself when he was talking to me. Only sometimes he broke out—"

"A man with a grievance against society, eh? A Communist perhaps?"

"I don't think so. I don't know—but I can't imagine him belonging to any party."

"He shared Dean Swift's opinion of his fellow men?"

The vicar looked startled. "How did you know that?"

Collier smiled. "I had a look at his books. There was no dust on *Gulliver's Travels*."

"Dear me," said the vicar. He seemed impressed. "I had no idea that policemen—but, of course, you have to be up in everything."

Collier laughed outright. "Well, more or less. And he never mentioned any relations to you, sir? You see our difficulty? We've got to get his background."

"I appreciate that. I'm sorry I can't help you. He never referred to his family. At least—he did mention his wife. He said she died in 1911, and added that if he had believed in a God he would have thanked him for that."

"Did he say why?"

"I thought he meant—before the War."

"I see." Collier stood up. "Thank you, sir. I've been taking up your time." He glanced towards the parrot who was moving with ineffable dignity and in a crab-like manner along his perch and stopping at intervals to bow to an imaginary audience. He wanted to conclude the interview on a lighter note so he asked if the bird could talk.

"Killick said he could, but I have never heard him. The—the police didn't know what to do with him so I offered to take care of him for the time being. I keep him in his cage though. Killick used to let him fly about the room."

"And the dogs?"

"Mrs. Fleming, just across the green from here, has very kindly taken charge of two of them. Her boy can exercise them. The other one—the mongrel—won't allow anybody to touch him. He—he haunts the churchyard," said the vicar in a low troubled voice. "I saw him just now lying on—on the grave. Toby's been over several times to try to tempt him with food, but he won't touch it. It—it's very painful."

He went with Collier to the door.

"I've met young Toby already," said Collier. "He seems a nice little chap."

Mr. Clare brightened. He indicated that he, too, approved of Toby. "He's often over here. I shall miss him when he goes back to school. I'm very fond of boys, Inspector. I had one of my own. You may have noticed his picture on my desk. If he had lived he would have done great things. He was gifted—well, well—greater love hath no man—you'll see his name with the others on our War Memorial in the churchyard. Good-bye."

"Thank you, sir. May I come in again if occurs to me? There may be some point you can clear up."

"Of course. Come when you like."

The vicar closed the door gently on his visitor and went back to his unfinished sermon.

Collier walked slowly and thoughtfully back to his car. He had decided that his next interview must be with Mrs. Yates. He spoke to the village postman who was just passing on his bicycle and who directed him. He found Mrs. Yates on her knees washing the stone floor of her picturesque but insanitary cottage. She got up and dusted a chair for him. Her manner was friendly and she gazed at him with unconcealed interest.

"You're the police, aren't you? A new one. We haven't seen you around before."

Collier knew news travels rapidly in villages. He smiled. "You've got it in one. I'm hoping to get some help from you, Mrs. Yates. You knew Mr. Killick pretty well."

"I wouldn't care to say that. He wasn't an easy man to know. I did a bit of cleaning and preparing vegetables and that for him."

"You had regular hours?"

"Yes. Eleven to one. I'd leave when I'd dished up his dinner, such as it was, and he'd stack the plates and that on a tray and take it down to the kitchen for me to wash up the next day. He lived on green stuff. Never no butcher's meat, not even for the dogs. They had to content theirselves with biscuits. I'd take them a bone sometimes on the sly. Not that he wasn't kind to they animals. He made a lot of fuss of them, being all alone like, poor gentleman."

"Did he have no friends to see him?"

"Never to my knowledge. I've only got to look out of this window to see the gate of the Grange across the green. Why, I've been watching your car standing there in the road this morning."

"Did he ever talk to you about his past life?"

"No, he didn't. But he was a very kind hearted gentleman. Took a great interest in my Tommy, he did—that's my son and some people think he's not exactly, but he's sharper than he looks. He's been doing odd jobs up at the Hall, and there was a lot of talk in the village when he started walking out with Miss Soper, and some says to me, 'Why don't you stop it, Car'line?' But when I told Mr. Killick he said he thought it'd be the making of Tommy, and Miss Soper was old enough to know her own mind and he'd give Tommy a ten pound note to buy hisself clothes for the wedding and a bit of furniture. I told him Sir Henry and her ladyship was upset at the idea of losing Florrie because she's the best cook they've ever had and she's been with them eight years. And he began to laugh. Gave me quite a turn, it did, for I'd never heard him laugh before. He always liked to hear about the goings on at the Hall. I hear a good bit from Florrie."

"Miss Soper is still cook at the Hall?"

"Yes. Her month isn't up yet. Banns were called for the first time last Sunday."

"He liked to hear about all the village doings?" suggested Collier.

"I wouldn't say that. He never subscribed for the new Parish Room nor for the blanket fund nor nothing. 'I'm not a lover of my fellow creatures,' he used to say, 'let 'em stew in their own juice,' he'd say, and sometimes things I couldn't bring myself to repeat but he always begged pardon when I told him I wasn't used to hearing such language. Quite the gentleman with me he was, or I wouldn't have stayed."

"But he liked the Webbers?"

"I wouldn't say that. He liked to hear about them, but he always seemed best pleased when something had gone wrong like."

"He and the vicar were friendly," said Collier.

"They were that. Though Mr. Killick he never darkened the doors of the church. But the vicar spent Monday evenings at the Grange regular. We all knew where to go for him if a sick person took a turn for the worse and wanted Parson on a Monday evening. Him and Mr. Killick played that game with the little red and black horses and that."

Collier was silent for a moment. Then he said, "I want you to recall the last day of Mr. Killick's life, Mrs. Yates. Was he just as usual?"

"He seemed in pretty good spirits for him. That was the time I told you he burst out laughing and promised me ten pounds for my Tommy. And later, when I took up his dinner he was sort of smiling to himself as if he d thought of something funny like.

Seems queer, don't it, with his death so near? Fair gives one the creeps."

Collier agreed. "Perhaps he'd had a letter with good news."

"Well, the postman did call that morning. He was coming away as I arrived. But Mr. Killick had been excited like for a day or two before that."

"Did he keep his correspondence?"

"I should think so. He had a whole lot of papers stuffed into the drawers of his writing table. Nice old mess that room was, but he wouldn't let me touch it barring shaking the mats once a week and laying the fire and that."

Collier, who had seen Sergeant Duffield waiting patiently at the end of the lane for the last ten minutes, rose to go. "Thanks for a most interesting chat, Mrs. Yates."

"Come again any time," said the lady graciously.

A shock headed youth with a vacant expression was fumbling with the latch of the gate as Collier went down the garden path. He stood aside, touching his cap as Collier passed. The detective wished him good morning, but he only grinned in reply.

"Who was that?" enquired Duffield as his superior officer joined him. "That's Tommy. He was at the vicarage last Wednesday about his banns."

"Well there's no accounting for tastes," said Duffield. "I got round the postmistress," he added placidly. "Mr. Killick had a letter with a foreign stamp on it on Wednesday."

"French? German?"

"Neither. One of those other places, she thought. It was either red or brown or yellow—or it might have been green. She didn't really notice because her little girl was crying."

"Anything else?"

"Yes. He didn't have many letters, but she had noticed the West Croydon postmark more than once."

"Good for her," said Collier more cheerfully. "He didn't like the Webbers, and he had a correspondent in Croydon. I wonder why he didn't like the Webbers. I think, Duffield, that we'll have a spot of bread and cheese at the pub—it's past one—and after that we'll buzz along to the Hall. The C.C. told me Sir Henry was up in the air about the disturbance to his game."

CHAPTER VI
THE COMMON DENOMINATOR

BEFORE he left the village, Collier went back to the Grange. He did not enter the house this time, but he walked round the neglected garden. It was surrounded by a seven foot stone wall much over-grown by ivy. There was only one door in it, that leading into the churchyard. Collier tried it and found that it was locked.

"I suppose Brett has the key. Any signs of an entry elsewhere, Duffield?"

The sergeant shook his head. "I've been all round. A man could climb over easy enough, but not without making footmarks in the damp earth and treading down some of this stuff." He eyed the tangled mass of vegetation in the borders disapprovingly.

"Can't be certain one way or another after a week," said Collier. "Anything in the potting shed?"

He unlatched the door and peered into the dark and musty interior of a small lean-to building. Something rustled in a corner, and Duffield switched on his pocket torch.

"A rat. There are several old packing cases there."

Collier went across to look at them and poked about in the mouldy straw. "I expect he brought his china and his books in these when he moved in." He bent to examine an old discoloured label nailed to the side of one of the smaller cases.

"Glass with care. S. Killick, Esq., The Larches, Oliphant Road, West Croydon. Write that down Duffield. We could have got his previous address, of course, but this is going to save us a bit of trouble. Come along. We mustn't keep Sir Henry waiting."

"Does he expect us?" enquired the literal sergeant.

Collier was settling himself in the driving seat of his car. "You never know," he said cryptically.

The grounds of the Hall were very well kept. The lodge gates and the lodge itself were spick and span. There was a magnificent show of late chrysanthemums in the borders facing the house, a solid red brick mansion dating back to the reign of Queen Anne. The door was opened by a butler of impressive appearance.

"Can I see Sir Henry Webber?"

"Sir Henry is away."

"When will he be coming back?"

"I could not say. Perhaps you will leave your card."

"Is Lady Webber at home?"

"Her ladyship is engaged."

Collier took a card from his case. "Will you give her this? You can say I shall not keep her long."

It was his official card. The butler's face changed slightly as he looked from it to the two men waiting on the step. He became definitely human. "It isn't—" He broke off. "I beg your pardon, sir. Please step inside. I will inform her ladyship." He left them standing in the hall.

Collier glanced about him. There was nothing with which a connoisseur of the Queen Anne period could have found fault. Sir Henry had had the house decorated and furnished throughout by a firm that employed experts on its staff.

"What do you think of it?" he asked Duffield.

"Smells of the Tottenham Court Road," said the sergeant most unjustly. Collier smiled. He knew what his subordinate meant.

The butler returned. "Her ladyship will see you if you will come this way."

He showed them into an octagon morning room whose walls were hung with portraits of Restoration Court Ladies after Lely. Electric flames flickered in the artificial logs on the hearth. The sergeant glanced up at the plump faintly smirking faces and the liberal expanses of flesh. The heavy lidded enigmatic eyes of my Lady Castlemaine seemed to follow him as he moved. "Gosh!" he said. "Eight of them."

Lady Webber came in. She was a handsome woman, no longer in her first youth. The hardness that was a characteristic of her face was accentuated by a very heavy make up. Her thin lips were scarlet, her eyebrows plucked to a line. Underlying the faint insolence that Collier divined was her habitual manner with her social inferiors there was something else. Was it fear? He could not be sure.

"You wanted to see me, Inspector?" She did not ask them to sit down and remained standing herself, as if to indicate that the interview must be very short. "I can't imagine why."

"I understand that Sir Henry is away from home?"

"Yes."

She was twisting his card about in her hands. Her face was a mask, but her hands betrayed her anxiety. Collier did not speak at once. As he expected she was unable to wait. He saw her moisten her painted lips.

"They should have applied directly to me, not to the police. I am prepared to pay whatever may be necessary. I don't want Sir Henry to be—to be troubled."

Collier guessed that she had been about to say "to be told."

"Money can't do everything, Lady Webber," he said quietly.

"Nonsense," she flashed. "I shan't haggle. He's only a child."

"I think we must be at cross purposes," he said. "The body of a man was found on Sir Henry's land and Mr. Killick of the Grange was fatally injured the same night. I am the Scotland Yard officer in charge of the cases, and I hoped Sir Henry might be able to give me some assistance."

"Oh, that—" she could not conceal her relief.

"Sir Henry is most annoyed at the high-handed action of the police. He says he hasn't a single pheasant left in Hammerpot woods. I wouldn't ask him for help if I were you, Inspector. That would be the last straw. And, in any case, he is away from home. Good afternoon."

Collier ignored this very plain intimation. "I don't want to annoy anybody, Lady Webber, but murder is a capital crime. Sir Henry, I understand, is a magistrate. I am sure we can rely on him to overlook any personal inconvenience he may have suffered. I wanted to ask if Mr. Killick was personally known to him?"

"I think not."

"Was he known to you, Lady Webber?"

"He was not. I never even heard of the man until I read about the murder in the paper."

"I see. Thank you." Collier believed that she was speaking the truth. He tried not to be disappointed. Another thread which might have been a clue had broken off short. Lady Webber had rung the bell and the butler had come to show them out. They were half way down the drive before he spoke. "She's worried, Duffield, but not about the murder. The rich have their troubles. What a comforting reflection for the deserving—and even the undeserving—poor. They may be outside our scope, but I'd like to get to know a little more about that family. And we're in luck after all, sergeant. It's the cook's afternoon out."

A stout woman in a bright blue coat with a fur collar was preceding them down the drive. Collier looked back and made sure that they could not longer be seen from the house.

"Step out, Duffield. We must catch her up, pass her, and be in the car and ready to give her a lift to the village. She'll jump at it. It's over a mile to the corner where she can catch a bus and her shoes are too tight."

"What do you know about the cook?" enquired Duffield.

"Nothing much. But she's engaged to Tommy who isn't exactly, and his mother worked for Mr. Killick, who liked to hear all the gossip from below stairs about the Webbers. Why? Lady Webber said she didn't know him, and I believed her. But she's afraid of something. Come along—"

The two men walked on quickly, passing the woman in the blue coat within a hundred yards of the lodge. They were tinkering with their car when she came out on the road and turned, as Collier had hoped she would, to the left. He let her cover another fifty yards before he slid into the driving seat and let in the clutch. "Cooks have to stand a lot. Her ankles are swollen and I'll bet that patent leather is drawing her poor feet."

He drove on and stopped. "Can I give you a lift?"

Florrie Soper eyed him suspiciously. Her broad red face was even redder than usual for she had hurried over her dressing and Collier had been right about her shoes. The second housemaid and the between maid were always getting lifts from young men.

She had heard them boasting of the fellows they picked up, but she—Florrie—wasn't that sort. On the other hand, her feet were burning and she had almost certainly lost the bus.

"I'm going to Brock Green."

"That's on our way. Hop in."

Florrie accepted the invitation, but they had not gone very far when the car stopped again. The driver pulled various levers without any result. "Bother," he said, "she's broken down again. Duffield, see what you can do, there's a good chap."

"Perhaps, I'd better walk on," said Florrie.

The driver, who was the younger and the better looking of the two and who, so far, had done all the talking, begged her to be patient. "He'll put it right in a few minutes. Will you have a cigarette?"

Florrie giggled. "I don't mind if I do. I like a gasper now and again, but her ladyship's ever so fussy. She says half the country house fires are caused by the servants smoking in bed. She's a tartar. I don't know how I've stuck her all these years, though it's a good place in a way. No stint—"

"Sir Henry's a rich man," suggested Collier.

"You've said it. But riches don't bring happiness."

Duffield, pretending to do something with a spanner at the back of the car, grinned appreciatively as he listened to the steady flow of Miss Super's conversation.

"There's not much love lost between him and her ladyship now, though Mr. Higgins—that's the butler—says he was mad about her at first. She's all for her two boys and especially the eldest. He was at a posh school, but he left a bit sudden like and now he's at one of them crammers before going to Sandhurst to learn to be a soldier. There's been a bit of talk and it wouldn't surprise me to hear he's got into some kind of mess. He's a young terror and that's a fact—"

Collier had heard enough. He raised his voice.

"Haven't you got that fixed, Duffield?"

Duffield took the hint. "I think she'll move now."

She did. Ten minutes later Florrie had been put down at the end of the lane leading to her future mother in law's cottage and Collier was driving back to Durchester.

"You might drop into some of the bars in the town to-night, Duffield, and pick up what you can about the Webbers. I can get the main facts of his career through official channels, but I'd like to hear how they're regarded locally."

"The eldest boy must be hot stuff. I rather fancy his mother thought we'd come about something he'd been up to," said the sergeant with the air of one making a discovery.

"I grasped that," said Collier. "The tigress in defence of her cub. When she learned we were on this case she lost interest. I don't think the Webber clue is going to lead us anywhere, but there isn't anything else at present. It's a very puzzling affair. If Killick had been killed first we should have felt tolerably certain that the man in the wood was a member of a gang and had been shot during a dispute over the loot. We must be thankful that young Toby trespassed in his search for conkers. If that body hadn't been found until the next day we should all be working on that theory."

Duffield cleared his throat. "I suppose it is quite certain that Killick was alive at seven that evening?" he said mildly.

Collier recovered from a skid that brought both their hearts into their mouths.

"It was your fault. You shouldn't give me such shocks. If the vicar isn't straight I'll eat my hat. We've got his evidence. He took back a book he borrowed."

"I know. The postmistress said old Mr. Clare was a saint, and she wasn't handing out many bouquets. But I got an impression from one and another that the dear old gentleman was a bit of a muddler. Apt to give out the wrong hymn numbers and all that, you know. He may be mistaken. I mean he may have thought he took back that book he borrowed on Wednesday evening, when really it was on Tuesday. One day must be very like another in these villages," added Duffield, betraying some ignorance of life in the country.

"Yes. But we've got the corroborative evidence of Tommy Yates, who's not exactly, and Florrie Soper, the cook from the Hall, who has probably shortened the life of this car's springs. He hurried back to the vicarage to see them about the putting up of their banns." Collier drew up by the roadside. "This is where I stopped yesterday to ask my way of an A.A. scout, and here I picked up Toby Fleming and his dogs. They were Killick's dogs really. Mrs. Fleming offered to give them a home for the time being. They might be able to tell us something if they could speak, eh?"

There were dense woods on either side of the road and a drift of dead leaves underfoot. Beyond the sere hedgerows the tree trunks loomed, grey and ghostly through the dank autumnal mist. Collier had switched off his engine and the silence was so profound that the sergeant could hear the ticking of the watch on his wrist. He looked at the stile and the notice board threatening trespassers with prosecution, and at the path that was lost almost immediately in the tangled undergrowth and he shivered involuntarily.

"It's turning colder. I don't like this place. I can't understand that kid going into these woods again after what happened."

"Neither can I," said Collier. "He was scared, too. Of course, he may have been daring himself to do it. I'll be seeing him again."

He drove on and neither of them spoke again until they reached their destination. Collier told the sergeant to order tea in their private sitting-room and left him to run the car into the hotel garage while he went into the station to buy an evening paper. He was coming away from the book-stall when he met Inspector Brett.

"Haven't arrested anybody yet then?" said the local man, conversationally.

"Not yet."

"Too bad," said Brett with such an evident desire to be annoying that Collier, who was tired after his long and on the whole unsatisfactory day, found it harder than usual to keep his temper. His efforts to establish friendly relations seemed to have failed but, in a way, he sympathised with Brett. He nodded and passed on.

He felt better after tea. Afterwards he and the sergeant smoked their pipes in amicable silence until Duffield got up, after glancing at the clock. "Time to start my pub crawl."

He came back soon after ten and sat down rather heavily.

"I've had three ports and one gin and bitters," he announced.

"And stood how many? Well, you've made a note, I suppose, for the expenses account. Did you get anything?"

Duffield sighed. "It doesn't suit me to drink between meals. I'll take a soda mint. And I'm tired of synthetic blondes. Sir Henry's free with his money in subscription lists, but he's not popular. Poachers have got heavier sentences since he's been on the bench. He's bought some land that has been practically open to the public for the last twenty years, woods where the local children went blackberrying autumn after autumn and nobody minded. He's given his keepers orders not only to chivvy the kids off but to confiscate the fruit they've picked. He may be within his rights but the people resent that. There are rumours about the elder boy, nothing definite, but one man said, 'If he was a poor man's son he'd be sent to Borstal. Sir Henry's hard enough on our lads when they get into trouble.'"

"Is that all?"

"Yes."

"Well, I rang up the Yard and got some general information. Sir Henry's senior partner in a firm that made a lot in the war. They got a big contract. He married in 1918 a Miss Beryl Leila Smith. They have two sons. The elder, Godfrey, is sixteen. The younger boy, Keith, is still at a preparatory school. He is thirteen. Sir Henry bought Brock Green Hall two years ago. Before that they had a place at Croydon."

"Croydon," said Duffield.

"Yes. You remember the address on the packing-case in the potting shed. Killick came from Croydon. Of course," he added, with the air of one who wants to be fair to all parties, "lots of people do. There may be nothing in it, but it's all we've got so far. I've heard it's a nice place. We'll have a look at it. Better turn in now. We'll make an early start."

CHAPTER VII
THE KNEELING WOMAN

THE Flemings were at breakfast when the boy from the post office leant his red painted bicycle against the fence and clattered up the garden path. The two Scottish terriers who had been sitting on either side of Toby, expectant of crumbs, rushed to the door, barking furiously. Toby followed to hold them by their collars while his mother read the telegram.

"It's from Uncle Gilbert's nurse. She says he's sinking fast and has asked for me. I ought to go—but how can I leave you here alone, Toby?"

"I'll be all right with Sandy and Mac. Don't you worry, Mother. There's plenty of tinned food. You go."

The boy waiting at the door scrabbled his feet impatiently.

"Any answer, please?"

"Oh—yes—half a minute."

Sandra scribbled an affirmative and let the boy go. Half an hour later she was hurrying along the road to catch the bus. Toby went with her with the two dogs on their leads.

"You'll come back to-night? I'll have a scrumptious supper ready for you," he promised.

"Oh, Toby darling, I don't know—I may have to stay the night. If the poor old thing is terribly pleased to see me and—and sort of clings, I shan't be able to tear myself away—"

"No. I see that," said Toby.

"I hate the idea of leaving you alone in the cottage. Mrs. Yates might come if you asked her," said Sandra doubtfully.

"I don't need any old woman to look after me," said Toby. He tried to laugh. "I'll borrow the parrot from the vicar and pretend to be Robinson Crusoe. Come on, Mother, we've got to run. I hear the bus."

They reached the corner just in time to stop it. "Good-bye, Toby. Take care of yourself."

He shouted "Come back as soon as you can—" but he was not sure that she heard him. He walked slowly back along the lane.

She had only gone for two or three days at most—he was sure that she would not consent to remain away longer than that. And he could manage quite well, and it would be fun getting his own meals, and there was nothing to be afraid of. But why couldn't poor old Uncle Gilbert have waited another week or two until he had gone back to school? He had slept pretty well the last three nights, but then he had known that his mother was in the next room with her door open so that she could hear and run to him and wake him up if he had a bad dream—the dream of the Thing that hid behind a tree while he stood, rooted to the ground and knowing that he would die of sheer terror if he caught so much as a glimpse of it. After the first night he had not called her. He had managed to wake himself and to lie sweating and shaking without making a sound until the blessed realisation came to him that it was only a particularly beastly nightmare and that he was safe. He did not want his mother to know how bad it had been because she was apt to worry over him anyhow and to make him take malt extract when he did not really need it. If she had known she would not have left him even to go to Uncle Gilbert.

"But I've got you, Sandy, and you, Mac."

Sandy the Cairn, who was the more demonstrative of the two, responded rapturously, and the boy's flagging spirits rose. He went home to wash the breakfast dishes and make the beds. The dogs ran up and downstairs and whined at closed doors, puzzled by Mrs. Fleming's absence. Toby gave them each a bone and shut them up in the kitchen. He had what was left of a loin of lamb and he wrapped it in a bit of paper and took it out with him. He was going to make one more effort to persuade Kim, the yellow mongrel, to leave his master's grave.

He crossed the green to the church. The children were in school and there was nobody about at that hour. He passed through the lych gate and stopped a minute by the War Memorial to replace some of the flowers that had been blown out of their jam jars during the gale the night before. There were chrysanthemums from the cottage gardens and a bunch of violets from the vicar's frame. He looked up at the list of names, but he was really thinking anxiously about Kim and whether he would like the mutton bone.

The War did not mean anything to Toby. It was over before he was born. He put the flowers back because Mr. Clare was always so jolly decent, and he was so keen on the Memorial.

He went slowly round the church, leaving the path and walking round the sunken mounds half-hidden in the long grass, past head stones new and old. There had not been a funeral since that of Mr. Killick. His was the only new grave. There were no fading wreaths on it. There had been nobody to send flowers. But Kim was there. He was lying down and he did not move as Toby came near. Always before he had slunk away with his tail between his legs to hide behind the shed where the sexton kept his tools until the boy had gone, leaving some food for him.

"I believe he's going to let me come up to him to-day," thought Toby hopefully. He went forward very slowly.

"Kim. Good old Kim. Good dog."

Mac and Sandy had not forgotten their master. They still got up uneasily and went from room to room to look for him and dragged on their leads, whimpering with excitement when they saw a man in the distance who might be him, but Kim—

Kim was lying very quietly on his side. The yellow of his coat blended with the colour of the upturned lumps of clay. His eyes were open and glazed. A small beetle was climbing laboriously over his shoulder. Kim had been faithful unto death.

Toby dropped his mutton bone and burst out crying. He was stumbling away blindly and still fumbling for his handkerchief when Mr. Clare came out of the vestry door. He saw the small figure wandering forlornly among the graves and hurried towards it.

"Toby! My dear boy—what is the matter?"

Toby swallowed hard. "I—I haven't got a handkerchief—"

"Here—take mine," said the vicar hastily. He waited while Toby blew his nose.

"Your mother—"

"She's all right." Toby gulped down another sob. "I know I'm an ass, but I did so want him to get over it. I mean—it's sort of sad, isn't it?"

"I don't understand."

Toby indicated the far corner of the churchyard with a backward jerk of his head. "Kim," he explained. "He's lying there dead. He never touched the food I brought him."

The vicar stood looking down at him. "The love that will go to any length. It's rare, even in dogs. I tell you what I'll do, Toby, presently. I'll get old Merton's spade and bury him in his master's grave."

"And will you say the burial service?"

"Well, some of it, perhaps. And don't upset yourself over this, my dear boy. You did your best and have nothing to regret. Suppose you come back to the vicarage with me and wash your face before you go home."

Toby brightened up. "May I clean out the parrot's cage?"

The vicar smiled faintly. "If you like. Watkins will be grateful to you. It's not a job she cares about. You'll have to be a keeper at the Zoo when you grow up, Toby, as you're so fond of animals."

"That's a wheeze," said Toby eagerly, "I never thought of it. I wonder if Mother'd let me. I must ask her."

He followed the vicar through the gate that opened on to a path that led through the shrubberies to the little greenhouse where Mr. Clare tended his arums for the altar and some white chrysanthemums in pots and a few tomato plants and a vine that bore little white grapes in September. From the greenhouse they entered the house by the study window, and Mr. Clare rang the bell for his housekeeper, while the parrot, seeing Toby, left his perch and began to clamber along the bars of his cage. Toby went to him and the bird arched his scrawny neck and closed his beady black eyes in ecstasy as the boy stroked his rumpled feathers.

"Fancy that," cried Mrs. Watkins, coming into the room, "and he's ever so spiteful with me! You've got a way with you, Master Toby." She went to get the cakes and lemonade the vicar had asked for.

"Go up to the bathroom and wash your face before she comes back," Mr. Clare said. Toby obeyed. Usually he thought washing rather unnecessary, but cold water was refreshing when one had been blubbing, and his hands smelt unpleasantly of mutton fat. He made an agreeable lather of soap and brisk use of the vicar's hair brush. He was looking remarkably pink and sleek when he returned to the study. There was a jug of lemonade and a glass and a plate of Mrs. Watkins' famous rock cakes on the table. The vicar was sitting in his shabby old chair by the fire, filling his pipe. His big sinewy hands, thickened with arthritis, were unsteady and shreds of tobacco dropped from his fingers on to the rug. He looked up with his friendly smile as the boy came in.

"Feeling better? That's right. Help yourself. Dost thou think because thou art virtuous there shall be no more cakes and lemonade? Where does that come from?"

Toby answered promptly. "*Twelfth Night*. We did it last term in our form. But it's ale really. Cakes and ale. I say, these are scrumptious," he added with his mouth full.

"Have another." The old man's eyes, those curiously childlike blue eyes, were very kind. "How's your mother? I should have asked before."

Toby explained that Mrs. Fleming had been called away and might not be back for a day or two.

"Dear me. And she's left you all alone? I don't think in her place"—he looked at the boy rather doubtfully. "You're very young—"

"I shall be all right. Thanks awfully for this, sir. I expect I ought to be getting back now."

The vicar seemed to be following another train of thought. He answered absently, "Very well, my dear."

Toby hesitated. "Please, Mr. Clare, do you hear confessions?"

The vicar, who had been gazing at the fire, turned his grey head slowly in his direction.

"Sometimes. Why?"

"And whatever it was you'd keep it secret? I mean—that's the rule, isn't it?"

"Certainly. Have you anything to confess, Toby?"

"Well, as a matter of fact I have—at least—it's more that I want advice," the boy said in a very low voice. "It's—it's about that chap that was shot."

"I see. Sit down, Toby, and tell me all about it. I'll promise not to repeat a single word without your leave. Is that good enough?"

"Yes, sir. Thank you, sir."

The vicar watched him rather intently as he picked out a low chair from those ranged against the wall and drew it forward. The pattern of life, he was thinking, threads crossing and recrossing to make the design. Everything meant—

"It's like this," began Toby. "I told the police the truth—but I didn't tell them everything. I told them he wasn't quite dead. Well, he was pretty bad, but he could speak—after a bit—it was hard for him—he tried and tried—and then he said 'Don't tell them. The kneeling woman.' He said some more that I couldn't understand and then two words that were quite plain. 'Hidden under." He repeated that. 'Hidden under'—and then a lot of mumbling, and then he sort of slid down, and I said I'd get help and I left him."

"The kneeling woman," said the vicar blankly. "The poor man's mind was wandering."

"I couldn't make head or tail of it," said Toby, "but he said not to tell, and I didn't feel like telling Brett. I didn't want to have to think about it. But the other day when I was mounting one of my brass rubbings I tumbled to it—what he meant, I mean—"

"'Oh"—the vicar still looked bewildered, "and what did he mean?"

"It's the brass," explained Toby, "the brass in that church in the wood. I was going to have a look at it that afternoon, but finding him of course I didn't. It's mentioned in the book on brasses Mother gave me for my birthday. It's somebody called Eleanor Chapman, with her children underneath all in a row, the boys on one side and the girls on the other and skulls over the ones that died in infancy. It's described in the book as a kneeling figure. I tried to get there the day before yesterday, but it was so foggy and getting late and so I—I turned back when I'd gone a little way into the wood, and when I got back to the road that Inspector from the Yard was there, and he gave me a lift home. He's jolly decent, I think."

"The brass to Eleanor Chapman," said the vicar, "it's in the chancel with a strip of matting over it. I should know. I hold a service there once a month. There's no congregation."

"Ought I to tell the Inspector from the Yard, Mr. Clare?"

The vicar did not answer immediately. Then he said "Yes. But it may not be easy for you as you didn't speak at once. I tell you what, Toby. I'll write him a note asking him to call here to-morrow morning at ten o'clock if that will suit him, and you can be here. Then if he is inclined to be cross I can back you up."

"Oh—thank you," said Toby. "I'm awfully glad I got it off my chest."

"Yes. Though I'm not sure that yours is the right interpretation," said the vicar. "The chancel brass. Dear, dear. I've let my pipe go out. Well, ten to-morrow, Toby, and I wouldn't mention it to anybody else in the meanwhile."

"Oh, I shan't. Thanks most awfully, sir."

"Wait a bit," said the vicar. "Do you think anybody could have seen you talking to this unfortunate man?"

"I don't know," said Toby uneasily. "I had a sort of feeling there might be. It's easy to hide in a wood."

"Just so. Well, Toby, I want you to promise you won't go beyond the village alone for the present. You can amuse yourself at home, can't you? Perhaps I could lend you a book—I've some volumes of Henry that belonged to my boy—"

"That's all right, thank you, sir. I'm making some shelves. I've heaps to do." He went towards the door, but paused on the way.

"What'll I do if the Inspector from the Yard comes to-day? Shall I ask him to come over here?"

The vicar thought a moment. "I shall be out this afternoon. I have to visit some of my sick people. I really don't think it will matter if we defer telling him until to-morrow morning. We must not attach too much importance to what the poor fellow said. He may not have meant the brass. But I tell you what I'll do. I have to visit one old man in that direction. I have left the church open hitherto for the benefit of students of ecclesiastical architecture—there's a fine bit of Saxon work in the nave—but I'll lock the door and bring the key along so that no unauthorised person can get in before your Inspector. And now, Toby, you'd better run along."

Chapter VIII
MR. KILLICK'S HOBBY

COLLIER did not go over to Brock Green that day. He had driven up to Croydon, taking the sergeant with him. He called first at the police station and saw the superintendent, who happened to be a personal friend of his, and explained his errand.

"I'm on the double murder near Durchester. The chap who was shot hasn't been identified yet, but the other was a man called Killick, a retired business man who'd bought a large old-fashioned house in the village and lived there alone but for a woman who came in for an hour or two daily. He lived here until a year ago, and so did the local bigwig who has a posh place a few miles out, Sir Henry Webber. I want to know if these two men were connected in any way."

"I see. We ought to be able to get that. Sir Henry Webber was very well known, of course. Plenty of money and spent it. He gave a lot away. Some of the charity bazaars and fêtes were held on his grounds."

"He was popular?"

The superintendent hesitated. "He should have been, but I'm afraid he wasn't very. There was a fuss about one of the maids who had got into trouble. The story goes that she was turned out at a moment's notice on a streaming wet night and had to walk two miles before she could get any conveyance. I don't know how much truth there was in the yarn. These things get exaggerated. But I should say from the little I saw of him that he could be ruthless, and so could she—her ladyship—I mean."

Collier grinned. "You don't have to tell me about her. I saw her yesterday."

"Did you ask her if she knew Killick?"

"Not directly. Yes, I did, though. She said no quite definitely to that, and I think she was telling the truth. But I didn't see her husband—"

"Where did Killick live?"

"The Larches, Oliphant Road.

The superintendent whistled. "So that's the man. I can't imagine him knowing the Webbers. He lived like a hermit. Seemed harmless enough. I remember on two or three occasions the constables on that beat got rather worked up about him because he kept a light burning all night in a sort of shed at the end of the garden. We kept an eye on the place for a bit, but nothing ever happened. He paid the tradesmen regularly and gave nobody cause to complain. Perhaps you'd like to have a look at the house. It has stood empty ever since he left. I've seen Battimore's board at the gate, so I expect they have the keys."

"Is it anywhere near Sir Henry's place?"

"No. It's the other side of Croydon. Frankly, Collier, I think the fact that they both migrated to the neighbourhood of Durchester is a pure coincidence. Still, anything we can do at any time—"

Battimore, the house agents in the High Street, produced the key of The Larches.

"It's a very nice property if you don't want all the latest improvements. It would want doing up, of course, but I think the owner would be willing to meet the reasonable requirements of a tenant taking the house on a fairly long lease."

It had evidently not yet occurred to the clerk in the office to connect the owner of the property with the crime he had read about in the papers or he would have shown more interest. Collier took the key and went back to his car.

The house proved to be an ugly barrack-like structure of slate and stucco, standing well back from the road and screened from it by unkempt shrubberies. The rooms were high pitched and most of them were darkened by windows whose panes were encrusted with the grime of years. Two rooms on the ground floor at the back were rather cleaner. Collier made a rapid survey of the house.

"Obviously he lived here as he did at Brock Green, furnished two or three rooms and kept the rest shut up. A detestable arrangement but sensible enough if you occupy a large house and don't keep servants. We'll have a look at this shed at the end of the garden where he burned a light all night."

On their way down the garden, which was choked with weeds, they passed some decaying wooden structures nailed to the back wall of a rickety fowl house.

"Rabbit hutches," said Duffield.

The shed itself was a portable building and in much better condition. It was lit by a large skylight and was fitted with a small sink furnished with a waste pipe running into the ground outside and served from a rain water tank. There were some fitted shelves, but any movable furniture had been taken away. Collier was chiefly interested in some fragments of broken glass that had been swept into a corner. "Reminds me of my school lab," he said. "I wonder if Mr. Killick's hobby was some form of chemical research. Why didn't he carry on with it at the Grange? Or am I getting too much from this stuff? We'll take that glass with us, Duffield. I fancy the manufacturers would be able to tell us if it's the kind that is used for retorts."

"He made scents, didn't he?" said Duffield, "and the muck women put on their faces."

"Yes, of course. The May Morning perfumery and cosmetics. Sounds charming, doesn't it." He turned the tap over the sink and a few drops of water, brown with rust, trickled out. "I think we'll take the key back to Battimore's. We'll drop it in their letter box. The young man in the office may have put two and two together by this time and I don't want to answer questions."

They carried out this programme, and then Collier went into a chemist's shop across the road, bought a tube of tooth paste, and asked the assistant if he stocked the May Morning products.

"Yes, sir. We've got the May Morning compacts and beauty sets, the May Morning perfumes; daisy, buttercup, clover, and meadow sweet in the two shilling and three and sixpenny sizes, and the May Morning hair remover, guaranteed to remove superfluous hair in ten minutes."

"That sounds rather drastic," said Collier.

"It's perfectly harmless. There are full instructions with each bottle. We have quite a good sale for it."

"Where is it made?"

The assistant looked at him doubtfully and asked him to wait a minute. He went away and after an interval an older man in the white overall of a dispenser came out of the room at the back of the shop.

"You were making some enquiries about the May Morning products? We can't be held responsible for any injury caused by misuse. There are full instructions—"

"That's all right," said Collier reassuringly. "I've no complaints to make."

The chemist looked relieved. "Well, I'm glad to hear it, though not surprised. The May Morning don't put out anything cheap or nasty. If they did we shouldn't deal with them."

"Quite. I want the address of the manufacturers, because I want to get some information through them about a former partner in the firm."

"Oh—I see. Well, there's no secret about it. Their traveller called about three weeks ago and we renewed our stock. The May Morning factory is in Warwickshire, Stratford-on-Avon. They issued a booklet advertising their cosmetics with quotations from Shakespeare's songs a year or two ago. Have we any of those booklets left, Mr. Collins? We haven't. Well, May Morning, Ltd., Stratford-on-Avon, will find them."

Collier went back to his car and climbed into the driver's seat beside Duffield.

"May morning and murder," he said as he let in the clutch. "It sounds incongruous, but they both begin with an M."

"Where are we going now?" asked Duffield patiently. It was past three o'clock and they not had any lunch.

Collier, glancing round, observed his subordinate's martyred expression and chuckled unfeelingly.

"You can look forward to high tea at the Station Hotel. We ought to get there between five and six." He accelerated in reply to a signal from a lorry in front.

He had been on the case for two days and he had accumulated a number of facts, but he could not feel that he had made any real progress. He had not even satisfied himself that the two crimes were related. He had been working a few weeks earlier on a shop murder. Superficially the crime bore some resemblance to the one he was tackling now. The old shop keeper had been killed like Mr. Killick by a blow from some blunt instrument that had fractured his skull, but the motive of the killer in the shop case had been obvious. He had robbed the till. The price of blood had been two pounds fourteen shillings and three pence half-penny, and the wretched youth who had committed the crime had spent it all in three days in treating chance-met acquaintances at dance halls and picture palaces. But there had been no such simple motive in either of these crimes.

Collier, sitting over the fire in his sitting-room at the Station Hotel that evening made another attempt at reconstruction. As usual when Duffield was with him he thought aloud and looked to the sergeant now and again for a comment or suggestion.

"The unknown man who looked like a foreigner. We'll call him X. We've no record of his finger-prints at the Yard, but he may belong to the underworld. If you can't be good be careful. He may have been careful. He had something in his possession, or had recently got rid of something that was badly wanted by Y, and probably Z. Had they arranged to meet in Hammerpot wood? It seems unlikely. The wood is preserved and the interview might be cut short by an irate gamekeeper at any moment. Did he, knowing that they were chasing him, get out of his car and run into the wood to either hide or destroy this thing they were after? It's a possible explanation. They followed, shot him down and searched him, leaving the loose change in his pockets but slitting his coat lining and removing his shoes. What sort of object would you sew into a lining or hide in your shoe, Duffield?"

"It might be a diamond, something of that sort," hazarded the sergeant. "Or some kind of paper."

"Well, it's not much use guessing, but I think we're safe in assuming that whatever it was Y and Z didn't find it."

"And then the kid came along looking for conkers." The sergeant drew at his pipe. "I think perhaps it was lucky for him he didn't arrive five minutes earlier," he said.

Collier was staring at the fire. "Y and Z went back to their car which they had left on the road on the western side of the wood—

the road that leads to Sir Henry Webber's place. The dead man's car or his motor cycle would be there, too, and it wouldn't do to leave it about as it might lead to his identification. Y takes charge of it and buzzes off. He'd want to get rid of it. Query. A deep pond. Make a note of that, Duffield. Get a list of all the ponds in the district and put the local people on to it."

"Very good, sir."

"Had they seen the finding of their victim by Toby? You're right, Duffield. That's important. I'd feel happier about the boy if I was sure—but of course they know now anyway. It was in the papers. Now there's a gap that we can't fill in. Those two shots were fired a little before four, and Killick was killed at any time after seven. If we assume that the Grange was the next objective it was a dark night and they may have waited in the churchyard or in the garden of the Grange itself until the coast was clear and they had seen the vicar go back—"

"Or suppose they were known to Mr. Killick. They may have been there when the vicar called. The two men may have quarrelled later—"

"They may have been there," said Collier, "but I don't think they quarrelled. Killick was struck down from behind as he was showing his visitors out. And then—the drawers of the writing table were turned out and most of their contents burned. Paper. I wonder if you're right, Duffield. It might be a will. And yet—no, we haven't really got a line on the thing yet."

He broke off as the Boots came in with a letter.

"Note for you, sir."

It had come by hand and was from the superintendent.

"Dear Mr. Collier," he wrote, "the enclosed came for you by the last post. I suppose we shall hear from you when you have any progress to report. They seem to think we can work miracles." He turned to the enclosure which was addressed in a sprawling unformed hand to Mr. Inspector Collyer, Pollice Station, Durchester.

"Gosh. It's from our young friend Toby Fleming."

"What does he want?"

"DEAR MR. INSPECTOR,

"I think perhaps you'll come to-day, but in case you don't will you please come to-morrow morning without fale as I have something to say and Mr. Clare thinks I ought at ten at the vicarage. I did want to do right, but it's differkult.

"Yours truly,

"CHRISTOPHER FLEMING."

Collier smiled as he re-read the note. "He came a cropper over *difficult*. I was going to look him up anyway. I felt sure the boy had something on his mind. He needed more careful handling than he got from Brett. Well, we shall see."

CHAPTER IX
NO HERO

WHEN Toby had written his letter to the Inspector he looked in his mother's desk for stamps and found none. That did not matter as he would have to go to the post office anyhow to post it, and he had fivepence left from his week's pocket money. The post office was also the general shop of the village and a recognised centre of social life, but, as it happened, there was no other customer there when Toby went in and, after buying his stamp and dropping his letter in the box, asked for an ounce of acid drops.

"Sure you don't mean a quarter, dearie?" Mrs. Beamish shook the sweets out of the jar with a lavish gesture. Toby Fleming was a favourite of hers. "Your ma's gone off and left you, I hear."

"I expect she'll be back to-morrow," said Toby. "I only want an ounce, please," he added rather anxiously.

"That's all right, son." She leaned over the counter to look at the two terriers. "You keep 'em on their leads, because of my cat," she warned him. "Poor Mr. Killick wasn't one to come down the village much. Kept himself to himself, but whenever I passed the Grange on my way to church I'd see those dogs looking through the gate and barking at passers by. There was another one. I've heard he won't leave the grave?"

Toby answered briefly. "He's dead.

"Well, there now. Did you ever!"

"He wouldn't eat."

"Have you had any trouble with these two?"

"They're always listening. I think they expect him to come back. But they're settling down. I'm hoping we'll be allowed to keep them."

Mrs. Beamish was evidently prepared with other questions but another customer came in and enabled Toby to escape.

He went home and made his midday meal of Heinz baked beans and tinned apricots, and spent the afternoon happily enough working at his shelves in the shed at the end of the garden. He went in when the light failed. The fire in the sitting-room had gone out and he relit it and presently was sitting down cosily to a good tea with jam and cakes, and carrying on a one-sided conversation with Mac and Sandy who sat on either side of him on the look out for crumbs.

Somebody had sent him *Treasure Island* for his birthday. Sandra had exclaimed when he undid the parcel. "Haven't you got that already? You haven't? My poor Toby, I've neglected your education shamefully." He had not begun it and this seemed a good opportunity. He cleared the table, put the dogs' biscuits in soak for their supper at seven, and settled down by the fire with what was left of his bag of sweets. The dogs had their meal in due course and Toby went back to his book. He could not leave it now, he wanted to know what was going to happen next.

But Pew and the blind beggar and Long John Silver are sinister company for a boy who is alone in a house at night for the first time in his life, and after a while Toby began to look round him rather uneasily at the door. Suppose it opened inch by inch? He started when a floor board creaked in the passage. His mother had not had time to do the lamps before she went. If the oil failed he might be left in the dark. In any case it was nine o'clock and past his usual bedtime. He went to the front door to let the dogs out for their last run. They rushed down the path together, barking frantically, but they always did that, and it meant nothing. But they were gone longer than usual, or perhaps it only seemed longer to Toby, who wanted to shut the door. The night was clammy and cold, with a fine rain falling, and the darkness was profound.

And it was still, so still that Toby's voice sounded unnaturally loud to himself when he called the dogs in. They came at last. He stopped to turn the key in the lock and shoot the bolts before he followed them into the living room. He saw then that they had got hold of something to eat in the garden. They were both licking their chops. When Toby began to scold them Mac turned his head away guiltily and Sandy rolled over on his back and waved his paws appealingly.

"I've half a mind to make you sleep downstairs," said Toby severely, but he knew he would not carry out his threat. He turned down the lamp, lit his candle and went up to his bedroom. Mac and Sandy ran up in front of him and were already curled up in their basket and fast asleep when he began to undress. Toby decided to get into bed before he said his prayers. On other nights Mac and Sandy had had games with him, running after him and trying to lick his bare feet. He spoke to them but evoked no response. They slept on, breathing stertorously. It was queer that they should be so tired when they had less exercise than on other days.

Toby got into bed, blew out the candle, and said his prayers. He was not worrying. He had written to the Inspector, and his mother would almost certainly be home again to-morrow. He snuggled down under his blankets and within ten minutes he, too, was sleeping. He was sleeping too soundly to hear the crash of broken glass in the room below, but it was at that moment that he began to dream. He dreamed that he was lying in a hole that had been scooped in the earth at the foot of a tree in Hammerpot woods. Two men were working with spades, filling in the hole. There were lumps of clay on his legs and on his chest. A light flashed up and vanished and something pressed down on his eyes. He tried to cry out but his mouth was too dry.

A man's voice said, "That will do. Keep quiet and you won't be hurt."

Toby's heart seemed to miss a beat. He realised that he was not dreaming now. He was awake and lying in his bed. The weight on his chest increased. His eyes had been covered by a bandage and a bit of his hair had been caught in the knot so that it hurt when he tried to move his head on the pillow.

"Now then," said the voice, "you know what we've come for. We saw you in the wood. What did he say to you?"

Toby's heart was thudding now like a machine out of gear under the heavy hand that held him down. He wasn't going to answer. Nothing would induce him to speak against his will. Things like this happened to all the heroes of all the adventure stories he had read. There was always one of the gang less brutal than the rest who intervened with "Let the kid alone. I like his grit—"

"What did he say?"

Another voice said something unintelligible. The weight on Toby's legs shifted a little. He heard a shuffling crackling sound which he later knew to have been the striking of a match. It was followed by an excruciating pain that flashed on a red hot wire of agony from the thumb of his left hand to his brain. The hand that had pressed him down on the bed was clamped over his mouth, stifling his cries. The pain faded away as he lost consciousness.

He woke again to find his head and hair drenched with water and his throat and lips burning. Somebody had been trying to give him brandy. He was shaking all over.

The voice said, "We don't want to hurt you again, What did he say? Quick—"

Toby gulped. 'He said 'Don't tell them. The kneeling woman. Hidden under—' That's all he said."

"What did he mean? Do you know?"

"No."

There was a murmur of conversation. Toby did not understand a word of it. He was hardly listening. He felt weak and dazed and his thumb was still hurting him, though now the pain was bearable.

The first voice said, "Do you swear that is all? Don't try to deceive us. We should find out and do something to make you sorry. You may get police protection after this, but you wouldn't get it for ever. We'd wait and then come—and you'd be sorry. Do you understand?"

"Yes."

"'Don't tell them. The kneeling woman. Hidden under.' That was all?"

"Yes."

"Why did he stop there?"

"His mouth filled with blood," said Toby faintly.

His eyes were bandaged but somehow he knew that his tormentor nodded, as if satisfied. "I believe that's true. He couldn't invent that."

The weights were lifted from Toby's legs and his chest. Stealthy sounds followed, the door of the room was softly opened and closed again, the stairs creaked.

Toby lay quite still for a while. He was feeling sick and his thumb ached persistently. Presently he was able to move a little. He turned over on his side and fumbled with his right hand at the knot of the bandage that had covered his eyes. He pulled it and threw it on the floor. He lay still again, huddled under his blankets and with his knees drawn up to his chin, and scalding tears filled his eyes slowly and overflowed and soaked into his pillow. He wasn't like the heroes in the adventure stories. He couldn't stand pain. He hadn't any grit, or any guts, or anything. He was a beastly funk, and a cry baby. "Look at me b-blubbing now," he mourned. As if the pillow wasn't wet enough already with the water those brutes had poured over him. He made an effort and turned the pillow over. On the other side it was almost dry. His anguished snufflings subsided gradually. He slept.

Collier started for Brock Green soon after breakfast, leaving Sergeant Duffield to make a few enquiries in the town regarding the foreigners on the list Brett had given him. He wanted to see Mrs. Fleming before he went to the vicarage, so he drove to the village by the road that passed the old forge and stopped his car at her gate. He was walking up the garden path when he noticed that the window of the living room was wide open and one pane of glass shattered. He looked up quickly, and his eyes, trained to observe every detail of a scene, noted the curtains that had not yet been drawn in the bedroom and that no smoke was issuing from the chimney. His lips tightened. Had he made a fearful—an irremediable mistake? He tried the door, found it locked, and did not waste time in knocking. He could get in by the window, but before he did so he took careful note of the footprints on the wet earth of the border.

Nothing had been disturbed in the living room. A few sparks still lived among the grey wood ash on the hearth. A lamp stood on the table and beside it lay a very sticky little paper bag that had held sweets and a copy of *Treasure Island*. He went to the foot of the stairs and called out.

"Is anybody up?"

There was no reply. Collier's spirits sank. He dreaded he knew not what. Mrs. Fleming had been nice to him. He had liked her, and he had liked the boy. Had he failed them by not realising that they were in danger?

He went quickly up the steep cottage stairs, lifted the latch of the door facing him, and went in. He caught his breath as he saw the small figure lying so still under the tumbled bed-clothes, and then as he leaned over it and heard the regular breathing he was conscious of an immense relief.

And yet—there was something wrong. And where was Mrs. Fleming? Toby's eyes opened. He gazed up into Collier's face for an instant without any sign of recognition. Then, as he tried to sit up, he winced.

"It hurts," he said. "It wasn't a dream then. I'm glad you've come."

Collier smiled at him reassuringly. "I'm here, and everything in the garden is lovely. But what happened exactly? Can you tell me?"

"They came in the night—two of them." Toby's face changed and his lips began to quiver as he remembered. "They—they made me tell them what I was going to tell you this morning. They tied something over my eyes, and they did this—"

Collier's eyes hardened as he looked at the angry red sore on the boy's thumb. It was the mark of a recent burn.

"We must put some dressing on this. Has your mother got a medicine chest? Where is your mother?"

"She's away. She went away yesterday to see poor Uncle Gilbert. We didn't think—and there were the dogs—" Toby broke off.

"Oh, please—will you see what's happened to Mac and Sandy?" he begged.

Collier went over to the dogs' basket, lifted Sandy out and set him on his legs. He fell over at once and lay where he fell.

"He's not dead?" cried Toby shrilly.

"No. I should say they've both been doped."

"They got hold of something in the garden last night just before I came up to bed."

Collier was frowning. "You shouldn't have been left here alone. Thank God it's no worse. How do you feel, apart from the thumb?"

Toby thought a moment. "Hungry."

Collier was sitting on the bed holding Toby's wrist and feeling for his pulse. "Splendid," he said. "Now, I've got a first-aid outfit in my car. I can go and fetch it and be back in three minutes. You won't mind being left?"

"No." Toby swallowed hard. "I—I suppose you think I'm an awful coward—telling them."

Collier shook his head. "No, I don't. Don't let that worry you, old man. I should probably cough up everything and a bit over myself if anybody applied a lighted match to me."

"You wouldn't," said Toby with conviction.

"Well, anyhow, don't brood. I'll fetch the lint and the doings and then you can wash and dress while I prepare a spot of breakfast."

"What time is it?"

"Twenty past nine. You'll feel better when you've wolfed down some of the eggs I'm going to scramble. We won't keep the vicar waiting, and we'll have the whole story then."

CHAPTER X
THE HIDING PLACE

COLLIER left Toby to eat his breakfast while he drove down the village to the post office where he remained for some twenty minutes shut up in the telephone call box.

"Two men broke into the Flemings' cottage last night. The boy was alone, and they forced him to repeat something that was said to him by the man who was shot in the woods. It sounds like gibberish to me but it may be a clue to the place where he hid what they were after. They had searched his clothing, you know, without taking his money. His pocket book was gone and everything that might have established his identity. They hadn't left the country. That's one thing. We'd almost certainly catch them if they made a bolt, with our men at all the ports, but I'm afraid they're too clever for that . . . yes, they hurt the kid, but not badly. It was a well planned job. Doped meat for the dogs. Rubber gloves of the kind one buys at Woolworth's. I found one behind a bush near the gate. Several footprints on the garden borders, but they won't be much use. . . . No. The boy didn't see them. They tied something over his eyes. Yes, I'll put the local people on to trying to trace their car. They must have used one. But it was a dark night."

He hurried back to his car and drove back to the cottage to pick up Toby who was waiting for him at the gate.

"Both dogs have been sick," he announced.

"You don't surprise me."

Collier drove round the green and, seeing the vicar's tall black figure bending over the flowers at the foot of the War Memorial, stopped at the lych gate and hailed him.

He straightened his back and stood for a moment looking towards them and shading his eyes with his hand before he replied.

"Ah, it's you, Inspector. Won't you drive on to the vicarage gate. Ring the bell and tell Mrs. Watkins I'm coming. I shan't be a minute."

They did as he asked and gave his housekeeper his message.

"I should hope so indeed," said Mrs. Watkins indignantly. "He's been out since before eight, in the church and messing about with the flowers. I said to him before he started, 'What about your breakfast, sir?' 'Never mind that,' he says. 'I'll have a cup of tea presently.' He ought to take more care of himself at his age."

She showed them into the study and left them. The vicar joined them almost at once, and made them welcome with anxious hospitality.

"Sit down, both of you. There's a good fire. Pleasant these chilly mornings, eh?" He spread his own hands, which were blue with cold, to the blaze. "Our church isn't heated, unfortunately. Well, Toby, this is the result of our conversation yesterday suppose. You got into touch with the Inspector as I suggested? Good. Open confession is good for the soul. You're going to make a clean breast of everything."

"He's done that already, Vicar. A good deal has happened since you saw Toby yesterday, Mr. Clare," said Collier, and added a brief account of Toby's nocturnal adventure.

The vicar did not conceal his horror. "My dear boy—you should not have been left alone—but your dear mother was not to know."

"I'll see that he gets adequate protection after this," said Collier. "And meanwhile, about these last words of the fellow who was shot, I haven't said much about it, Toby, but you weren't playing the game in keeping them to yourself."

"I know," mumbled Toby, looking chastened. Collier turned to the vicar. "Do you agree with Toby that the kneeling woman may be a brass in the chancel of the church in Hammerpot woods?"

It was the vicar's turn to look guilty. "I'm so sorry, Inspector. I thought with Toby that it would be best to lock the church door and bring away the key. Usually it is kept hanging on a nail in the porch. I was going out that way to visit a sick man. It slipped my memory. I was trying to comfort and reassure old Tasker. He's not long for this world. I forgot. Peccavi. Peccavi."

Collier's lips tightened, but he only said rather dryly, "It's a pity, certainly,"

"You should have tied a knot in your handkerchief, sir," said Toby. "Are we going to the church now to look, Mr. Collier?"

"We are. You will come with us, Vicar?"

"If I may. I am greatly interested."

"Come along then."

Mrs. Watkins, coming up the kitchen stairs with tea and butter and a boiled egg for her master, heard the front door closed and was just in time to see the two men going down the drive, with Toby running on in front to open the gate and scramble into the back of the car. His spirits, which had been temporarily damped by Collier's censure, were rising again.

"Have you got a theory, Mr. Collier?

"I'm trying to collect facts, Toby. Theories are dangerous things. Just hand over that rug for the vicar."

"You must not pamper me, Inspector," said the old man gaily.

The rain clouds had vanished during the night and the sky was a pale clear blue. The thatched roofs of the cottages round the green were steaming in the heat of the sun, and the woods that had looked so dreary in the falling rain were glowing with the gold of birch and chestnut leaves and the copper of the beeches.

Collier stopped his car, at a word from the vicar, at a gate on the left hand side of the road.

A path leading into the wood was littered for a hundred yards with cigarette cartons, banana skins, orange peel, and torn paper.

"This is a favourite picnic place with the Durchester people during the summer, but not, of course, at this time of the year. I hear Sir Henry Webber has tried to stop it, but it is difficult because this path through the wood is a right of way. It leads to the church and then on to the lower road."

"Do all these people come to visit the church!"

The vicar smiled faintly. "I hardly think so. A few may just look inside. But the greater number are probably unaware of its existence. It is hidden from the road by a turn in the path."

"Why was it built in a wood?" asked Collier.

"It was attached to a priory, but the monastic buildings have disappeared, though I fancy you might come across some of the foundations if you poked about among these clumps of briars. Probably the stones and bricks were carted away to build some of the cottages at Brock Green, including yours, Toby."

Toby had lingered behind to fill his pockets with nuts, and had just rejoined them.

They had come to the church. It was so small, so old and grey, with its lichen-stained buttresses and its roof of Horsham stones that it looked more like some animal, with a back humped against wind and weather, a hedgehog or a badger crouching in its bed of nettles and osiers, than the work of men's hands. The vicar turned the door handle and the door swung back on creaking hinges. The interior was lighter than Collier had expected, for the windows were filled with clear glass. It had a musty smell. The old box pews filled the nave, and there was a three decker pulpit of worm-eaten oak. The altar was bare.

"I keep the altar vessels locked up in the cupboard in the vestry," the vicar explained, "and only put them out when I hold a service. The brass, you see, is on the floor in the chancel a little to the left of the altar."

Toby had seen it first and was already kneeling on the stone floor beside it. He looked up eagerly as the two men approached.

"It's not the best period, of course, but it's jolly good. You'll let me take a rubbing of it some time, Mr. Clare? I was coming to give it the once over, you know, that day—"

"You told the Durchester police you were looking for conkers," Collier reminded him.

"Well, that's why I left the footpath. What do you think we're going to find under this, Inspector? It might be a clue to hidden treasure."

The brass represented a woman wearing the voluminous gown and starched ruff of the late sixteenth century. She was kneeling at a fald stool, and her four boys and five girls were ranged decorously in a kneeling row behind her. The name of Eleanor Chapman and the date 1578 were just decipherable in the worn lettering at the foot of the panel.

Collier was examining the three screws that attached the sheet of metal to the stone beneath. There were numerous scratches on the surface and the screws were loose in their sockets, so loose that he got them up easily with his pocket knife.

"We're a day late for the fair, I fancy," he said as he cautiously lifted the panel.

"Nothing!" said Toby. "What a swizzle! I wish I hadn't told them!"

Collier was examining the under part of the brass. "I'll have to take this away with me and have it examined for finger prints, Vicar. You shall have it back when we've done with it."

"I fear I am to blame for forgetting to lock the church door yesterday afternoon," said the vicar.

"Don't let that worry you, sir. They'd have got in anyhow. What I can't understand—" he checked himself. "I must take this to Durchester, but I'll run you back to the village first."

They left the church together, Collier carrying the brass.

"It's lucky it's a small one," said Toby. "There's one eight feet long at Cowfold. It was clever of them to guess what he meant by the kneeling woman, wasn't it."

"Yes," said Collier. "That's an interesting point, Toby. It may even narrow the field of search." He glanced round at the vicar who was lagging a little. "Will you take my arm, sir?"

"Thank you. Thank you. I confess I should be glad of it. I feel a little tired."

Collier suited his pace to that of the old man and they went slowly back to the road. Toby, who had several questions to ask, was restrained by something aloof in the Inspector's manner. He was quick to realise that Collier did not want to be talked to just then.

Collier was disappointed at the negative results of their expedition. He was acquiring facts, but the case, as a whole, was as great a puzzle as ever. And yet he had learned something. The impression left on the under part of the brass was that of a long envelope of the type used by lawyers for holding documents. Was it for this that two men had died? It was maddening to think that if he had known what he knew now a day earlier he might have the solution of the mystery in his hand. He was silent during the drive back to the village. Mr. Clare was set down at the vicarage gate.

"I hope you've forgiven me for being so inept," he said humbly.

"My own memory isn't infallible, sir. May I come in again some time if I think you can help me? You knew Mr. Killick better than anyone else about here."

"Yes. I suppose I did. Come any time."

Collier sat for a moment with his hands on the steering wheel, watching the tall figure in shabby clerical black trudging rather wearily up the drive. He had just remembered that Mr. Clare had not had the cup of tea his housekeeper was to have brought him.

Nearly twelve o'clock, and he was still fasting. No wonder the poor old gentleman had looked rather blue about the lips.

"He wants looking after, Toby."

"Mother says all men do. Please, Mr. Collier, Mother's come back. I can see her standing at the gate."

"It's a long way off. Are you sure?"

"Yes. May I go, please."

He was struggling with the door handle.

"Stay where you are. I can drive round and get there more quickly than if you ran across the green."

Sandra Fleming moved forward impulsively as the car stopped in front of her gate. Toby hurled himself out and ran to her. Collier waited to turn off the engine before he followed. It was an odd fact that Mrs. Fleming, though she was so simple and natural herself, always made him feel clumsy and ill at ease. "Thank God you've come." she said.

"Were you alarmed?" He knew as he uttered the words that it was a foolish question.

"I was terrified. The broken window, and a fire burning and the remains of breakfast on the table, and nobody there. It was like the mystery of the *Marie Celeste*. I found the dogs upstairs, and they seemed very sorry for themselves, and they'd been sick on your bedroom carpet, Toby."

"They'd been drugged."

"Good Heavens."

"May I come in and explain?" said Collier.

"Please. I do want to know. Toby, darling, why is your hand bandaged?"

"He'll tell you. I want to see the dogs."

He ran up the path to the cottage. His mother and Collier followed.

"Toby, never mind the dogs now. They've both had some milk I warmed for them, and they've gone back to their basket.

Put another log on the fire, dear. Did you have any difficulty in lighting it?"

"The Inspector lit it. He cooked the breakfast, too. You see, I was still in bed when he came."

"I don't see," said Sandra. She looked at Collier.

"It was like this," he began.

Sandra listened to his account of all that had happened since he received Toby's letter the evening before. She did not speak again until he had done. She was holding Toby's right hand, the uninjured hand, rather tightly in both her own.

"I ought never to have gone," she said.

"You couldn't have foreseen such a thing. I didn't. They won't come again. They've got what they wanted. But I'll feel happier if you will consent to have a man here at night until we've cleared this up," said Collier.

"Thank you. I won't say no. I shan't feel very safe until you've caught those brutes. Do you mean a policeman?"

"Yes. I'll see the local superintendent about it, and send a glazier along to get your window mended."

He got to his feet. "I must get back to Durchester now." His obvious embarrassment made him seem younger than usual. Sandra, who had risen too, found herself wondering how old policemen had to be before they were made Inspectors. She smiled as she held out her hand.

"Thank you for looking after Toby."

"But I didn't. I am ashamed of my carelessness," he said earnestly.

"Come and see us again."

She wondered if she was being wise when she saw how his face lit up.

"May I? Thanks awfully. I will."

He found it difficult to prevent his thoughts from straying as he drove back to Durchester by the lower road, stopping at the A.A. box on the way. He found the sergeant in their private sitting-room at the Station Hotel.

"You look as if you'd got on to something, Inspector."

"Do I? Well, let's have dinner first. Then we'll swop yarns."

The sergeant agreed and they went down to the farmer's ordinary, which, as it was market day, was crowded, and consumed boiled beef and carrots and currant dumpling washed down with beer from the local brewery.

When they were upstairs again, sitting by the fire, and had filled their pipes the sergeant said, "I've been through that list."

Collier prepared to listen sympathetically. No one knew better than he did what hard and thankless work was entailed by the routine of their profession. He had done a good deal of it in his time. He remembered how he had called on every ironmonger in Birmingham to enquire after a customer who had come in during the previous March to buy an unusually long screw, and his search through the slums of Portsmouth for a woman of about forty with a slight cast in her left eye.

Duffield produced his notebook and turned over the pages.

"The organ grinder lives in Hodder's Rents, name Contarini Giuseppe. He came from Naples, has been forty years in England, and his wife was English. He has his regular beats. The constable I spoke to said he would be playing down Dominion Road this morning, and he was. He's an old man and walks lame. He plays along the London Road and in Park Crescent on Wednesday afternoons, and he gets a cup of tea from the cook at Number 17. He was there as usual the Wednesday before last, at the time of the murder. The chap who used to play the violin at the cinema was operated on three weeks ago for appendicitis and is still in the Cottage Hospital. The teacher of languages is a Professor Muller. He calls himself a Swiss. The police haven't anything against him. He lives in quiet lodgings and his landlady speaks highly of him. He teaches French and German in all the schools round about and has a motor bicycle to get from place to place. He attends a girls' school at Leatherhead on Wednesday mornings. He has that afternoon free. His landlady says that the Wednesday before last he was out all day and did not return until between one and two in the morning. He told her he had gone up to London from Leatherhead and had visited a theatre. She saw the programme lying about in his room. It was a play called *The Three Sisters*, by some foreign author, at the Old Vic. That's an alibi I suppose, but it's not a very good one."

"Did you see Muller?"

"No. He was out teaching somewhere."

"No. A theatre programme is easily come by. He has a motor cycle, and he would pass the Hammerpot woods coming from Leatherhead. The time of his absence would cover both murders. We'll bear the professor in mind. Go on, Duffield."

"Then there is a chap called Constantine who keeps an antique shop in the High Street. I went in there to ask the price of a brass doorknocker. He's a picturesque old party with a long white beard, a black velvet coat and a skull cap. Very courtly manners. I didn't get much out of him, but I'd heard already that he keeps no assistant. His daughter helps him in the shop. She was educated away somewhere and has not been home long. She's a handsome girl, very dark. Their nationality is English, but I should say their actual place of origin was either the Levant or the Balkans."

"What about the Wednesday before last?"

"Wednesday is early closing. They live over the shop and have a woman to come in the mornings. I got some of this from her husband in the bar of the Red Lion. The Constantines have an Austin Seven. The daughter drives it. They usually go out in it on Wednesday afternoons and Sundays. It is kept in a lock-up garage. On the other hand I don't think either of them could have killed Mr. Killick. Constantine is old and physically very frail. I noticed his hands particularly, they looked almost transparent; and the girl isn't the athletic type of young woman."

"You are assuming that there was only one murderer?"

"Yes. The two crimes must be part of the same job. They must be connected," argued Duffield.

"I can't believe that two entirely separate crimes of violence were committed within a few miles and a few hours of one another in this quiet countryside."

"I'm inclined to agree with you. And yet the pieces don't fit."

"Might not Killick himself have shot the man in the wood, and then been done in later by other members of the gang?" suggested Duffield. "He didn't run a car, but he may have taken long walks."

Collier shook his head. "In that case what became of the car or cars? What became of the pistol and of the dead man's shoes? I'm not ruling that out altogether, though. It isn't impossible. But you haven't heard my story."

He related all that he had learned during that morning. Duffield listened with rather less than his usual stolidity.

"If only we'd been on the spot last night," he sighed.

"How do you suppose that paper got hidden under the brass?"

Collier answered slowly. "Well, I imagine it was in the possession, of the unknown man, and he knew it might be taken from him. He hurried into the wood and took refuge in the church. It struck him that under the brass would be a good hiding place. You can take it up and relay it in less than five minutes. I timed myself this morning. Then he left the church and hurried through the wood. The others caught up with him. He was shot and his body searched. Then Toby came along and the murderers retreated. For all they knew the boy might have had others with him. Probably he owes his life to their uncertainty on that point, though you will have noticed that they didn't proceed to extremes last night. They didn't kill the dogs. They might have given them strychnine. I think I can see how the paper came to be hidden where it was. What I can't understand is how these two men were so quick in grasping the meaning of the dying man's last words. I don't mind betting a penny to a pound that not one person in a hundred in Durchester or the country round about knows anything about an old memorial brass in a derelict church."

"Unless it had been used by the gang before as a hiding place."

"That's a possibility. But, in that case, wouldn't they have gone there without taking the considerable risk of breaking into the Flemings' cottage and making the boy tell them what the dying man had said to him?"

"I'd like to see the brass," said Duffield.

"You shall." The Inspector fetched it from his room and laid it on the table, taking care not to rub the surface. "You notice the new scratches where screws were loosened." They turned the panel over and displayed the under side. "Here you see where something was pressed against the metal, removing the faint film of dust. A long envelope."

"The kneeling woman," said Duffield. "And they jumped to it." He grinned. "I fancy archaeologists are a law abiding crowd, as a rule. Somebody who knows about church brasses. That ought to help. In our list old Constantine seems the most likely."

"We've got to find out if any of these people were out during last night," his chief reminded him.

"Oh, gosh, so we have."

"Yes," said Collier grimly. "I'll see the Constantines myself. I'm going round to the station now."

CHAPTER XI
THE CHAFF AND THE GRAIN

THE Chief Constable received Collier rather coolly.

"I wondered when you would recall our existence," he said. " I rang up the Station Hotel yesterday, but was informed that you had been out all day. I hope you have come to report progress?"

"I'm sorry, sir. I haven't anything very definite as yet. I should only be wasting your time."

"Well, don't do that," said Captain Lowther sourly. "You're in charge. It's your pigeon now."

"But you were good enough to promise any help I might require," Collier reminded him.

"So you've come for help? Brett said you would. We shall give it, of course."

"Thank you, sir. I want a man on duty at Mrs. Fleming's house at Brock Green as soon as it gets dark—say, five o'clock—I don't mean to stay up all night. She has a spare room."

"Mrs. Fleming? That is the mother of the boy who found the dead man?"

"Yes. The house was entered last night by two men who compelled the boy to give them certain details concerning the crime."

"Details. What details?"

Collier hesitated. He did not want to get Toby into trouble with the local authorities, but he did not see how he could withhold information from the Chief Constable if he asked for it. He answered reluctantly.

"The motive for the murder seems to have been a paper which the man who was shot had hidden. He was still conscious when the boy found him. He said 'Don't tell them. The kneeling woman. Hidden under—' The boy was forced to repeat those words to the men who broke into the cottage last night."

Captain Lowther frowned. "He never said a word of this to Brett. We have his statement."

"He says he wasn't actually asked if the man spoke to him."

The Chief Constable sprang up and walked about the room. "He withheld important information. It looks bad. Who are these Flemings? They may be implicated in this affair."

"I don't think so, sir. He is only twelve, and young for his age in some ways. It was a terrifying experience. He needed careful handling. He took refuge in silence."

"The kneeling woman. What the hell does it mean anyway? It doesn't make sense."

"It's a brass in that church in the wood."

"Good lord! Well, what more do you want?"

"Well, sir, I did ring up your superintendent from an A.A. box on the road on my way here from Brock Green. I think he's notified all the police in your district of what I want. We've got to find out if two men boarded any early morning train within a fifteen mile radius of Brock Green or were seen on the road. The chances are they had their own car. They took a big risk, and they pulled it off."

"It gives you some light on the motive, eh?"

"Yes. Possession of some paper. I've brought the brass with me, sir. I want both sides photographed and tested for fingerprints. Not that I expect to get any."

"Very well. That'll be enough to keep my fellows from dying of inanition," said Captain Lowther with heavy sarcasm. "What are you doing yourself, if I may ask?"

"Some enquiries in the town, sir. These men had considerable knowledge of the locality. It's rather remarkable. Would you have guessed the kneeling woman riddle, sir?"

"I should not. Brasses! Good lord, no. You think the solution is to be found in the district then?"

"I don't say that. I may have to go up to Warwickshire to-morrow."

"Oh? Well—you're responsible for the conduct of this enquiry, Inspector. Good afternoon."

Collier found his way to the High Street in the older and less frequented part of the town. The antique dealer's shop was half way down the hill to the river. He stood for a moment looking at the Sheraton chairs, the Dutch landscape, black with age, the battered silver chalice, the Paisley shawl covering a table and the tray of old-fashioned jewellery in the window before he entered the shop.

A young woman was sitting behind the counter mending a bit of Flemish point lace. She had a creamy white skin and intensely dark eyes, and a mass of blue black hair was knotted at the nape of her neck. Her dress, clumsily made of some thick black material, would have made most girls of her age unhappy, but she seemed serenely unconscious of her own appearance.

"What is the price of that chalice?"

"Twelve pounds. It is Flemish work. Fifteenth century. Shall I get it out of the window for you to see?"

"No, thanks. I couldn't give so much. I'm interested in ecclesiastical art. Is there anything worth seeing about here?"

"They would tell you in the local guide."

"I must get one. I'd heard something about a church in the woods."

"You mean at Hammerpot? Yes, that is very old. But here is my father. He will tell you. Father, the gentleman was speaking of Botolphs."

Constantine was very tall, very bent, and obviously frail. He leaned heavily on a stick and it was evident that his sight was bad for he wore dark glasses. His white beard was trimmed to a point. His appearance was striking and it was easy to see that he must have been remarkably handsome in his youth. He made Collier a little bow.

"A student of architecture, sir? The church in the woods is worth a visit. There is some Saxon stonework, and a fine sixteenth century brass in the chancel. We have often been there in the summer eh, Alma, in the old days. But the present owner of the woods objects to picnic parties."

"A pity to spoil a beauty spot by committing a murder," said Collier.

Constantine turned his head towards him. " Murder? What murder? Have you heard of a murder, Alma? My sight is failing. I have to rely on my daughter to read me the local paper."

"It was some time ago, Father. You wouldn't have been interested," she said quickly.

Collier changed the subject. "You've got some good stuff here."

The old man rose eagerly to the bait, and for ten minutes they discussed Sheraton furniture and Waterford glass. Then Collier took his leave. "Come in whenever you like and have a look round," said Constantine. His daughter said nothing.

Collier walked back to the side street where he had parked his car. Why had the murder which had been the talk of the neighbourhood for the last ten days, been kept from old Constantine? Or was his ignorance assumed? He would certainly pay another visit to the antique shop.

He was returning to Brock Green by the lower road. He ran his car on to the grass by the roadside just before he emerged from the woods. He would allow himself a few minutes to go over his notes of the case. There was the time factor. The shooting took place at about ten minutes to four on Wednesday. Simon Killick was murdered some time after seven the same evening. Query. Did Killick shoot the man in Hammerpot wood, and did he meet his death subsequently at the hands of the dead man's friends? That was possible. No pistol had been found. There was no evidence so far as to who was the original owner of the document that had been hidden under the brass. Killick's bureau had been searched, but not his clothing. The search at the Grange had been incomplete. Strange that men who had slit the pockets and the coat lining of their victim in the wood a few hours earlier had not adopted the same procedure again. Had their nerve failed them? The howling of the dogs shut up on the floor above would prevent them from hearing any other sounds. They were impatient to get away from that house of death, and so they had vanished into the night out of which they had come leaving no trace, but the bureau emptied and contents burned on the hearth in the living room. Killick, who was a retired manufacturer of scents and cosmetics, had made a hobby of chemical research, but not lately. Query. Had he followed the Webbers from Croydon? Sir Henry Webber is away. Was his coming to the Grange, within three miles of the Webbers' place, a coincidence? Lady Webber had shown no interest in the case, but her indifference might be assumed.

"There may have been some connection between Killick and Sir Henry," thought Collier. "I'll have to go into that."

Had both crimes been committed by the same man? It seemed reasonable to assume that the two men involved had gone on from the woods to the Grange. They had been admitted by Killick. They might have been expected. He had received a letter with a foreign stamp on it that morning, but that might have nothing to do with the visit. What was certain was that there had been no struggle. He had been struck down apparently as he was showing his visitors out. Killick himself must have shut the dogs up in his bedroom. It would be a natural thing to do if one were anticipating a visit from strangers. Practically every man and woman in the village had been questioned by Brett without result. No one had seen any strangers about the place. That was hardly surprising. The night had been dark and wet. There was no street lighting in Brock Green. It would be easy to come to the Grange and to leave it again unseen. Perhaps, after shooting the man in the wood they had gone to Killick for shelter, claiming his assistance. If he refused it the rest might have followed. Would they have dared to leave their car in the road outside the Grange? The vicar would not have seen it, for he had gone to the Grange by the short cut across the churchyard, but Tommy Yates and his future bride, the cook from Brock Hall, had called at the vicarage about seven, had left about twenty minutes later. Miss Soper would have to get back to the Hall by ten. They might have noticed a strange car, but—again he reminded himself that the night had been dark. Tommy was half-witted. Miss Soper was sharp enough, but she had just had her banns put up, and probably she would have been too flustered to be very observant. They were both witnesses of the type Collier had come to know only too well by experience, the type that is quite unable to distinguish between the chaff and the grain of their experience. It would be his job to do the winnowing. He had planned to call on Mrs. Yates at about the hour her son would be coming back from his work as under gardener and odd man at the Hall. He looked at his watch and decided that it was time to drive on. He left his car at the gate of the Flemings' cottage and walked down the lane. His timing had been accurate for a shambling figure was just wheeling a bicycle up Mrs. Yates' well scoured brick path. Collier caught up with him.

"Good evening, Yates. I want a word with you."

The youth grinned foolishly. "Ar. But they calls me Tommy. I'll just put my bike in the shed."

"All right. I'll go in."

He entered the warm, lamp-lit kitchen. The table was laid for tea and Mrs. Yates was frying bloaters over an oil stove.

"If it isn't the 'tec from the Yard. Come in, Mister," she said. Her future daughter-in-law was sitting by the fire. She had kicked off her shoes.

"Still feeling your feet, Miss Soper?"

"You've said it. I'm heavy on 'em, and cooking you can't sit down. Seems to make the pastry go flat. You gave me a lift the other day. Been to call on her ladyship, hadn't you? Higgins told me. She got the wind up thinking her darling Harold was in trouble again. He's a terror, he is. Both boys are. Mind you, they take after her. Hard as nails, she is She don't interfere with me of course. She knows her place and I knows mine. They won't get a better cook in a month of Sundays. When they started their games with my Tommy I warned her I wouldn't stand for it, and she put a stop to it. They can trap the birds and get up to their nasty tricks. She don't care." Miss Soper paused for breath. "Are you really a 'tec?"

Collier smiled. "I am."

"Fancy that. I've read a lot of Edgar Wallace. I'm a great reader. Will you give me your autograph?"

Mrs. Yates giggled delightedly. It was evident that she admired her future daughter-in-law. "You've got a nerve, Florrie Soper. Fancy asking him that."

"Well, he's come here to pump us, hasn't he?" said Florrie shrewdly. "He won't mind doing a little thing like that in return."

"Of course," said Collier, "I'd be delighted. You shall have it now." He produced his fountain pen. "There's just one thing, Miss Soper. I'd be glad if you didn't mention me and our meeting in this friendly way to anyone up at the Hall, or indeed to anybody outside these four walls. I know I can rely on your discretion. And you, too, Mrs. Yates"—he turned to the older woman. "It's for your own sakes I am saying this. It wouldn't do—it might not be very safe for you if it appeared that you knew more than other people about what happened ten days ago."

Both women looked startled and Florrie Soper's fat face had lost some of its high colour.

"What d'you mean by safe?" she asked with an attempt at defiance. "We don't know no more than other people.

"I know that," he said soothingly. "I'm only warning you to be careful. It's one thing to read about murders in a story book, Miss Soper, and another to have one committed within a few hundred yards of where one happens to be."

Tommy Yates came in, nodded to his mother and his affianced, and sat down at the table. Mrs. Yates turned the bloaters out of the frying pan on to a plate and set it before him. Florrie Soper paid no attention to him whatever. Her eyes were fixed on the detective.

"What d'you mean by a few hundred yards?"

"You were at the vicarage about seven. We don't know exactly when the crime was committed."

"It wasn't until after eight anyway, and Tommy and Miss Soper was in the bus going back to the Hall by then," said Mrs. Yates. "They caught the five to eight at the cross roads, didn't you, Florrie?"

"Yes," said the other eagerly. "The conductor would remember. Him and me was talking about a bad half crown he'd had given him that morning."

"But how can you prove that it wasn't until after eight?" said Collier, concealing his inward excitement. Was this visit going to be even more fruitful than he had dared to hope?

Mrs. Yates answered. "Because of Uncle Daniel. Well, then, you can hear what he has to say. He'll be home by now." She picked up one of Miss Soper's badly trodden over shoes and rapped on the party wall with the heel. There was a rumble in reply and after an interval they heard the click of the gate.

"He's coming in. He'll tell you."

Tommy ate his bloaters and munched bread and butter washed down with strong tea. He did not seem to be listening to what was being said. His round red face expressed nothing but a bovine contentment, an animal enjoyment of his food. Collier glanced from him to the stout and plain but by no means unintelligent woman who had made up her mind to marry him, and wondered. But Miss Soper's choice of a husband could hardly have any bearing on the case. He was recalled to the present by the arrival of Uncle Daniel, a rather grimy old man wearing steel rimmed spectacles and the leather apron of his trade.

"I ha'n't finished soleing your boots, Car'line, if that's what you want," he rumbled, and then he saw Collier. "I didn't know you had company."

"Sit down, Uncle Daniel," said Mrs. Yates hospitably, "I'll get you a glass of my elder wine,"

"I won't say no to that." His little eyes twinkled behind his glasses as he peered round at Collier.

"We gets lots of strangers about these days. Is the gentleman one of these newspaper writers?"

"You can tell Uncle Daniel anything," said Mrs. Yates. "It won't go no further."

"Very well," said Collier. "I've come down from Scotland Yard about these murders. Your neighbour here was saying that Mr. Killick was still alive some time after eight, and that you could prove it. What about it?"

Mrs. Yates had produced a bottle of elder wine and some glasses. "Have a drink first."

"I will," said Uncle Daniel, "I wasn't overfond of the police in my young days. If a man can't have a rabbit pie now and again what's the use of being an Englishman? Might as well be one of they foreigners living on frogs." He drank his wine in one gulp and act down the glass. Collier, who had sipped his cautiously and whose eyes were still watering, could only suppose his throat was made of the same material as his apron.

"Well," he smiled. "Speaking unofficially I don't see much harm in a bit of poaching, especially if it all happened years ago."

"I'm too rheumatic these days. I'll never see the moon rise over Hammerpot woods again. But you haven't called me in to talk about that."

Collier brought him back to the point. "Mrs. Yates says you can prove Mr. Killick was alive until past eight."

"Ah, so I can. I'd mended a pair of shoes for him and I was taking them over that night. I know the time cause I've got a wireless and I was listening up to eight o'clock. The announcer says he was switching us over to Covent Garden and I've no use for all that foreign squalling so I switched off he, and I wrapped the shoes in a bit of paper and took them under my arm and off I went across the green. It was dark but I know my way"—he stopped and gazed at the bottle of elder wine.

"You'll have just a drop more?" said Mrs. Yates, taking the hint.

"I don't mind if I do."

Collier restrained his impatience. He realised that the old man could not be hurried. He would tell his story in his own way.

"I didn't tell that there Inspector Brett when he come nosing round. I don't hold with that lot at Durchester. But you're different. I went to the front door and knocked same as I had before when I'd brought back the shoes I'd mended, and I heard the dogs barking upstairs. I waited a bit and knocked again, and then I heard Mr. Killick. He said, 'Go away now. I'm busy.' So of course I went. I thought I'd ask Car'line Yates to take the shoes over for me when she went to work in the morning. You had them with you, didn't you, Car'line, when you ran back to get the police?"

"That's right," she confirmed him, "and I've got them still in the scullery. I don't rightly know what to do with them."

"Thank you," said Collier. "That's clear enough. And you could swear to the time?"

"It was somewhere between eight and half past. I made a round like and it was half past by the Red Lion clock when I walked into the bar. Call it ten minutes from the Grange to the Red Lion at my rate of walking."

"I've written all that down. Will you sign it and your friends can witness it."

Uncle Daniel was willing to sign. "But it's all foolishness," he said bluntly.

Collier did not argue the point.

"Talking of time, I must be going, or I'll miss that bus," said Miss Soper.

Collier stood up. "I'll run you back as far as the park gates," he said. After cordial leave takings all round he walked with her up the lane to where he had left his car. He took her as far as the gates of Brock Hall, as he had promised, and then returned to the village. He could see a light shining in the sitting-room window of the Forge and he meant to round off his day by spending a few minutes there with Mrs. Fleming and Toby, but he had to call at the vicarage first.

It was very dark in the drive between the high banks of laurels, but a dim light showed through the frosted glass of the fanlight over the door. He rang and after an interval the door was opened on the chain by the housekeeper.

"It's only me, Mrs. Watkins."

"Oh—did you want to come in? The vicar's in his study. He don't like to be disturbed."

That's all right. I just wanted to ask you—Wednesday's your evening out, isn't it?"

"No. Thursday."

"But you were out the night of the murder?"

"I'd gone down the village to see my niece who was expecting, but I wasn't gone long. I come up the drive just as the vicar was showing Tommy Yates and that cook from the Hall out. I'd told him I'd be in plenty of time to get his supper at a quarter to eight and so I was."

"Did you go out again later?"

"Me?" there was a trace of indignation in Mrs. Watkins' manner. "Not likely. I was never one for gadding. And the vicar's stomach was upset and he wasn't any too well. He had his supper, a cup of hot milk, and cheese and biscuits and an apple, and then he went off to bed, and I took him up a hot water bottle."

The study door opened and the vicar came out.

"Who is it, Mrs. Watkins? My friend the Inspector. Don't keep him out there in the cold."

"It's all right, sir. I can't come in."

"But you must have wanted something?"

Collier smiled. "I'm testing alibis. Mrs. Watkins has a good one and so have you."

"Have we? Splendid. That's a weight off my mind." He began to chuckle and checked himself. "I oughtn't to laugh," he said remorsefully. "Nothing to laugh at. Poor Killick. Poor Killick." His voice had dropped and coming out of the dimness of the hall, sounded mournful enough to appease his old friend's shade.

"You'd better go back to the study fire," said the housekeeper reproachfully. "You've got a cold as it is. You'll catch your death."

"Oh—very well. Good night, Inspector."

"Good night."

CHAPTER XII
THE POLICE ARE HUMAN

MRS. Fleming and Toby were playing Ludo. A glazier had come over from Durchester early in the afternoon and had mended the broken window. Later, when they had just finished tea, a very large and very shy young man had presented himself. He was carrying a brown paper parcel. He had explained diffidently that he had come to spend the night.

"Those are my orders, madam. But I don't want to intrude. I mean—"

"I'm very glad to have you," she said. "It was very kind of the Inspector to think of it. I'll show you your room."

She had left him in the tiny bedroom under the eaves, solemnly undoing the parcel which probably contained a toothbrush and a suit of pyjamas. She went down again to find Toby, crimson with suppressed laughter. "Toby, be quiet! If he thinks you're making fun of him he'll be hurt. And it's very ungrateful. You know we shouldn't feel a bit safe here to-night without somebody."

"Yes. But why does he dither? Does he think you'll bite?"

"Hush, he's coming."

They sat down to Ludo, but the minutes and their guardian remained upstairs. Sandra was uneasy. "I hope he doesn't think he must spend the evening in that wretched little room without a fire. He's terribly shy, poor boy. Toby, you go up and ask him if he'll join us in a game."

"All right. Or he might tell us about a policeman's life."

Toby went up. He had not returned when she heard a car stop at the gate and a moment later there was a knock at the door. She went to open it.

"It's me," said Collier, smiling. "May I come in just for a minute?"

"Please do."

He followed her into the pleasant homely room. She saw his tired face relax as he looked about him. "They've mended the window? Good. And they were to send up a man—he should have been here."

"He is. He's upstairs. Toby's just gone up to ask him if he plays Ludo."

Collier looked at her doubtfully. "He can patrol the garden if you'd rather."

"On a wet night in November? Don't be absurd. We're going to try to make him feel at home."

"Very kind of you," said Collier rather formally. "I expect he's quite a decent young chap. Well, I'll be getting along. Good night, Mrs. Fleming."

He had meant to stay longer. He had intended to allow himself half an hour's rest, to sit in one of Mrs. Fleming's comfortable chairs listening to her and Toby and watching the two eager face, so much alike, in the flickering firelight. But he couldn't do that with one of Brett's underlings looking on. And—he had thought she liked him; he had made one of those mistakes that make one hot with humiliation when one recalls them. She had been nice to him, but she was nice to everyone. She did not distinguish between him and the awkward clumping youth, a newcomer to the local force, whose heavy tread he heard coming down the stairs.

"Have the dogs recovered from the dope! Splendid"—he bent to pat the head of Mac who had got out of his basket to greet him. "I'll let myself out. Please don't trouble."

Toby, bursting into the room, with the young constable following sheepishly in his wake, found his mother playing rather absently with the dice on the Ludo board.

"I say, Mother, he'd like to play. But where's the Inspector? I thought I heard him. It was him, wasn't it?"

"Yes."

Toby looked disappointed. "Couldn't he have stayed?"

"Why should he?" said Sandra rather sharply. "He's a busy man. And we've told him all we can."

"Oh, that. But I thought he seemed matey," persisted Toby.

"Nonsense, darling. Inspectors from Scotland Yard are very grand people, aren't they, Mr.—"

"Quilter," said the young constable, blushing.

"Come on," said Toby, "if we're going to play."

Collier, meanwhile, was driving back to Durchester. The rain was dimming the windscreen and he set the wiper in motion. He hardly knew how much of his irritation was due to physical fatigue. Had he been ungracious just now to Mrs. Fleming? She had been smiling when she opened the door, and her smile had faded. Had he—"Oh, hell!" said Collier aloud. He couldn't even drive fast with all these leaves on the road. Two men dead, and he was no nearer a solution than he had been when he first took over the case. Of course he was at a disadvantage. A week has passed before the local authorities called up the Yard. The scent was stone cold. He had not seen either of the victims, only their photographs taken after death. How little those helped. And yet—

Collier came out of a skid that had nearly landed him in the ditch and concentrated his attention on the road. But there was a gleam in his eye and his spirits were rising and instead of going directly to the Station Hotel as he had intended he called at the police station. Both the Chief Constable and Inspector Brett had gone home. So had the Superintendent, but the sergeant on duty in the charge room was able to supply him with copies of the photographs taken in the mortuary of its most recent occupants. He did not look at them then and there, that would do later. He drove on to the hotel and garaged his car. Duffield was waiting for him in their sitting-room.

"Any news? Will it keep? Good. We'll have some grub first."

He hardly spoke again until the waiter had cleared the table and brought in the coffee. Duffield had not tried to make conversation. He ate his supper placidly and thought about the bulbs he meant to plant in his little back garden. But now and again his small shrewd eyes were fixed on his colleague's face and when they were alone again he delivered himself of an unexpected remark.

"You know you take things too hard, Inspector."

Collier, who had been staring gloomily at the grounds in his coffee cup, looked up quickly. "What do you mean?"

Duffield tried to explain. "It's like actors feeling their parts too much. If a chap acting Lear, for instance, really felt all he's supposed to feel he'd be dead in a week. He doesn't. It's just his job. And with us—it's our job to catch the crooks and the murderers. We do our best—but if we fail you care too much."

"You may be right. Once I've started I hate to fail. Why are you saying this, Duffield? You aren't hopeful of our success in this case? It's true that I go for things, as the Yankees say, bald-headed. I can't help it. Did you find out if Muller or the Constantines were out last night?"

"Muller went out after his supper. He told his landlady he was going to the Palladium picture house in the London Road. She didn't hear him come in. He has a latch key. She goes to bed about ten and is rather deaf. His bed-sitting-room is on the ground floor, so his fellow lodgers wouldn't be likely to hear him either. I couldn't find out anything about the Constantines. Their lock-up garage isn't overlooked."

Collier had taken a packet from his coat pocket and was arranging its contents on the table in front of him. There were three time exposures of Killick taken as he lay in the police mortuary, and three of the man who was still unidentified. Collier was concentrating his attention on the latter. He beckoned to Duffield, who came and looked over his shoulder,

"The chap who works the camera here isn't too bad," he conceded. "There's something—gosh—"

"You've seen it, too?" said Collier quickly.

"It's the upper part of the face," said the sergeant. He pointed a stubby forefinger at the finely marked black brows and the heavy lidded eyes with their sweep of long black lashes. "The girl in the antique shop. Old Constantine's daughter."

Collier nodded. "It was her father's face that seemed vaguely familiar. It came to me as I was driving. That's why I called at the station for these photographs. Let's see what the police surgeon had to say about the deceased." He turned over the pages of his notes on the case. "Height, five feet, eight inches. Inclined to corpulence. Evidently a man of sedentary habits. No organic disease. Hands remarkably fine and well kept. Age anything between twenty-eight and forty. That's a big margin, but the men of Central and Eastern Europe age quicker than Englishmen. Yes, there's a likeness, but it doesn't follow that he's actually related to the Constantines. It may be a racial resemblance. That will have to be followed up."

The town hall clock was striking nine as he walked down the old High Street the following morning. Milk bottles were still standing the pavement in front of the fishmonger's. Farther along the street there were no signs of life at that hour, but Alma Constantine was just unlocking the shop door as Collier cane up. She looked at him with the gentle gravity that had impressed him before and stood back to allow him to pass in.

"Have you come for the chalice?"

"No." He laid one of the photographs he had brought with him before her on the counter. "Do you recognise that?"

He saw something like a grey shadow pass over the creamy pallor of throat and cheek and brow. The counter was between them and she stood, leaning both hands on it, and answered without lifting her eyes.

"Who is it? Why do you ask?"

Before Collier could answer her father called to her from the room at the back.

"Who is it so early, Alma? A customer?"

She called back. "All right, Father. I can manage"—then she turned hurriedly to the young man. "Not here. Meet me down by the bridge in half an hour."

Collier hesitated.

"Please," the soft dark eyes besought him. "He mustn't know. It would kill him."

"Very well," he said, "I'll wait for you."

He went down the hill to the bridge and leaned on the parapet, watching the water flow under the arches. Presently, Alma Constantine came down the hill and went down the steps on to the towing path. Collier followed her.

"Shall we sit down?"

"Yes. But I must not stay long. I have to do my shopping."

He was looking at her. The grey shadow had passed but there was something rigid in her attitude that he had not noticed previously.

"I'm so sorry," he said. "I'm afraid I gave you a shock just now. You recognised the person whose picture I showed you."

She moistened her lips before she spoke. "I don't say that. It frightened me. He looked so stiff—so unnatural."

"Didn't you realise," he said gently, "it was taken after death?"

He heard her gasp. "Death—" she whispered.

"Was it—your brother?"

"How did you know?" she cried. And then, "No. I won't answer. What right have you? I shouldn't have come—"

She seemed about to rise but he laid a hand on her arm. An old woman carrying a bundle of laundry stared at them curiously.

"I'm sorry," said Collier again, "but you had really better be frank with me, Miss Constantine. I am a police officer"—he produced his card and gave it to her. She looked at it vaguely through a mist of tears. "I am here making enquiries in connection with the double murder that was committed near here ten days ago."

She was fumbling in her handbag for her handkerchief. He waited a moment, looking away from her at the pollard willows along the towing path and the reflection of the bridge on the river.

"Thank you," she said faintly.

He turned back to her. "Didn't it ever occur to you that the man who was found shot in Hammerpot wood might be your brother?"

"I—I was afraid it might be. But I couldn't be sure—"

"You had reason to believe that he was in the neighbourhood at that time?"

"Yes. He met me on Wednesday morning in the market. I hadn't expected him. He said he had come down by an early train—on business. He just asked how Father was and if we were all right. You see—he never came to the house. Father and he quarrelled years ago. He—I think it was something about politics—they didn't think alike. But Michael loved us just the same."

"He didn't tell you why he had come down here?"

"No. But he said I wasn't to worry if the shop was doing badly because soon he would have a lot of money and could help us."

"He said that, did he?"

"Yes. But you must not think Michael was mixed up in anything shady. He wasn't like that. He was full of enthusiasm and wanted to do away with tyranny and injustice—"

"How long were you together on the Wednesday morning, Miss Constantine?"

"Only a few minutes. He said he would write in a day or two, but I haven't heard anything."

"Would he have known of the brass in the church in Hammerpot wood?"

"The brass? Oh yes. He showed it me long ago. He used to stay with us sometimes before he and Father quarrelled. Why?

What has the brass to do with it? He—he wasn't killed in the church, was he?"

"No. Never mind that now. Could you swear to your brother's identity from this photograph, Miss Constantine? Wait a minute. I'll show you two more taken from different angles."

She took the prints from him and looked at them closely.

"I am almost sure," she said at last. "I couldn't swear to it."

"Can you remember what clothes he was wearing?"

She thought for a moment. "He had a dark grey frieze overcoat over a navy blue suit."

"And his tie?"

"It would have been black. He never wore coloured ties. Does that agree with—" She could not go on.

He nodded. "Yes. That tallies with the list I have. The clothing worn by the deceased is in the possession of the police, naturally. It had no distinguishing marks. Did he live abroad chiefly, Miss Constantine?"

"I don't know. He was very reticent about his affairs. I was not in his confidence. I know he was devoting his life to something that seemed to him terribly important. I mean, apart from what he did to earn his living."

"And what was that exactly?"

"Well, he was in partnership with Father until they quarrelled. He was a dealer in antiques. He went about the country to sales."

"After the quarrel he set up on his own. Had he a place in London?"

"I can't tell you. He may have worked for another firm. He never said."

"Your father has been naturalised for some time?"

"Yes. As soon as he could after he came over to England and that was thirty-five years ago."

"You may think it strange," she said, "but it's a fact that I don't know. When my mother was alive they used to talk in their own language and my brother Michael learned it, but she died when I was born, and after that he had an English housekeeper and nothing but English spoken. And he never speaks of the past. I think he has some fearful memories. He was a refugee. I think it may have been one of the Balkan countries, but I may be wrong."

"Thank you. That may be helpful. One never knows. Did it strike you that your brother was nervous or uneasy, that the business to which he referred might be distasteful—or dangerous?"

"Not at all. He seemed pleased, as if he had had good news."

"He was a good deal older than you are?"

"Oh yes. Thirteen years. He was thirty-two. I am nineteen. I've told you all I can. Please—you'll keep it from my father, won't you," she pleaded.

"I'm afraid I can't promise that," he said gently. "There's no need to broadcast this information at once, but it will have to come out eventually. You want us to bring the murderers to justice, don't you?"

She sighed. "I suppose so. But Michael had gone his own way. I want to spare my father. He—you have seen him. He isn't strong."

"You've been frank with me, Miss Constantine," Collier said. "I'll do all I can in return. You can break the bad news to him yourself if you would rather, or you can be present when I tell him. And I can give you twenty-four hours to think it over. I have to follow up another line of enquiry to-day. I'll call at the shop to-morrow morning if I'm not detained elsewhere."

"Very well," she said submissively.

"There's just one other question," he said. "Did you know Mr. Killick at all?"

"No. I never heard of him before I read his name in the papers. You—you don't think it was he who killed my brother?"

"We have no proof one way or the other. We're still looking for the motive in both cases. I won't keep you any longer, Miss Constantine. You want to get back to the shop. Don't worry more than you must. The police are quite human, you know. We won't make things harder for you if we can help it," he sad earnestly.

They were both standing now. Alma looked at him, hesitated, and held out her hand.

"Thank you," she said. "I believe you really mean that."

*

Collier hurried back to the hotel and put through a trunk call. The special branch might know something about Michael Constantine if his main activities were, as his sister thought, political. Then he had a brief conversation with Duffield.

"We've identified the man in the wood. A son of old Constantine, the antique dealer. He came down for the day on business. He met his sister and was in high spirits. Seemed to think it was going to be a paying proposition. I want you to hire a motor cycle, sergeant, and park it where you will be able to get hold of it at once if the Constantines go out in their car. You're to keep a watch on the shop and follow them if they go out. I think they're O.K. but one can't be certain. I had to show my hand to the girl."

"Very good, sir."

"Will you need a local man to relieve you?"

"No. There's a bun shop a little farther down the street where I can get some grub."

"I'll ask them to send somebody along for the night shift."

"You don't really trust them then?" said Duffield.

"I did while I was with her. But she's so darned good looking. We're all apt to be soft with a pretty woman, Duffield. She cried. I don't want to be had for a mug. She knew the picture right enough. She turned grey. But it's just possible that the person she's concerned about isn't the victim but the killer. Anyway—you know your job."

CHAPTER XIII
MAY MORNING PRODUCTS

THE factory and offices of the May Morning products were on the Evesham road a mile out of the town of Stratford. Collier asked for the manager and sent in his card. The afternoon was drawing in and the lights were on in the work rooms. He heard a rumble of machines and caught a glimpse through glass doors of girls in white overalls bending over their tasks. He was not kept waiting long but was shown into a small room where an alert youngish man rose from a roll top desk to receive him.

"Please sit down, Inspector. Will you have a cigarette? We don't allow smoking elsewhere, but it's all right in here with the door shut."

Collier grinned. "Are lipsticks explosive?"

The manager laughed. "Hardly. There's no danger really, but we would rather be over careful than risk an accident. Safety first. Some of the ingredients used in the manufacture of our perfumes might be inflammable. I hope your visit doesn't mean that any of our people have got into trouble, Inspector—"

"No. I just wanted a little information which I thought you would be able to supply about Mr. Killick."

"Killick"—the manager gazed at him blankly for a moment. Then a light seemed to dawn on him. "Oh—Killick—he was one of the original partners in the firm; but he retired years ago, just after the War, I think. I never met him. It was before my time. What do you want to know about him?"

Collier saw that the manager had not read any of the accounts of the murder, or, if he had, had failed to make the connection.

"Is there anybody here who would remember him?" he asked.

The manager reflected. "Most of our workers are young girls who come here when they leave school and leave us to get married. Some of the men have been here longer though. Wait a bit—" He rang a bell and asked the young woman who answered it to send up Baines.

"Mr. Killick's not been stepping outside the law, I hope," he said with a smile.

Collier saw no object in making a mystery of his object in coming so far. He answered bluntly, "He's been murdered."

"Good Heavens!"

The workman he had sent for came in before he could say more. He was a little old man with shaggy grey hair, his hands and his overalls blackened with machine oil and coal dust. Collier gathered that he was in charge of the furnaces.

"Baines, you've been here a long time. You remember Mr. Killick?"

"Yes, sir."

"He used to work in the laboratory himself, didn't he?" asked Collier.

The old man looked towards him. "Yes, sir. He was a first class hand at all that. He invented some of our standard scents. In his time we were always putting something new on the market like."

"Why did he retire? Was it a breakdown in health?"

"It was the death of his son, sir. He was killed at the front. He had only the one boy, and he didn't join up, not at first. There was some talk of his being a conchy, but I don't know if that was so. Anyways, when the news came poor Mr. Killick shut himself up and wasn't seen about the place for several days. But afterwards he bore up bravely as so many of us had to. It wasn't until eighteen months later, some time after the Armistice, that he got real queer. Something happened. Giles, who's commissionaire now at the Illyria picture house, knew more about it than anyone, but he won't talk. It was hushed up, whatever it was, and the poor gentleman gave up coming to the works and went right away, and so far as I know he's never been back since."

The manager, who had been listening with unconcealed interest, intervened. "What do you mean by queer, Baines? Did he go off his rocker?"

"I wouldn't say that, sir. We was all sorry for the poor gentleman. He was well liked at the works. We were sorry—specially those who remembered him as he used to be before those blasted Jerries started messing things up. The world's never been the same since."

"He was popular with the workers, you say? So far as you know he never made an enemy here?"

"Oh, laws, no, sir. He was always fair. Not weak. He'd sack you, but never without warning, and never without a good reason. He hadn't no enemies."

"I see. Thank you."

"That will do, thank you, Baines," said the manager. Half a crown changed hands, and the old furnace man shuffled out.

"Surely you didn't suspect a vendetta dating back to the time Killick left here?" said the manager. "That would be very un-English."

"Quite," said Collier. "But Killick appeared to be eccentric. He had been living the life of a recluse. We wanted to find out the reason. It was conceivable that he was trying to keep out of somebody's way. Lying low. What some people call the science of detection is simply the accumulation of apparently irrelevant and unimportant facts."

He took leave of the manager and walked back from the May Morning works to the town. It was his first visit to Stratford and he looked with admiration at the picturesque old timbered houses and the Clopton bridge spanning the famous river, but he had no time for sight-seeing. An errand boy directed him to the recently opened Illyria picture house. The commissionaire, a big man in a gaudy uniform, with a row of medals on his chest, was on duty in the vestibule, but there was nobody in the box office.

"Your name is Giles, I believe? You were employed at the May Morning factory?"

"No, sir. I was a gardener at one time."

"I see. You were a gardener to Mr. Killick before the War?"

"That's right." He looked at Collier enquiringly. "Would you be a friend of Mr. Killick's, sir? I've often wondered how he was getting on."

"He died recently, and as nothing was known about him where he was living, I have come to make a few enquiries. They told me at the May Morning works that you knew him well. I'd be glad of any particulars."

Giles was silent for a moment. Then he said, "Who might you be, sir? A lawyer?"

"No. I am a police officer. The fact is, Giles, Mr. Killick was murdered. He was found lying dead in a passage of his house. We don't know why or by whom he was attacked. There may be something in his past life to help us."

"Well, that's bad news and no mistake," said Giles heavily. "Poor Mr. Killick. He was a good master to me. 'You'll find your job waiting when you come back,' he said when I rejoined. I'd been in the army before, you see, sir. And he was as good as his word. He had one of those houses on the Tiddington Road with a garden sloping down to the river. We had a rare show of roses. I never took a regular place after he sold the house and went away, just went out jobbing, and I had to give that up on account of my chest, having been gassed, you see, sir, so I was glad to get taken on here. Though, between you and me, this fancy uniform gives me the jim-jams."

"Oh I don't know," said Collier, smiling, "it's a bit of colour on a grey November afternoon. So many of us rely on the pictures for colour in our lives, Giles. Mr. Killick lost his only son in the War, didn't he?"

The question seemed a harmless one, but it had a curious effect on the commissionaire. It turned the easy flow of his reminiscences off at the tap. He became abruptly monosyllabic.

"Yes, sir."

"He took it very hard, didn't he?"

"Yes."

Collier hesitated. He did not want to inflict needless pain, and it was obvious that he had touched on a sore spot. It seemed unlikely that young Killick's death in Flanders could have any bearing on a crime committed seventeen years later. But one never knew.

"Look here," he began. But a young person with lips of sealing wax red had taken her place in the box office, and people were coming into the vestibule to buy their tickets. "Sorry, sir," said Giles, "I've got to attend to my job. If the boss was to catch me talking I'd get the sack."

Collier nodded. "All right. I'll be seeing you again later."

He took a stroll through the town, dined at the Arden Hotel, and spent half an hour on the bridge watching the lights reflected in the dark water. He was far from easy in his mind. He might be wasting valuable time. But it was clear that Giles knew something regarding Killick that he did not want to tell. He had not been able to form any very distinct mental picture of Mr. Killick, but, on the whole reports were favourable. He had been liked at the works. As an employer of labour he had been just and apparently sympathetic. Giles, obviously, had been fond of his master. There had been a break in his life when he left Stratford. Until then he had been normal. At Croydon he had lived like a hermit. He had worked at all hours of the night in his laboratory. Was he still experimenting on behalf of the May Morning products? Collier looked at his watch, and leaving the bridge and the mass of the new theatre dark against the starry sky, walked back up Sheep Street, and reached the Illyria picture house just as the audience was coming out. He joined Giles as the latter emerged, wearing an overcoat over his garish uniform.

"What was the big trouble, Giles? It was something more than his son's death?"

"I've been thinking things over, sir. I'm not going to answer that. Mr. Killick wouldn't want me to, I'm sure. He was good to me, and I'm not going to repay him by blabbing about his concerns."

"Don't you want his murderer brought to justice, Giles?"

"Of course I do. But what happened those years ago is a different matter."

"You cannot be sure of that."

"I can." He stopped at the door of one of the old houses.

"This is where I live. I won't ask you to come in. It's late. I'm sorry to seem disobliging, but I've made up my mind."

"Very well," said Collier. He knew when he was beaten. "Good night."

"Good night, sir."

Collier went back to Town the next day and called the Yard to report to his superintendent. Cardew put aside the work on which he had been engaged and prepared to listen.

"Any chance of an arrest within the next day or two?"

"None whatever, I should say, sir. But perhaps things may begin to move now that I've identified the man in the wood. Can the special branch help us there?"

"To some extent, yes. He has acted as a traveller and agent for one or two firms selling peasant embroideries. He has been in several of the Balkan countries, and especially in Jugo-Slavia, collecting the stuff from the villages. He may also be in touch with some of the local political organisations, secret societies and terrorists, but, if so, his activities have been well camouflaged.

He has been under observation at times, but nothing has been proved against him. And I must say that a sleepy little town in one of the sleepiest counties seems an unlikely venue for people of that sort."

"Yes, sir. But, if I'm right, Killick was the storm centre."

"Beware of theories, Collier. Curb that imagination of yours."

"Yes, sir," said Collier obediently, "I haven't actually got a theory yet. I'm feeling my way."

"Did you try to get any light on Killick's past from anyone else when Giles failed you?"

"Yes. Seventeen years is a long time. But there was a tobacconist in Bridge Street who remembered him and his son. He said the boy was an art student and showed great talent. His father idolised him. He—the boy—seemed very shy and reserved, but they were obviously mutually devoted. The old man was simply stunned with grief when his son was killed, but he carried on as usual. The actual break-down occurred some time later, after the Armistice. The tobacconist said, 'It was about the time Giles, who had been their gardener and was an N.C.O. in the same regiment as young Killick, came home.' He seemed to think that Giles' return brought the whole tragedy back—but I fancy there's more to it than that, though whether it has anything to do with this case—"

The superintendent made a note. "We'll get in touch with the military authorities and get Giles' record and young Killick's. I don't know what you have in mind, Collier. Do you think Killick was being blackmailed by some organisation of which Constantine was a member, and that he killed Constantine and was done in later by other people in the gang?"

"It's possible," said Collier, "but it's over four miles from Hammerpot woods to his house, and he seems to have been a man of sedentary habits. He hadn't a car or even a push bike. He could have covered the distance on foot easily in the time, of course. Constantine was shot at about four, and Killick was in when the vicar called a few minutes before seven to return a book he had borrowed."

"The vicar was the last to see him alive?"

"I thought so, but I was mistaken. The village cobbler, known locally as Uncle Daniel, went to the Grange some time between eight and half past with a pair of shoes he had soled. Killick called out to him that he was busy and that he was to come again another time. That gives the vicar an absolutely unshakable alibi, for his housekeeper can prove that he went up to bed directly after supper. Not that he's ever been in my list of suspects," Collier added with a half smile. "He's a man of the highest character, universally respected."

"Just so. But you're right to make no exceptions." The Superintendent was looking through Collier's notes on the case.

"This choice of the memorial brass as a hiding place may be explained by the fact that Constantine lived for a while at Durchester and was interested in such things. But the men who broke into the Flemings' house the other night must have known of it, too, or they couldn't have understood the dying man's reference to a kneeling woman. I'd keep that in mind if I were you, Collier. You did well to leave Duffield to keep watch on old Constantine and his daughter. It wouldn't surprise me to learn that they were both in this up to the neck. Good-bye." He reached for the papers he had been studying when Collier came in. "Shut the door after you."

Chapter XIV
BOYS WILL BE BOYS

Lady Webber had sent Marples with the Lanchester to fetch her younger boy Kenneth home from his preparatory school for the half-term holiday. The elder boy, Harold, had not gone back to the famous public school where his name had been entered at birth, and been placed in the care of an Army coach who received a few youths, described as delicate or backward, under his own roof, and prepared them to enter Sandhurst. Among the servants at Brock Hall it was generally agreed that if Master Harold had belonged to the working class he would have been sent to Borstal. Both boys were superficially attractive, having inherited their mother's pink and white colouring and corn-coloured hair. They were a bitter disappointment to their father, who had been proud of them when they were sturdy, rosy cheeked babies, and his not infrequent quarrels with his wife were often concerned with her determination that her darlings should never suffer any consequences of their misdeeds.

Kenneth arrived on Friday evening in time to have dinner with his mother.

"I've ordered all the things you like best, darling. Cook's made a special sort of sweet with lots of cream. Your father's away."

"Good egg," said Kenneth.

"You ought not to say that, dear."

"Well, you know he does nothing but preach. A chap gets fed up. I say, mum, can we run up to Town to-morrow and have lunch at a restaurant, and go to a theatre?"

"Darling, I'm so sorry. You'll have to amuse yourself at home. It's a long standing engagement. I have to take a stall at a bazaar. The Duchess will be opening it at twelve so I must be there early, and I shall have to leave here directly after breakfast. That's really why I suggested that you should bring a friend with you so that you would have somebody to play with."

"None of the chaps I wanted could come. How absolutely rotten!"

He brooded. "Couldn't Harold come home for the week-end? Then we could play tennis and knock the balls about on the billiard table."

"You know your father has forbidden you to touch the billiard table. You always cut the cloth—"

"All right. But what about Harold?"

"I'm afraid not, dear. It's against the rules for any of the pupils to go away during the term. Mr. Renny has to be very strict. You know, Harold really was very naughty. Your father was terribly upset."

"What did he do exactly?"

"We won't talk about it, Kenneth," said Lady Webber sharply, and Kenneth, who knew exactly how far he could go with his mother, said no more.

Lady Webber returned to the subject later in the drawing-room.

"It's a pity we don't know any boys of about your age in this neighbourhood who could come over to play with you."

"There is one as a matter of fact," said Kenneth. "He's one of the chaps who didn't come back at the beginning of the term because of measles but he'll be turning up next half I suppose. It's young Fleming, and I remember hearing him tell Parkes Major that he lived at a place called Brock Green now."

"What sort of boy is he?"

Kenneth, who had sometimes joined with kindred spirits in twisting Toby Fleming's arms and treading on his toes, smiled thoughtfully.

"Not bad. I wouldn't cross the road for him if there was anybody else. He swots at books and is a rabbit at games. But he'd do."

"Is he quiet and well behaved? I shall have to put you on your honour not to get into mischief, Kenneth."

"Oh, he's a regular plaster saint," said the boy with a grin.

Lady Webber frowned a little. "I suppose his people are all right or he wouldn't be at that school. I seem to have heard the name lately, but they aren't on my visiting list."

"I believe his mother's a widow and fairly hard up. He's one of the chaps that are always short of tin. You needn't get him if you don't want to, Mother. I don't really care."

"I'll think it over," she said.

The next morning at breakfast she told him she would drive round by Brock Green on her way to Durchester to catch the London express.

"You can come with me and we can pick this boy up and Marples will bring you both home after seeing me off. By the way, Kenneth, did I hear you at the telephone just now?"

"No, Mother."

Sandra Fleming, answering the door, was rather overwhelmed by the unexpected appearance of a very beautiful woman in velvet and sables.

"I am Lady Webber. You are Mrs. Fleming! Thank you, I won't come in. I'm in a hurry, rushing to catch a train up to Town. But my son tells me that your boy is one of his school friends, and I thought it would be so nice for Kenneth if your boy would spend the day with him, and they can have such fun together. I have to be away unfortunately and the poor child will be terribly dull if he hasn't a companion. Your boy would be sent home in the car, of course."

"I see." Sandra, who had heard of the Webbers only as the rich newcomers to the neighbourhood who had bought Brock Hall, flushed with pleasure. "Toby will love it. But he's only got his old suit on. Will there be time for him to change?"

"I'm afraid not, but it won't matter a bit. They'll just be running about in the park. Can he come now? I don't want to miss my train—"

"I'll fetch him."

If Sandra had been an old-fashioned mother she would almost certainly have declined Lady Webber's invitation, but she was modern enough to have read a good deal about repressions and complexes and she was always on her guard, trying not to be possessive and to yield to the temptation to keep Toby to herself. Lady Webber's assured manner could easily become insolent. She was gracious merely to serve her own ends, and if she had come to ask Sandra to lunch the latter would have had no difficulty whatever in saying no. But the Webbers were rich, and Sir Henry had influence. They might be able to help Toby later on—and he had not had another boy to play with for months. So she hurried down the garden to the shed where Toby was happily engaged in sawing wood, with Mac and Sandy looking on.

"Darling, Lady Webber has called to fetch you back to the Hall to spend the day with her boy. She says he's at the same school. You never told me. Come quickly and wash your hands. There isn't time to change into your other suit. She's waiting—"

Toby gazed at her appalled. "Mother! You haven't said I'd go—"

"Yes, I have. It'll be a nice change for you. They'll send you back in their car. I'll take care of the dogs."

"Mother—" His heart sank. He had to face the fact that, however unconsciously, she had betrayed him to the enemy. You could never be certain with grown ups, he thought bitterly.

It did not seem possible to make them understand that you didn't necessarily enjoy being with people because they were round about the same age. That beast Piggy Webber.

"Mother, I don't want to—"

"Nonsense, darling. I've said you'd be delighted. Come along—" said Sandra firmly. She thought, "He's clinging to me too much. It isn't healthy. I mustn't give way."

Reluctantly Toby laid down his saw and glanced round him wistfully at his beloved workshop. He had been so happy only five minutes ago. Of course, he could not explain. He could not tell his mother that Webber was one of the boys who bullied him at school. It had not been so bad last term because he had entered into a defensive alliance with another boy, Harley Major. But he wouldn't have Harley at Brock Hall. He followed his mother up the path. She shut the dogs into the sitting-room while he washed his hands under the tap in the scullery, and came back with a hair brush.

"There. You're fairly tidy now. Put on your overcoat."

She went with him down to the gate and smiled at the rosy cheeked schoolboy sitting beside the uniformed chauffeur. Kenneth smiled back at her. He was in high spirits. He grinned at Toby. "Hallo, Fleming."

"Hallo," said Toby.

Lady Webber was holding the door open for him to get in with her.

"So good of you to let him come," she said sweetly to Sandra, who, now that it was too late, was looking rather unhappy. "Durchester station, Marples, we must not linger. I don't want to lose my train."

The huge glittering car slid away, leaving Sandra, standing at her gate, with a confused impression of carnations in a silver vase, fur rugs, fur coats, and smiles that were somehow not reassuring. She went slowly back to the sitting-room where the dogs were whining to be let out. Why had she let him go? He had not wanted to, and the house, without him, felt cold and empty, Lady Webber, meanwhile, was still being gracious. She had made room for Toby beside her and covered his knees with a part of the chinchilla rug. She had enquired his age and noted, with satisfaction, that he was not nearly so tall nor so sturdy for his years as her Kenneth. Further enquiries elicited the fact that Toby was very little use at cricket or football.

"Kenneth is good at both," said Lady Webber complacently.

Toby agreed. "They all say Webber's jolly good."

Both boys went on to the platform at the station and saw Lady Webber into her train. Toby did not like her, but he was sorry to see her go. He dreaded the prospect of spending the rest of the day alone with Piggy.

"We'll go to Corney's in the High Street and have coffee and cakes," said Kenneth, as they went back to the car, but in this he was disappointed. Marples said that her ladyship's orders were that they were to go straight back to the Hall and he was not to be moved either by persuasions or by threats.

"Oh, all right," said Kenneth at last, furiously banging the door after him as he scrambled in after Toby. "He hates me," he explained. "Our servants are a ghastly crew of sneaks and tell-tales. I'll pay him out some day, see if I don't." He relapsed into a sulky silence from which he only roused himself as they were passing up the avenue to the house. "Can you roller skate?"

"Yes. A little."

"You can have Harold's skates then. We'll practise a bit on the hard court. It'll be more fun than tennis as I know you can't play for nuts."

The rest of the morning was spent on the hard court. Toby soon discovered that the other boy's main object was to make him lose his balance by barging against him unexpectedly. He developed defensive tactics, but Kenneth was the heavier of the two and more at home on his skates, and the younger boy had several nasty falls. Toby was very hot and rather white about the lips when the parlourmaid came out to say that lunch would be ready in five minutes if the young gentlemen would like to come in and wash.

"You'd better lay a third place," ordered Kenneth.

"What for, Master Kenneth?"

"Never you mind. You just lay it."

"I'm expecting my brother Harold," he explained to Toby as they walked back to the house together. "I rang him up before breakfast and he said he'd borrow a motor bike and buzz along."

"He's at school, isn't he?"

"Not now. There was some sort of shindy. He's with an Army Coach. Harold's no end of a sport," boasted his younger brother. "We'll have some fun this afternoon when he comes."

Harold arrived just as they were sitting down to lunch. He was a handsome boy, with a fair, flushed face, heavy-lidded blue eyes, and a mop of corn-coloured hair. He greeted his admiring younger brother with easy good humour and Toby with a condescending nod.

"Well, it'll be something to have some decent food again. The cooking at the place I'm at is putrid. No, Higgins," as the butler was about to fill his glass with lemonade. Keep that for the kids. I'll have claret."

"I'm sorry, Master Harold—"

"What d'you mean, sorry?"

"I couldn't give you claret, sir, without Sir Henry's permission or her ladyship's."

"Rot," said Harold angrily, but something in the butler's expression warned him that he was not likely to get his own way. He and Kenneth ate heartily. Toby's nerves had affected his digestion. He could hardly force himself to swallow a few mouthfuls.

After lunch Harold led the way into a large room built out at the side of the house.

"This is our den, Fleming."

Toby looked about him. There was a bagatelle board and some book-shelves were filled with tattered copies of boys' books. Cricket bats, tennis rackets and fishing rods were stacked in the corners.

"Like to see my stamp album?" asked Kenneth.

Looking at stamps seemed to offer less scope for the kind of persecution he expected than roller skating so he said, "Oh, rather!" with genuine enthusiasm. Kenneth, who liked to boast about his possessions got out his album. Harold, who had produced a packet of cigarettes and lit one with an elaborate show of ease, was loafing about the room with his hands in his pockets. He chose a moment when the younger boys' heads were both bent over the stamp album to throw the half smoked cigarette into the fire.

"I say, this is pretty slow," he complained. "What about going into the park and playing Indians?"

Kenneth looked up quickly and caught his brother's eye. They exchanged slow smiles of anticipated satisfaction. Toby, quick to feel the danger ahead, said, "I'd like to look through these stamps first," in a voice that he tried hard to keep steady.

"All right." Harold's attention had been drawn to a brown paper parcel on a side table by the open window. "What's this? Chocs, by gum." He had thrown the crumpled brown paper into the fender where it flared up, caught by a falling spark from the grate, before he untied the rose coloured satin ribbon that was wound round the box and lifted the lid, and flicked off the sheet of silver paper. Kenneth jumped up and went over to him.

"I say, how scrumptious! Don't wolf them all, you pig."

"Pig yourself," said his elder indistinctly. "I'll have a hard centre this time. It's so difficult to tell. Didn't you know they were here?"

"Hadn't an earthly. I suppose Mother got them for me yesterday and forgot to say."

Harold raised his voice. "Will you have a chocolate, Fleming?"

"No, thanks," said Toby. He was still feeling rather sick, but he knew if he said so they would probably force him to eat some. He sat staring forlornly at the stamps of Nicaragua. He couldn't go home yet. Not for hours and hours. And they were planning something. The other two were whispering together. Kenneth giggled. Then Harold, after hunting in a cupboard and making a collection of odds and ends that included a torn fishing net and a length of fine cord, signified that they were ready.

"Come on, Fleming, you've been slacking on that sofa long enough. You're always a slacker, Kenneth tells me. Bad habit. You'll have to break yourself of it."

They passed through a gate in the rose garden and were in the park. "Now I'll tell you the game and the rules," said Harold. "Kenneth and I are chiefs of the Blackfeet tribe, and you're a spy of an enemy tribe. Do you see that oak tree bigger than the others? If you get to that before we catch you you'll be safe. It's no use running to it. You've got to take cover. There's plenty of bracken and undergrowth. Kenneth and I are going to shut our eyes and count two hundred slowly to give you a start. After that look out for yourself." He smiled down at Toby and licked his lips. You know Indian tortures are pretty bad," he said gently.

Toby gasped but said nothing. So that was the meaning of the cord and the net. Indian tortures. He went very white. Harold, seeing that he was afraid, laughed delightedly. "Now then, we're going to start." He shut his eyes. "One, two, three—"

Toby cast a hunted look about him and darted off into the woods on their left, plunging through the rain sodden bracken and stumbling over the roots of trees. Could he hide so that they would not find him? How long would it take them to count two hundred? Less than four minutes even if they did not cheat. Would they really keep their eyes shut? He wouldn't trust either of them. Piggy was bad enough at school, but the torments devised by him there were necessarily brief. A bell rang, and he had to stop. But here—Higgins, the butler, watched them from the dining-room window until they passed out of sight.

"I wonder what they're up to," he said doubtfully. "Well, it's no business of mine."

Toby had already lost sight of the tree that was to be his sanctuary. In any case he knew well enough that if he reached it they would say it was the wrong one. He wasn't really being given a chance. He reached a clump of undergrowth and crouched down behind a holly bush. Hope died in his heart as he heard the yells of the red Indian braves drawing nearer. Harold and Kenneth hurled themselves on him with whoops of triumph. His struggles ceased after a hearty hack on the shin from the elder boy.

"What shall we do with him?" enquired Kenneth, as they hauled him away between them.

"There's that stump of the silver birch in the clearing. We'll tie him to that. Indian prisoners are always tied to stakes."

The Webber boys were enjoying themselves. It was rather disappointing that their captive showed so little fight. Failing that he would have been more amusing if he had cried and begged for mercy. Still, from the red Indian standpoint he was living up to the best traditions of silent endurance. They had both seen a red Indian film founded on one of Fenimore Cooper's novels during the holidays. The recollection of it enabled them to give a picturesque gloss to their natural desire to hurt something weaker than themselves. It was an instinct they had inherited from the woman who, at that moment, was selling a satin sofa cushion to a Royal personage who was making several purchases at her stall.

The war dance round the stake was good exercise for a cold November afternoon but the victim was shivering in his bonds. He tried to speak once. "I say, you chaps—"

They were not listening, but they were tired of dancing. "What shall we do next?"

"Tell the squaws to collect brushwood for the fire. Have you got a penknife, Ken? We ought to run pine splinters under his nails. They always do that."

They moved away together. Kenneth lowered his voice. "He's simply dithering," he said gleefully.

Harold licked his lips. "I know."

"He thinks you really are going to go to do it."

"Well, we are, aren't we? Tell you what, Ken, I'll offer him half a crown if he'll let me run a splinter right up his nail without making a sound. I bet he won't be able to stick it."

Kenneth glanced rather doubtfully at his elder brother. Harold's handsome face was flushed and his heavy lidded blue eyes were blazing. Harold was queer sometimes. "He might kick up a row afterwards. Perhaps we'd better untie him now and go back to the house. It must be nearly tea time," he suggested.

"Rot. We haven't nearly done with him. He's a beastly little funk and deserves all he's going to get," said Harold impatiently. "You collect the stick for the fire while I get the splinters ready. Ouch"—he winced and stood quite still for a moment. Kenneth stared. "What's the matter?"

"Gripes," replied his elder tersely. "Don't stop there gaping."

Kenneth glanced round rather doubtfully at the forlorn little trussed-up figure in the middle of the clearing. "Why is he hanging his head down like that?" he asked rather anxiously. He not sorry for Toby, but he was beginning to be uneasy about the possible consequences to himself if they went too far. "He—he couldn't die could he, Harold? It wouldn't kill a person to be tied up?"

Harold laughed contemptuously. "Of course not, you young ass. He's shamming to get a rise out of us. You—" He did not go on. His handsome ruddy face had turned a queer streaky colour. He bent forward with his hands at his waist. "Oh gosh—" he muttered.

Kenneth began to be frightened. "What is it, Harold? Do you feel bad?"

"It's nothing," gasped Harold. "At least—help me back to the house, will you—the pain's—rotten."

Chapter XV
CONSEQUENCES

"Better now?" said a voice.

Toby opened his eyes and saw two faces bending over him by the light of a stable lanthorn. He recognised Higgins, the butler, and Marples, the chauffeur. He was still in the clearing, but it was quite dark. Toby, struggling to a sitting position, saw the jagged stump only a few yards away and a mass of cut ropes lying on the ground. He tried to remember what had happened. Kenneth and his brother had been dancing round him and they had gone away and left him. The pain in his arms had been unbearable and everything had gone black. His wrists were aching now and he felt numb with cold.

"Please," he said shakily, "I want to go home."

The two men exchanged glances. Higgins nodded. "Fetch the car, Marples. I can get him along to the avenue from here. Be as quick as you can."

Marples ran off and the butler helped Toby to his feet.

"You hold on to me," he said kindly. "Lean as heavily as you like. That's right." He cleared his throat. "I suppose you know that if you tell your mother all about this it'll mean a whole lot of trouble?"

Toby said nothing.

"They didn't ought to have treated you so," said Higgins, "but why did you let them tie you up?"

"I couldn't help it. There were two of them, and Harold's twice my size."

"Well"—Higgins suppressed his own private opinion of the young Webbers—"you mustn't take it too seriously, Master Toby, because it was just a game, and you'd all have been in to tea, and none the worse, if Master Harold hadn't come over queer and his brother had to help him back to the house, and when they were in Master Kenneth began to feel bad, too. The housekeeper did what she could for them, but we've rung up the doctor and he may be along any minute. I asked Master Kenneth what had become of you when he seemed a little easier about half an hour ago, and then he said you were in the clearing, and tied up, so Marples and I came along at once. And now you know everything."

"I see," said Toby. "What's the matter with them?"

"Over eating," said the butler curtly. "They've both been terribly sick."

He helped Toby down a bank on to the smooth tarred surface of the avenue. "Here's Marples with the car. Now you won't upset your ma by telling her too much, will you?"

Toby said nothing.

The car had stopped and Higgins helped him to get in. "The stiffness will pass off," he said anxiously. "I've talked to Master Toby, Marples. He's a sensible boy, he knows that least said soonest mended. All right. Drive on."

Higgins was looking towards the lodge. The headlights of another car coming up the drive dazzled his eyes. He signalled to the driver to stop and moved forward.

"Is it Doctor Harrison? I am Sir Henry's butler. Sir Henry and her ladyship being away I am responsible. I'm glad you've come, doctor. The young gentlemen are very poorly."

"Get in," said the doctor sharply. "I'll give you a lift back to the house. What are you doing wandering about without a hat or overcoat on a night like this?"

"The young gentlemen had a young friend spending the day, sir. I was sending him home in her ladyship's car."

The doctor grunted. He thought the butler seemed very flurried. "How old are the boys?"

"Sixteen and thirteen, sir."

"And they've eaten something that's upset them? Don't look so tragic, man. We'll soon put that to rights," said the doctor cheerfully, but his professional optimism seemed to have no effect on Higgins, who left one of the under servants to take the doctor upstairs while he hurried to the telephone. He had failed to get into touch with Lady Webber, who had left Wanborough House, where the Bazaar was being held, before he rang up. And Sir Henry was not at his club.

Marples, meanwhile, had put Toby down at his garden gate and had waited to see the door of the cottage open and Mrs. Fleming come out before he drove on to meet the train by which Lady Webber had told him she would return from Town. He was waiting on the platform, an imposing figure in his dark green uniform, when the train came in. Lady Webber hardly glanced at him. She had had a tiring day but it had been very satisfactory on the whole. The Duchess had been very gracious, and people who mattered had been friendly, while she had been successful in avoiding others who might have been tiresome. She sank back with a sigh of satisfaction as the car started and, opening her handbag, looked at herself earnestly in her mirror before touching the thin red curve of her lips with lipstick. She really looked absurdly young. Just as well that she had no daughter. It would have been very annoying to have a girl to bring out. She touched the burnished golden curls clustering over her ears caressingly with her gloved finger-tips before she picked up the speaking tube.

"I rather thought Master Kenneth would come to meet me. Is that boy still at the house?"

"No, my lady. I took him home on my way." Marples hesitated. Like the rest of the servants he disliked his mistress more than his master. Of the two Sir Henry was far more considerate.

"I think perhaps I should tell you, my lady, that neither of the young gentlemen are very well. Higgins rang up a doctor."

"Why? What happened?" she asked sharply.

"I haven't seen them myself, my lady, and from what I hear it seems to be a bad bilious attack."

She frowned. "You didn't let them go to the confectioner's?"

"No, my lady. I drove straight back to the Hall."

"You took young Fleming home in that state! I don't know what his mother will think—"

"I wasn't referring to him, my lady. Master Harold was home for lunch."

"Harold—" She pressed her lips together as she hung up the speaking tube. If Harold could be sent back to his crammer's before Sir Henry returned no great harm would be done. He must not have another row with his father so soon after the last. She took a cigarette from her case and leaned back, smoking thoughtfully.

The lodge gates were open. The car swept up the avenue and stopped at the foot of the steps. Higgins was at the door.

"Oh, my lady—"

"Where are the boys?" Marples had tried to prepare her, but she had not really grasped what he was saying.

Higgins began to speak, but her attention diverted from him to a strange man who was just coming down the stairs. He was looking at her, not respectfully or admiringly, but with an expression she was unable to define.

"Lady Webber? I am Doctor Harrison. Your butler rang me up. Your housekeeper and one of the maids have been helping me, but I must have a trained nurse. It might be better if you sent your car into Durchester to fetch her—"

Violet Webber's colour was fixed, but he saw her eyes dilate. "Does that mean that my boys are seriously ill? It's very sudden. Kenneth was perfectly well when I left home this morning."

"Very likely," he said curtly. "Will you see about the car while I ring up the nursing home?"

She looked after him angrily as he crossed the hall to the telephone. Horrid little man, taking advantage of his position. She turned to Higgins who was hovering in the background.

"Tell Marples to bring the car out of the garage again. He has to fetch the nurse." She passed into the octagonal sitting-room in which she had interviewed the detective from Scotland Yard a few days previously. But she was not thinking of him now. Brock Hall was centrally heated and she was beginning to feel too warm. She slipped out of her fur coat and stood with her back to the hearth while she drew off her gloves. One of them split across the back as she tugged at it.

The doctor had spoken to Higgins and was crossing the hall. She called him back.

He came a little way into the room. "I must go back to my patients, Lady Webber."

"Yes, of course," she said coldly. She was annoyed but not really frightened yet. "Are they sickening for something? But they have not been together since the end of the summer holidays. Is it something they have eaten?"

"I think so. That will have to be enquired into—" He turned quickly as a white-faced maid servant appeared on the threshold.

"Please, sir, you're wanted."

"All right. I'm coming."

"I'll come with you," said Lady Webber.

He was running up the stairs. She followed him, moving with her usual deliberate grace. The Webbers were never ill. It seemed to her that the doctor was making an unnecessary fuss.

Higgins was left alone in the large, brightly lit hall. He stood at the foot of the stairs, listening to the muffled sounds on the floor above. The parlourmaid came through from the servants' quarters with a tray of glasses.

"Cook says what about dinner, Mr. Higgins?"

He shook his head. "I don't suppose her ladyship will want any. Tell her to keep something hot to send up on a tray later." A thought struck him. "Ask her not to throw away anything that was left over from lunch."

He went into the octagonal room to switch off the lights Lady Webber had left burning. The eight courtly ladies, fingering their long curls with taper fingers, gazed down at him with coldly smiling eyes. He picked up the fur coat from the floor and hung it over the back of a chair before he went back to his post at the foot of the stairs.

Lady Webber, meanwhile, was standing by Harold's bedside. Mabel, the first housemaid, was sponging his face and hands.

"He's a bit easier now, my lady."

"Is he?" she said huskily. She was appalled at the change in him. His face was grey and sunken, his eyes were red-rimmed. They met hers with a vacant scare. She was quite unused to sick rooms and her chief desire was to get away. There was a murmur of voices on the landing and a woman in nurse's uniform came in.

"The doctor would like a word with you, Lady Webber. He is on the landing."

"Very well." She bent over Harold and touched his cheek with her lips. "My poor darling, you'll soon be better."

She went out quickly. "Doctor, this is terrible. Please do everything possible. Expense is no object. There's no need for the boys to share a nurse. We must have another one for Kenneth."

"Unfortunately the local supply of nurses is limited, Lady Webber. I have asked for another but she can't be here before the morning. The butler tells me he has tried to get in touch with Sir Henry and failed. Perhaps you will know where he may be found. He should be here."

"I have no idea," she said. "I suppose Higgins tried his club. He has his letters forwarded there. I believe he was going to Paris on business, but that was a fortnight ago."

"Hasn't he written?"

"No. He's not a good correspondent. He hates fuss and so do I. He often goes away like this," she added irritably. "It's quite usual."

"I see. Then I think, Lady Webber, we ought to get in touch with the B.B.C. and ask them to broadcast an S.O.S. for him at 9.30."

He saw the knuckles of the hand resting on the balustrade whiten.

"Is it—as bad as that?"

"Both the boys are dangerously ill, Lady Webber. I'd like to ring up my partner."

"Get a specialist down from Town if you think it's any use."

"I want somebody who can be here within a hour. Look here, Lady Webber, I must not leave the boys. Will you ring up Doctor Mackintosh? You'll find him in the telephone directory. Tell him it's urgent. Tell him we may need oxygen. And then get the B.B.C. and ask them to broadcast for you."

"Very well," she said dully.

Two hours after midnight lights were still burning all over the house. Doctor Mackintosh had arrived some hours previously and was upstairs with his colleague. Higgins opened the door when his master arrived a little before three o'clock.

"Thank God you've come. Sir Henry," he said as he helped him off with his coat.

"What was it? An accident?"

"No, sir. It seems like food poisoning. There's two doctors with them and a nurse. We've done all we can, sir."

"Where is her ladyship?"

"She's lying down, sir." Higgins, after a glance at his master's rigid face, added rather hastily, "She was quite worn out."

Sir Henry was twenty years older than his beautiful wife, a big burly man with a rugged face and a shock of iron grey hair. The strain of his long drive and the anxiety he had suffered had added another ten years to his age. The butler, watching him slowly mount the stairs, thought for the first time that he was an old man. His boys had given him very little cause to be proud of them, but he was their father.

As he reached the landing Doctor Harrison came out of Harold's room. He was coatless and his shirt sleeves were rolled up to the elbow. Sir Henry's heart sank at the sight of his haggard face. He tried to ask a question. "How—how—"

The doctor seemed equally at a loss. He stared at Sir Henry for a moment in silence before he said, "Sir Henry Webber?"

"Yes."

Harrison wiped his face with his handkerchief. His hands were trembling. "You're just too late for the elder boy," he said bluntly. "He died five minutes ago."

Sir Henry heard his own voice saying "What of?" It sounded a long way off.

"Heart failure from general shock was the immediate cause, but both the boys have been suffering from acute internal inflammation. I shall have to ask you to communicate with the police, Sir Henry."

"Good Heavens! Why?"

"The symptoms are those of arsenical poisoning."

Sir Henry said nothing for a long minute. In the silence both men could hear the ticking of the clock in the hall below.

"It's incredible," said Sir Henry at last. "Why should—but there'll be time for that. How is Kenneth? Can he be saved?"

"My partner, Doctor Mackintosh, and the nurse are with him now. We are doing all we can, but—"

He stepped back a pace and opened the door of Kenneth's room. Sir Henry went in and the little group standing by the bedside made way for him.

"Kenneth," he stammered, "my dear boy—" Kenneth had always been his favourite. "He doesn't know me," he muttered. "Terrible. Terrible!"

But the boy's pale lips were moving. His father, bending over him, heard him making the painful effort to articulate.

"Fleming—"

It came clearly, not a whisper but a cry. The doctor and the nurse hurried forward and Sir Henry was thrust aside.

Chapter XVI
THE OPEN WINDOW

COLLIER was awakened by the rattle of the blind being jerked up by an impatient hand. He had been dreaming a confused dream in which the brass of the kneeling woman, Alma Constantine, and the May Morning products all had their parts. He sat up and stared at the intruder, who was no less a person than Inspector Brett.

"I say"—his voice was deceptively mild. "Did you knock?"

"I did. And you said 'Come in' but I suppose you weren't really awake. Look here," Brett cleared his throat and turned rather red. "I wasn't over civil when you came, I know. I'll admit I was peeved with the Chief for calling you in. But I've got over that."

"Splendid," said Collier cordially. This was just what he had wanted. "But"—he glanced unobtrusively at the watch ticking away on the chair by his bedside—it was not yet eight. Couldn't Brett have waited until after breakfast? Unless, of course—he was wide awake now. "More trouble?" he asked.

"Yes."

Collier sprang out of bed and grabbed his clothes. "Tell me about it while I dress." Duffield had had nothing to report when he returned. He had kept a watch on the antique shop, but neither Constantine nor his daughter had left the premises. The Flemings should have been safe enough with a constable on guard. Yet it was clear that Brett was badly shaken. Mechanically he tested the temperature of the water. Couldn't go out without shaving. Brett was prowling restlessly about the room.

"I've told them downstairs to have your breakfast ready. I thought you'd like to come along with me. Of course, it may have nothing whatever to do with the Killick case. In fact, I can't imagine any possible connection. But when the superintendent rang up he seemed to think you should be told—"

"For the Lord's sake, Brett, don't beat about the bush. You don't have to apologise for letting me in on this."

"Oh, all right." Brett was surprised by his colleague's unexpected vehemence. This fellow from the Yard seemed a nervy sort of chap. "The trouble's at Brock Hall. Sir Henry Webber has two sons. The younger lad came home yesterday morning for his half term holiday and the elder brother, who was with an Army coach, arrived in time for lunch. They were both taken ill about tea time. Their parents were away. The butler got the wind up and sent for Doctor Harrison, and after a bit he got his partner to join him and they had a nurse. They seem to have done their best, but both the boys died during the night. Doctor Harrison rang us up before he left the Hall and his partner is remaining there to meet us. Of course there'll be a post-mortem and an inquest. The point is—it's rather unusual. The doctors seem to have made up their minds without waiting for the analysis that will give us proof of arsenical poisoning. The question is who would do such a thing, and why? A man like Sir Henry who has made a large fortune in business, has probably made a few enemies in his time, but a thing like this seems so malignant."

Collier gave his chin a final scrape and wiped his razor.

"Mightn't it have been an accident?"

"That remains to be seen. You need not come with me if you don't want to. I know you've got your hands full—but Sir Henry asked if you were still here."

Brett had let the cat out of the bag. Collier realised that he would not have been called on if Sir Henry himself had not asked for him. "That's all right, he said. "I'll come. It's on my road anyway. I was going to Brock Green. You have a car? I'll follow you in mine. I'll rejoin you downstairs in two minutes, Inspector. I must just have a word with Duffield."

Brett took the hint and went down to the dining-room. He sat with Collier and smoked a pipe while the latter ate his breakfast. "Doctor Harrison is sending the usual samples to the county analyst. We should hear to-morrow if arsenic is present. Harrison thinks they were both stiff with it. Medical men don't generally burn their boats like that. He'll feel a prize ass if it turns out to be something else, but he seems certain."

"Are there any other children?"

"No. Pretty ghastly for the parents. Well, if you're ready we might start."

He led the way outside. Collier glanced at his watch before he climbed into the driving seat of his car. Exactly twenty-five minutes since he woke to another day.

They were admitted by Higgins, who looked wan and tremulous and had cut himself while shaving, and were shown into the morning-room where the bereaved father awaited them. He, too, was haggard and heavy-eyed. He was sitting at his desk writing. He nodded to them without rising and indicated that they should sit down.

"You are the police?"

Brett answered, introducing himself and his companion.

"You have heard what has happened," he said harshly. "I only got back at three o'clock this morning. The B.B.C. broadcast an S.O.S. at 9.30. My wife was in London all yesterday, and both boys were seriously ill and the doctor was here when she came home. I have questioned the servants and I have drawn certain conclusions, but I don't want to influence you. I want the truth. The case is in your hands from now on."

Brett answered. "I'd like a word with the doctors first."

"I'm sorry. They left half an hour ago. They did not think any good purpose would be served by their remaining. The nurse is still here. I asked her to remain in attendance on my wife, who is, of course, prostrated by the shock. I have instructed the butler to take you to the morning-room. You can interview the staff there."

He dismissed them with another nod and resumed his writing. Higgins was waiting in the hall to show them to their allotted quarters. Brett asked for the nurse.

"Pretty cool customer, what?" he said, when they were alone. "All cut and dried. No Absalom, my son, my son, about him."

"He looked all in," said Collier. "He's got his feelings well under control, but he's hard hit, Brett. Make no mistake about that. I wouldn't care to have that man for my enemy. He's bitter as gall and one can't blame him."

"He's got his knife into someone about this if that remark of his about having drawn certain conclusions meant anything, but I thought I'd leave it at that. I want to take an unprejudiced view," said Brett. Collier was silent. In Brett's place he would have followed that up, but he was only there on sufferance.

The nurse, a thin woman with a skin that looked as if it had been scrubbed, came in with a rustle of starched linen.

Brett waved her to a chair. "We want to hear all you can tell us about this affair, nurse."

She answered succinctly. "Certainly. I am on the staff of St. Audrey's nursing home in Durchester. I had just come in from the Pictures and was going on duty when Matron told me Doctor Harrison had rung up from Brock Hall for a nurse, and a car was being sent. Both boys were vomiting almost incessantly and were on the verge of collapse. The housekeeper and one of the maids helped me through the night. We did our best, but the elder boy died at twenty minutes to three and the younger boy on the stroke of six."

"Did Lady Webber assist in the nursing?"

"No. She had seen the boys when she came back from London just before I arrived. She is quite unused to illness and she was very much upset. I saw her again a little before midnight. She told me she knew they were in good hands and that everything possible was being done and that she meant to take some aspirin and go to bed."

"Did she ask you to fetch her if there was a change for the worse?"

The nurse looked down her nose. "She did not. She did not wake until the maid took in her early tea."

"Who broke the news to her?"

"Sir Henry himself, I believe."

Brett cleared his throat. He was wondering if he had been wise in asking the man from the Yard to come with him. True, his superintendent had not given him much choice in the matter, and, so far, he felt tolerably certain, Collier could not have found any fault with his methods. Since a fairly strong hint he had received from his superintendent he had been consciously endeavouring to curb his tendency to browbeat witnesses.

"What do you think the two boys died of, nurse?"

She answered primly. "It isn't for me to say."

"Were the symptoms similar to those of any patient you've had before?"

They both saw her shudder. "No. And I hope I never see anything like it again. It was awful."

"Did either of them say anything that threw any light on the cause of their illness? I mean—'Oh, nurse, those berries we ate in the wood'—something like that?"

"No." She paused as if uncertain. "Just at the last the younger boy called out a name—the name of the schoolfellow who had been spending the day with him. His father was present and the doctor. He cried out 'Fleming!' quite loudly. It gave us all a shock, I think. Of course, I didn't know what he meant. And he never spoke after that."

"Fleming," said Brett. "Would that be the boy who found the body in Hammerpot wood? I suppose it must be. Odd how he keeps on cropping up. I shouldn't have thought he'd have been at a posh school, the sort of place Sir Henry would send his boys to. Well, all this is quite informal, nurse. I'm not asking you to sign statements or anything of that sort this morning. You're staying on with her ladyship?"

"Only until another nurse can be sent out here. I'm not made of iron, Inspector," said the nurse tartly. "I'm going back to St. Audrey's to get a few hours' sleep."

"Could we see Lady Webber now?"

"No. The doctor gave her a sleeping draught. In any case she was in London all yesterday. She can't tell you anything."

"Thank you, nurse." He held the door open for her and beckoned to the butler who was waiting in the hall.

"You next. We want to hear everything you can tell us about yesterday."

"Very good, sir."

"Now I'm not asking for a formal statement, Higgins, as I told the nurse just now. There will have to be an inquest and the police have got to know a lot more than will ever be made public, so don't be afraid to speak out here. Between you and me and the gatepost I've heard rumours about the young Webbers. They were inclined to be mischievous, weren't they?"

"They were—-uncommonly self willed," Higgins admitted.

"Is it a fact that the elder boy was expelled from his school?"

"I couldn't say, Inspector. I'm only a servant."

"All right. We'll leave that, but there's been a rumour that one of the younger boys, as the result of persistent bullying, tried to commit suicide, and that the principal responsibility was traced to Webber."

"I never heard the reason why Master Harold didn't go back to his school," said Higgins slowly.

"Does the reason given strike you as improbable?"

"No. I mean—I couldn't say."

"All right. Now what about this boy Fleming who came here yesterday to spend the day? Was it his first visit to the Hall?"

"Yes. Her ladyship thought Master Kenneth would be dull by himself, and when he said a boy he knew at his school was living down the village she said he might have him to play with. Master Kenneth went with her ladyship in the car to the station, and on the way they picked up young Fleming. Master Kenneth had wanted his brother to come home for the week-end, but her ladyship wouldn't allow it."

"But he did come."

"Master Kenneth rang him up before her ladyship came down to breakfast. Master Kenneth and young Fleming spent the morning roller skating on the hard tennis court."

"Did they get on well together?

"Master Kenneth was enjoying himself. I heard him shouting and laughing. I don't know so much about the other boy. He was smaller and not so used to skating. I fancy he had a good many falls. I noticed he looked rather white when they came in to lunch, and he didn't eat much, just crumbled the food on his plate. Master Harold turned up in time for lunch."

"What did they have to eat?"

"Fried sole, roast chicken with brussels sprouts and fried potatoes, and a favourite sweet of Master Kenneth's, sponge cakes with jam and cream. It was all good wholesome stuff, Inspector. The housekeeper and me had what was left afterwards warmed up for our own lunch, and we're none the worse."

"What happened after lunch?"

"The young gentlemen went to their own sitting-room. It's on the ground floor and was built about fifty years ago for a billiard room. The boys keep their games and their books and that there. They stayed there about half an hour and then they went out into the park. I saw them from the landing window as they crossed the open space in front of the house towards the woods." He hesitated before he added. "The Webber boys had got young Fleming between them. I mean, they were holding his arms."

"Did he seem to be going willingly?"

"Well—it's hard to say."

"What happened after that?"

"I saw no more of them until between four and half-past. I was in the hall when Master Kenneth and his brother came in together. Master Harold was leaning on his brother and groaning. I thought for a moment that they were up to some trick, play acting, but then the elder boy doubled up and let out a scream. Mabel came running and I sent her for Mrs. Simmons, and between us we got them up to their rooms and put them to bed. They both needed constant attention. We were all badly scared. I tried to get in touch with her ladyship and with Sir Henry, and then I rang up the doctor."

"What became of Fleming?"

"I wondered about that, and when Master Kenneth seemed a little easier I asked him. He said, 'We left him in the wood. Harold was so bad, we didn't stop to untie him.' Well, that worried me a bit. Mrs. Simmons and Mabel were with the boys and Marples would have to be going into Durchester before long to meet the train her ladyship was coming back by. I sent for him and we went down the park together. We found young Fleming down in the clearing and he came round nicely and I talked to him a bit and Marples took him home in the car."

"What do you mean by came round nicely, Higgins?"

Again the butler hesitated. "He was tied up to a tree stump. They would have untied him when they all came in to tea and nobody been any the worse, but—you see how it was—they'd left him. He'd been there a couple of hours, and what with the discomfort of the ropes, and the cold and the dark, the poor kid was all in."

"So I should think," said Brett dryly. Neither he nor Collier attempted to hide their disgust.

Higgins looked from one to the other. "I haven't told Sir Henry. Her ladyship always found excuses for them when they got up to their tricks, but he didn't. I told the little chap it'd only upset his poor mother if he complained, and he hadn't any hurts that couldn't be put right by a good night's rest. The less said the better, I thought." It was obvious that the old butler's chief concern was to spare his master's feeling as far as possible.

"Can't make any promises," said Brett, "I'd like to see the room where the boys spent that half hour before they left the house. It's not been cleaned or interfered with since, I hope."

"It should have been, but the maids are behind with their work. This way, gentlemen."

They found the play-room just as the boys had left it after lunch the previous day. Higgins went back to the hall, leaving them to their work. The stamp album was still lying open on the table. Its pages were stirred by the wind blowing in from the open window. The sill was wet and there was a damp stain on the carpet where rain had come in during the night. There was a small table in front of the window. Its cloth had slipped off and was lying on the ground between the table legs and the wall. The white paint of the window sill was smeared with mud and marked with numerous scratches.

"I expect the boys came in and out this way rather than by the door," said Brett with a half laugh. He was turning away when Collier recalled him. He had stooped and picked up two crumpled scraps of tinsel paper. He held them out on the palm of his hand.

"These may be important. There are several more in the waste paper basket."

"Wrappings from chocolates, eh? And they must have been eaten yesterday, or the paper wouldn't be here. You're right." He felt that he was being magnanimous as he said it, for the man from the Yard had been getting on his nerves and he had been trying to think of some way of getting rid of him. "I think we'll have Higgins in about this."

He rang the bell and the butler appeared.

"The boys were eating chocolates in here yesterday, Higgins. Can you tell us what became of the box?"

The butler looked about him. "I couldn't say, sir. I don't see it anywhere about."

"Would it be one belonging to Lady Webber?"

"I shouldn't think so. Her ladyship never touches chocolates."

"She may have bought a box as a treat for the boy when he came home."

"She may, but not to my knowledge. She didn't like him to eat sweets, though of course he bought them whenever he could."

"Perhaps young Fleming brought the box with him."

"Not if it was a large box," said the butler firmly. "He wasn't carrying anything when he got out of the car."

"It's more likely to have been brought by Harold," said Collier.

"We must not make too much of the chocolates," said Brett rather impatiently.

"No. But the complete disappearance of the box is curious. They may have eaten the lot and thrown the box into the fire before they went down to the woods, but in that case I should have expected to find a good many more of the paper wrappings. There are only five here. Two were on the floor and three in the waste paper basket. Is this table covered with a cloth, Higgins?"

"Yes." He moved forward to replace it but Collier stopped him.

"I notice several finger-prints on the polished top of this table, Brett. Four on the edge nearest the window are particularly interesting. Suppose you were outside on the garden path. Anything placed on the farther side of the table would be out of reach but it might be brought nearer if you pulled at the cloth. But the table is highly polished and the cloth might slip right off, bearing the desired object with it. You would have to lean far over the sill to retrieve it, and to prevent yourself from falling head first into the room you might rest one hand heavily on the edge of the table."

The butler looked bewildered, but Brett's eyes gleamed. "You think the box was planted by somebody who got it back when the mischief had been done?"

"It's possible. Would it be easy to open this window from outside, Higgins?"

"The young gentlemen often did with the blade of a penknife. That was during the day. I always put the catch down when I made my last round at night. I didn't last night, though."

"That will do for the present, Higgins. No one is to come into this room, you understand. I shall want to see the chauffeur next. I'm coming back to the morning-room. Send him up when I ring."

"Very good, Inspector."

When the butler had left them Brett turned to his colleague from the Yard.

"What's your opinion of this business, so far, Inspector? Has it any connection with the job that's brought you down here from

London? Because, if it hasn't, I oughtn't to keep you here wasting your valuable time."

For Brett, usually so heavy-handed, this was really tactful.

"I wouldn't call it waste," said Collier amiably. "I'm always glad of a chance to see a good man at work. One gets set in one's own ways, and it's helpful to watch other people's methods."

To his relief the local man swallowed this. He even looked pleased. "I don't go in for frills. I just go straight on. It's the best way. And not too much talk. Now, in your place, if you don't mind my saying so, I wouldn't have said all that about the table in front of Higgins. I'd seen it all, naturally, and drawn much the same conclusions—though I make certain reservations—but he hadn't. We can't be sure of him, you know."

"I daresay you're right," said Collier with charming humility.

"You've got the case well in hand. You'll be busy with your assistants when they arrive getting all the prints in this room, and the prints of every person under this roof, I may as well buzz off. I was going to Brock Green. Can I help you by getting a statement from young Toby? That'll have to be done."

He would have liked to have added, "He and I are friends and he'll tell me more than he would you," but he knew that if he did Brett would probably insist on interviewing Toby himself.

"It's not a—" began Brett, and broke off with a startled exclamation. "What's the matter?"

Collier had turned white. "Good God!" he said. "Why didn't I think of it before? The chocolates! He may have eaten them, too."

Brett, to do him justice, was almost equally horrified. "You'd better go at once."

The advice was superfluous. Collier had gone. Brett followed, only stopping to lock the door of the play-room and pocket the key. He was going to carry out the programme suggested by Collier, and to do that he had to ring up the station at Durchester. He could hear Collier's car hurtling down the avenue as he picked up the receiver.

Sir Henry came out of his study as he hung it up a few minutes later.

CHAPTER XVII
TOBY

COLLIER sprang out of his car at the gate of the Forge Cottage and ran up the path. Sandra Fleming opened the door for him before he could knock.

"I saw you from the window. Please come in."

"How's Toby?"

"Still sleeping, so we must be quiet. I've got his breakfast tray ready to take up when he wakes. The poor boy had an awful time with those hooligans at the Hall. I shall never forgive myself for making him go. But I had no idea—"

She had led the way into the living room. "Please sit down, Mr. Collier."

"Thank you."

She had set his worst fears at rest. She was looking at him curiously. "I thought something perfectly ghastly had happened when I saw you running up the path."

"You weren't far out," he said gravely

"Oh!" she said rather faintly. "In connection with—with those murders?"

"I wish you'd tell me first what happened to Toby yesterday. I understand that he was brought back here by the chauffeur. Is that right?"

"Yes. It was after dark and our faithful watchdog—Quilter, I mean—had just arrived on his bicycle when the Webber's car drove up and dropped Toby at the gate. He simply crawled in. He was white as a sheet. I asked him what had happened, and he said they had been ragging and he was tired and had a headache and wanted to go to bed. It seemed the best thing, but I saw that he had a hot bath first. Mr. Collier, he's simply covered with bruises. I almost think I ought to write to Lady Webber and complain, though I know Toby would hate me to do that."

"He didn't give you any details?"

"No. I gave him a couple of aspirins with a cup of hot milk. I thought a good long sleep was the best thing."

Yes. I'm afraid I shall have to ask him a questions presently."

"Why?"

"You have not seen any of your neighbours to speak to this morning? I thought not. It must be all over the village by now. Prepare for a shock, Mrs. Fleming."

She sat, her small work-worn hands pressed together, her steady grey eyes, so like Toby's, fixed on his face.

"What is it?"

He told her.

She had listened, at first incredulous, and then with unconcealed horror. "Poisoned! But who would do such a thing? And you think chocolates? But then—"

Collier saw the awful fear that had brought him driving like a madman through the lanes from the Hall to the village flash through her mind. "Toby," she gasped. "My darling—he may have eaten them, too."

He went to her quickly as she rose shakily to her feet. She had gone white to the lips. "Don't worry, Mrs. Fleming. I thought of that. But I'm sure Toby's safe. He would have felt the effects before now."

"Are you certain? The aspirins I gave him might have delayed the action."

"No."

"Oh," she sighed. "I don't know what I'd do without you. You're so—so solid. But I must run up and look at him."

"I'll come too if I may," he said.

He followed her up the steep little staircase. She whispered a warning to him to mind his head. In Toby's room the ceiling sloped down to the lattice window. Mac, the Cairn terrier, was lying curled up at the foot of the bed. He wagged his tail as they approached. Toby was sleeping quietly.

"He's all right. Don't wake him," murmured Collier. She nodded, and they left the room on tiptoe, but Toby was calling his mother before they reached the foot of the stairs.

She called back to him. "Don't get up. I'm bringing your breakfast." The kettle was simmering on the hob. "He'll want me to stay with him," she said as she made the tea. "You won't mind being left?" They smiled at each other as he answered, "Not a bit."

But when Sandra had gone upstairs with her tray and the Inspector had resumed his seat by the fire and filled his pipe his smile had vanished and his face betrayed his real feelings. The chocolates. That was only a guess. There was no actual proof as yet that the chocolates had been the medium used. Until the post mortem on the two boys had been held there was no proof that they had actually died of arsenical poisoning. There were other possibilities. But, in fact, he had little doubt that murder had been committed. Was there any connection between this crime and the deaths of Constantine and of Killick? Brett had asked him that question and he had evaded answering it. Was it just a strange coincidence that had involved Toby Fleming in both cases? His presence in Hammerpot wood and at the Hall was accounted for. The motive in the first case, which seemed to be a struggle in the first case, which seemed to be a struggle for the possession of the paper hidden under the brass of the kneeling woman, could not be held operative in the death of two schoolboys. There was another point. Harold's return home had been unexpected. Until he turned up at lunch time his younger brother Kenneth had been the only member of the household who had anticipated his coming. Did that mean that his death had not been planned? Or—another possibility—had he brought the chocolates with him and would the criminal be found among his fellow pupils at the crammer's? Or had the killer missed his mark? Was Toby the intended victim? Collier frowned as he considered this point. He had assumed hitherto that the two men who had entered the cottage and forced Toby to repeat Constantine's dying words had found the paper they were seeking under the brass, and were satisfied. But perhaps that episode had been less simple than he had imagined. He looked at his watch. So much had happened since he got up that morning that he was surprised to find it was only just after eleven. He wanted to ring up headquarters. They might have the information he had asked for about young Killick's army record by this time. He went to the foot of the stairs and called up.

"Mrs. Fleming."

"Yes."

"I'm going on to the post office. I want to put through a trunk call. I'd like a word with Toby when I come back."

"All right. He'll be downstairs by then."

The post office was at the farther end of the village. It was also a general shop, and several customers who were buying groceries stared with undisguised curiosity as Collier came in and immured himself in the dark cupboard that contained the telephone. It took him nearly twenty minutes to get through, and then he was told that the information he required had been sent to him through the post.

Deliberately he had refrained from mentioning the tragedy at Brock Hall. It was not his pigeon. The Yard would be apprised of it, if at all, by the Chief Constable. He would have to be careful not to take too much upon himself. He drove back to the Forge Cottage. Sandra Fleming was at the gate and obviously waiting for him. He could hear the dogs barking inside.

"Oh, Mr. Collier," she burst out before he could speak, "they've taken him away!"

He saw that she was on the verge of tears.

"What do you mean?"

"Toby. That policeman from Durchester—the one who barks at you. He said Toby must answer some questions at the police station. I begged him to wait until you came back, but that made him worse. He—he sounded so harsh. I know Toby's afraid of him."

Collier bit his lip. "Toby has done no wrong Mrs. Fleming. He has nothing to fear from the police. It won't be as bad as you think."

"But did you know he would be fetched away?"

"No. I thought I'd get the boy to talk to me here, and that they'd be satisfied with that. But this isn't really my case, Mrs. Fleming."

"If you could have gone with him," she said wistfully. "You would have given him confidence."

"I'll go now if you like," he said.

He thought Inspector Brett might have waited for him, but he realised that Mrs. Fleming and Toby's outspoken preference for himself had annoyed the local man. He would have to try and smooth him down again when they met. He was a little doubtful of the wisdom of his offer, but Sandra was so much cheered by it that he felt rewarded. Apart from his very human wish to please he felt very strongly that Toby needed very careful handling.

"Look here," he said, "why not come with me? Bring the dogs if you can't leave them behind. I'll park you at a café while I go to the police station and hand Toby over to you when they've done with him. They've got a Harold Lloyd film running at the Palladium. Take him to that before you come home. You both need distraction."

This seemed a good plan to Sandra. She ran in to get her hat and coat and came back with Mac and Sandy tugging at their leads. Twenty minutes later Collier was knocking at the door of the superintendent's room.

There were three men present, the Chief Constable, the superintendent, and Inspector Brett. Toby's examination had only just begun with some well meant hortatory remarks by the Chief Constable, to which Toby, sitting on the extreme edge of his chair, listened with a great appearance of docility, while the superintendent played with his fountain pen and Brett controlled his impatience.

Collier was received civilly but without any signs of enthusiasm. Captain Lowther shook hands with him, the superintendent nodded, and Brett affected to be rearranging some loose leaves in his note book, while Toby looked hopefully towards the man whom he regarded as his friend.

"We hope to get some useful information from this young man," began the Chief Constable. "I've just been telling him that we expect the truth and nothing but the truth. Small boys have a habit of romancing, but that won't do here. Inspector Brett, you know what you want."

The Inspector looked hard at Toby. "You remember the potting shed at the bottom of the kitchen garden at Brock Hall?"

"Yes. We left our skates there."

"That was just before lunch?"

"Yes."

"You had been roller skating on the hard tennis court for some time?"

"Yes."

"Kenneth Webber had knocked you down several times, hadn't he?"

"Well—he barged into me. I can't skate very well."

"Did you notice a tin of weed killer in the shed?"

"Yes. On a shelf. Kenneth pointed it out to me. He said, 'That's deadly poison. Wouldn't it be a lark to give old Barn owl some.'"

"Who is old Barn owl?"

"He's one of the masters at our school. He gives us maths. He's pretty foul," said Toby judicially.

"You went back to the house for lunch and met Kenneth's elder brother. After lunch you all three went into the playroom. Is that right?"

"Yes."

"Tell us what happened then?"

"Kenneth showed me his stamp album. Harold found a box of chocolates on a table and he and Kenneth started stuffing."

"Did you have any?"

"No. They did ask me, but I didn't want any. I was feeling rather rotten and I was afraid of being sick."

"What table was this box on?"

"It was near an open window."

"Was it a large box? Can you describe it?"

"I didn't see it close to, but it looked like a half pound box and it was just plain white with a bit of pink ribbon tied round it. Harold chucked the ribbon into the fire with some of the packing stuff."

"What happened after that?"

"They said we should play Indians. I wasn't keen because I knew it meant getting knocked about, so I said I wanted to go on looking at the stamps, but they made me come."

"Had you any sweets of your own with you?"

"I had a few acid drops in a paper bag in my pocket."

He was giving his answers readily, but he seemed to become aware of increasing tension for he looked about him doubtfully at the grave faces of his audience.

"You were going down to the park?"

"Yes.

"And on the way you went into the potting shed again."

"No."

"The ropes the Webbers used to tie you to the tree stump were kept in the shed."

The Chief Constable leaned forward across his desk. "You need not answer questions if you don't want to, Toby. I should have told you if I had realised the drift—" He glanced at Collier. "We are in a difficult position. I don't want to take advantage of this witness's youth and inexperience."

Collier was silent for a moment. He was making up his mind. Finally he said, "I don't think Toby has anything to hide. Go on, Toby."

The boy moistened his lips. There was something here that he did not understand. He struggled on, stumbling a little now over some words.

"There was some rope in the playroom. Harold brought that along. We passed the potting shed but we didn't go in. They pointed out a tree that was home and shut their eyes while they counted two hundred. I hid behind some bushes but they soon found me, and I was tied up. They did a war dance and all that and then they went away to get wood for a fire. Oh—they took my acid drops out of my pocket and ate them before they went."

"At your invitation?"

"No. They just found them and helped themselves. They—they'd been pretty beastly to me, hacking me on the shins and pinching and all that." He looked round him again, this time defiantly. "I can't say I'm sorry they're dead," he said.

Collier groaned in spirit. Could the others be trusted to see that the boy would never have said that if he had been guilty?

Brett leaned back. "And that's that," he said. "We've corroboration of some of the details. I picked up the paper bag that contained the acid drops on the ground by the tree stump in the park little more than an hour ago."

The superintended seemed about to speak but Collier intervened.

"I fancy Toby has told you all he knows, and his mother is waiting for him at the Cadena Café in the High Street. You know where he lives. He is within easy reach whenever you want him. May I hand him over to his mother and then come back?"

Brett opened his mouth to speak and shut it again without saying anything. Captain Lowther hesitated. "You accept the responsibility?"

"Yes. Come along, Toby."

The boy jumped up eagerly, and they left the room together.

Collier spoke over his shoulder as they went out. "I'll be back in five minutes."

He was true to his word. He spoke directly to the Chief Constable. "I hope you didn't think I was too high-handed, sir. I could see he had no idea that he was being suspected of having murdered the Webber boys, and I wanted to get him away before he tumbled to it. He's a sensitive little chap and I don't know what his reactions might be."

"Sir Henry is convinced of his guilt," said Brett.

"He may be. But Sir Henry has never so much as laid eyes on him," said Collier hotly. "Because his own boys were a couple of young toughs he thinks all boys are like Habakkuk, *capable de tout*."

Brett reddened. "You've got to admit the motive and the opportunity."

"Rot!" said Collier violently, and then, realising he was losing his temper, he made an effort.

"I beg your pardon, Brett. I've seen more of the boy than you have. I'm prepared to stake any reputation I may have that Sir Henry's wrong. I still think the chocolates were the medium. In any case you've nothing to lose by leaving the boy alone for a bit. He'll be there when you want him."

"I leave it to the Chief," said Brett stiffly.

"We don't want to commit ourselves before we've heard the result of the post mortem," said Captain Lowther. "I gather that your theory is that young Fleming shifted some of the weed killer into his bag of acid drops while the other boys were routing about for rope in the potting shed. Fortunately you found the bag. It can be analysed."

Meanwhile Mrs. Fleming and Toby were having lunch at the Cadena Café and Toby was giving his mother a description of his interview with the police. Sandra said very little. She was reproaching herself bitterly for having allowed Toby to go to Brock Hall. If only she could live the last twenty-four hours over again.

"Inspector Collier was jolly decent all through," Toby was saying. "And there's no need to look so upset, Mother. It was quite all right really—though I do rather wish I hadn't told them about Kenneth and his brother kicking me on the shin bones and all that. I mean—one doesn't want to be a sneak." And then, more cheerfully, "Only I thought as they were dead it couldn't get them into any sort of mess." He was silent for a moment, evidently immersed in the intricacies of a schoolboy's code of honour. When he resumed it was with the air of one making a discovery.

"They kept on about the weed killer and my acid drops. Do you suppose they think I might have done the dirty work?"

"Of course not, darling," she said. "Don't be absurd."

"Am I?" he said. He broke off to give Mac, who was sitting up and waving his shaggy little forepaws imploringly, a piece of ham. "I suppose I could have done it if I'd thought of it. I was hating them both."

"Toby," she cried, "for Heaven's sake don't talk like that."

He looked up, surprised by her vehemence. "Well, I did," he argued. "You don't know what I had to put up with last term from Webber, and I wasn't the only one. But I wouldn't be such a priceless ass as to try to murder him."

"Of course not," she said again, "but don't keep on saying how much you disliked them. After all, they're dead."

"What difference does that make?" enquired Toby, "but I don't want to go on jawing about them. I'd rather forget them." He paused for a moment and added with a slight change of manner, "Mother, you do know I wouldn't do a rotten thing like that, don't you?"

"Yes, dear. And now we'll drop the subject. Mr. Collier suggested we should go to see Harold Lloyd at the Palladium."

"A jolly good wheeze," said Toby with enthusiasm. "Come on. They start the first house at one thirty. I say, Mother, I do like him awfully, don't you?"

"Harold Lloyd? Yes, he's good."

"I meant the Inspector."

Chapter XVIII
AN ARREST

COLLIER resisted the temptation to join the Flemings at lunch. He had realised that it might be better if he did not identify himself too openly with them. He had gone quite far enough already. At one point in the discussion in the superintendent's room Captain Lowther had asked him if the boy and his mother were personal friends of his.

"I met them for the first time ten days ago."

"I see," said the Chief Constable. "And you've no actual knowledge of their antecedents?"

"None."

Before he got up to go he had been given a rather strong hint that he should stick to his own case and leave the Brock Hall poisoning mystery to the local police. The horrid business was public property now. Newsboys were running across the market square as he left the station, with pink posters, sticky from the press, wrapped about them.

TERRIBLE TRAGEDY:
DEATH OF SIR HENRY WEBBER'S SONS.

He saw Alma Constantine at the door of the antique shop, buying a paper, as he went down the High Street. She had it spread out on the counter and was reading it when he entered. He had been delayed by the faithful Duffield, who had stepped out of a doorway to make his report. He had a confession to make. The girl had taken out the car soon after noon on the previous day. He had followed on a motor cycle to the outskirts of the town.

"And then—I had to swerve to avoid a lorry coming out of the gas works. I skidded into the hedge. No bones broken, but by the time I got straightened out it was hopeless. I thought the best thing I could do was to come back here and see when she came back."

"And when did she?"

"Half an hour ago."

Collier made no comment. Duffield had been unlucky. It couldn't be helped. He noticed as he entered the shop that Alma glanced at the door leading to the back of the house before she looked at him. It was closed. She was wearing the same clumsily made dress of some dark woollen material. Collier met her direct unsmiling gaze with an equal steadiness.

"Does your father know what I told you the other day?"

"Yes."

He laid a finger on the paper spread on the counter between them. "You've read what happened yesterday at Brock Hall?"

"Yes."

"What do you know of the Webbers?"

"The Webbers?" She seemed surprised. "Sir Henry bought a Buhl table off us a few months ago. She comes in sometimes to price things, but she never buys. Why?"

"Oh, nothing. You've been away, haven't you?"

"I suppose you've been having us watched. Father and I don't mind. We've never had any trouble with the police and if my brother Michael is dead he's safe. Father wanted me to go up to London to see my aunt Zoe. He hoped she might have seen my brother since—since what happened here. Michael was often at her place. So I drove up yesterday and stayed the night with her. But she couldn't tell me anything. He's not been there for over three weeks."

"I'd like your aunt's name and address."

"Her name is Michaelis. Since my uncle's death she has run a boarding-house in Russell Square. Most of her guests are medical or law students, Egyptians and Indians, and she gets some foreigners, too."

He saw that she attached no significance to this fact and he was careful to show no elation as he jotted down the address in his notebook. He thanked her again and took his leave. On his way up the street he stopped to speak to Duffield.

All right. You can call it a day. I'm going back to the hotel."

"Shall I come with you?"

"No. The less we're seen about together the better."

As he walked on he pondered the case. As it happened he had heard of Madame Michaelis. There had been an unexplained explosion in the basement of her house in Russell Square some eighteen earlier. It had been put down to an escape of gas but the police had had their doubts. The occupant of the room in which it had occurred, a Jugo-Slavian political exile, had been killed by the fall of the mantelpiece. The special branch at the Yard might know more about Madame's guests. Collier had gathered that there were idealists among them whose impatience with a sadly imperfect world might lead to attempts to improve matters with sawed off shot guns or nitro-glycerine. The May Morning products. Chemical experiments. It looked as if the pieces of the puzzle were fitting into their places at last, thought Collier as he waited for the traffic lights to turn green. He had left his car parked outside the police station. He went back to it and drove to the hotel which, at that hour of the afternoon, was practically deserted. The postman came in while he was shut up in the telephone booth at the entrance waiting to be put through to his chief at the Yard. He saw, through the glass door, the brassy-haired young woman in the office putting the letters in the rack.

"Hallo . . . is that you, sir? Yes, Collier speaking. I've got a line on Constantine at last. Yes, the man who was shot in Hammerpot woods. His aunt is Madame Michaelis who runs a boarding-house in Russell Square . . . yes, that place. Will you find out if any of her boarders were away on—you know the relevant dates, and if any have left since last Wednesday week? No, I don't suppose there's much hope of making an arrest. They'll be God knows where by this time . . . Thanks for those kind words, sir . . ." he was grinning as he hung up the receiver. Good old Cardew. He never let his men down. He was beginning to be very conscious of having missed his lunch. He spoke to the girl in the office, asking that tea might be sent up to his sitting-room, took the letter that had come for him from the rack, and went upstairs in the lift.

Duffield, coming in an hour later, learned from the boots that his friend had just gone out again in his car.

Sir Henry Webber was in his study, sitting alone in the fire-light, when the butler brought in Collier's official card.

"Yes, of course I'll see him," he said. "Show him in here."

He could bear anything better than inaction and since the police had concluded their examination and had left the house had seemed intolerably silent. Earlier in the day he had been fully occupied. He had made all the necessary arrangements for the funeral over the telephone. There had been a great deal to be done. The inquest was to be opened the following morning. The Chief Constable had assured him that the proceedings would be purely formal and would only last a few minutes, and they could start on the long drive to Golders Green at noon. He would be alone, of course. Violet, characteristically, was relying on dope to see her through. She would remain in bed, drowsy, semi-conscious, until it was all over. Well, she wasn't the sort of person one wanted to have about when one was in trouble anyway, he reflected grimly. He turned his head wearily as the visitor came forward and switched on the reading lamp at his elbow.

"Inspector Collier, is it? You came with the local man this morning but I noticed he did all the talking. I'd heard there was a man down from the Yard about that other affair and I asked for him. Why weren't you pulling your weight?"

"The local people have got this case in hand, Sir Henry. We have to be careful not to overlap. We can't intervene unless we're formally invited. I really came because I thought it just possible that there might be some connection between these cases."

"Sit down," said Sir Henry gruffly. "Will you have a drink first? You'll find whisky and a syphon on that table. No? Very well then. You realise now, I imagine, that this case has nothing whatever to do with anything that happened before yesterday. My sons were poisoned by the boy who was brought here to play with them. That fact has got to be established so that no suspicion may rest on innocent persons. I have never been blind to my sons' faults, Inspector. They had unfortunate tendencies, which I tried to check. Harold was expelled from his public school last term for bullying a younger boy. His victim tried to commit suicide. I have no doubt that this other boy, young Fleming, was driven momentarily over the border line of sanity. No doubt that will be taken into account at the trial. I presume he can be tried, though they tell me he is only twelve."

"I gather that the analysis of the paper bag that the acid drops will establish his guilt—or his innocence," said Collier. He spoke without heat. It was obvious that Sir Henry was trying to be just. Collier found him more likeable than he had expected. He felt very sorry for him. However unsatisfactory his sons might have been, their loss was a heavy blow. Collier thought he had aged in the few hours that had elapsed since he had first seen him.

"It's not my pigeon, sir, but I feel I ought to say I don't believe young Fleming is the culprit."

"What's your alternative?"

"There are several. It might be one of the servants—or one of your elder son's fellow pupils. I understand that you had sent him to one of those places that take young fellows who are described as backward or difficult."

He spoke bluntly but Sir Henry did not take offence. Indeed he looked at the younger man with more interest than he had yet shown.

"Unlicked cubs, and some of them probably with criminal tendencies. I suppose the police will make enquiries there?"

"I think you'll find Inspector Brett thorough. But what I really came about-and I hope you'll forgive my intrusion at this time, but I have to get on with my job—what I came for was to ask if at any time during the War you served with the South West Loam-shire Regiment?"

Sir Henry stared. "Me? No. I never was in the army. I was doing work of national importance at home. What's the idea?"

"Well, sir, the son of Hugh Killick, the man who was murdered ten days ago, was in that regiment. I thought you might remember him, perhaps."

"Why should I? What are you driving at?"

"You didn't know Killick personally, or know anything about him?"

"Not a thing. He was a complete stranger to me. I never so much as heard of him until I read about his death. I read of that with interest because I saw he lived in the village not three miles from my place."

"Thank you," said Collier. "I accept that. But the fact remains, Sir Henry, that Killick took a great interest in you and your family."

"Did he? That's queer. How do you get that?"

"I can't tell you that, Sir Henry. But it wasn't a friendly interest."

Webber laughed harshly. "I've had my share of enemies. Men I've had to dismiss for incompetence or dishonesty, people who've failed where I succeeded, men who've gone under because they weren't strong enough to stand up. I don't recall anybody of that name."

"He was at one time a partner in a firm manufacturing scents and cosmetics, the May Morning products. It still carries on though he retired some years ago. Does that help at all?"

Sir Henry shook his head. "Not at all. Cosmetics. Good Lord. The fellow ought to have been a millionaire. What was he like?"

"A lonely, embittered man, living the life of a recluse. The vicar of Brock Green was his only friend."

"What? The Reverend Mr. Clare? We're not church goers, but he's been here now and then to get subscriptions for his parish activities. A charming old gentleman with courtly manners." Sir Henry smiled grimly at some recollection. "My wife tried to be rude to him, but he simply didn't understand. One of the saints of God—but as he admitted he couldn't play bridge he has never been asked to dinner here."

Collier was silent for a minute. He saw no reason to disbelieve anything that Sir Henry had said throughout their interview. He had drawn a blank, and that was that. He decided that the interest Killick had shown in the gossip about the Webbers retailed to him by his charwoman was of no importance. At most it showed a not uncommon kink, the dislike of the comparative failure for others more successful.

Sir Henry spoke again. "I can't follow your train of thought, inspector. You seem to be suggesting that Killick was an enemy of mine. But, assuming that was the case he can't have killed my sons. You're not going to tell me the dead can return to dabble with arsenic?"

"No, sir. I'll be quite candid. I had a feeling these cases might be related though I couldn't see how or why. I've changed my mind. I apologise for troubling you."

He stood up to go.

"Just a minute," said Sir Henry. "You're not working on my case?"

"No, Sir Henry. The local people have that in hand."

"If I ask you one or two questions unofficially, will you answer them?"

"If I can, certainly. But I hope you won't quote me to my colleagues. One has to be careful not to butt in."

"I understand that. I may tell you that I've heard all about the Fleming boy's statement. Captain Lowther rang me up and told me just now. You said, didn't you, that one of Harold's fellow pupils at his crammer's might have poisoned some chocolates in a box that Harold brought with him. I'll grant that is possible. But how do you account for the disappearance of the box? They were in the playroom for about twenty minutes after lunch. I suppose Harold and Kenneth could have eaten a pound of chocolates between them in that time and burnt the box—but Fleming was present, and according to him Harold burnt the paper covering the top layer and the pink ribbon that tied only the box. There seems no reason why he should tell a lie about that."

"I have never taken the theory that the murder was committed by one of your elder son's fellow pupils very seriously," said Collier. "One has to consider every possibility. I think it is tolerably certain that the boys left the partly finished box of chocolates on the table by the open window when they went out, and that subsequently someone came along the path—which is not overlooked by any window in the house—and got at the box by pulling off the table cloth and the box with it and then picking up the box from where it lay between the table and the wall. To avoid overbalancing he gripped the edge of the table with his left hand. The police have got those prints and it may lead them to the criminal if the culprit is a member of your staff. I heard that all the servants had submitted to having their finger prints taken?"

"Yes. But when could this have been done?"

"The boys left the playroom between half past two and three in the afternoon. Higgins was too flustered to think of his usual routine and the window was left open all night. No one went near the place until Inspector Brett and I went in this morning about nine o'clock. The box might have been taken at any time during those eighteen hours."

"A big margin," said Sir Henry. "Thank you, Inspector. We can only hope the truth will be brought to light."

Collier bowed and was moving towards the door when the telephone bell rang on Sir Henry's desk. Sir Henry took up the receiver.

"Just a moment, Inspector. I had one further question to ask."

"Very good, Sir Henry."

Collier, waiting by the door, saw a gleam in the deep-set eyes, but he could make little of the one-sided conversation that ensued.

"Yes. . . . I hear you. Oh, good work. Yes, I hope so. . . . Thank you for telling me. Yes, I'd be glad to hear. . . . Goodbye."

He turned to Collier when he had rung off,

"That was Captain Lowther. They've made an arrest."

"Really?"

"It's a young man called Yates who is employed on the estate as an odd job man and under gardener."

"Did the Chief Constable mention what evidence he had?"

"Yes. Yates comes to work here on a bicycle. Yesterday morning he arrived at the lodge gates at the same time as the postman and they rode up the avenue together. The postman noticed that he had a small oblong parcel tied to the carrier of his bicycle. They parted at the entrance to the stable yard and the postman went round to the front door to deliver the letters. When he came back two or three minutes later Yates' bicycle was leaning against the wall, but the parcel had gone. He saw Yates in the distance walking along the path through the shrubberies. That path would lead him round to the playroom."

"What does Yates say about it?"

"Nothing."

"Yates," said Collier. "Good Lord! That would be Tommy Yates. He's what they call a natural, weak in the upper storey—"

"That's the chap," said Webber. "My boys used to rag him. I had to speak to them about it. That doesn't help him much, does it. Supplies a motive." He sighed heavily. "It will be gone into to-morrow at the inquest. God! I wish it was over. Good night, Inspector."

He seemed to have forgotten the question he had been about to ask and Collier did not remind him. He glanced back as he reached the door. Sir Henry was standing, leaning one arm on the mantelpiece and gazing moodily down at the fire blazing on the hearth.

A tragic figure, thought Collier, in his grief and his loneliness.

"Excuse me, Inspector."

The butler had hurried after him across the hall. "About this arrest."

Collier had long ceased to be surprised at the rapidity with which news travels in country pieces. In Africa there are drums, in England there are errand boys. "You've heard then?" he said.

"Twenty minutes ago from the lad who brought the fish for dinner. Cook's in a way about it, Inspector. She and Yates had their banns called for the second time last Sunday. She's throwing herself away, but it's no use arguing with women."

"Tell her not to worry. If he's innocent he's safe enough."

"She'd like a word with you, Inspector, She's in the house-keeper's room just down this passage."

"It's nothing to do with me. I'm not responsible," said Collier hastily. He did not feel inclined for an altercation with Miss Florrie Soper.

"That's all right, sir. Inspector Brett made it quite clear this morning that he was in charge of the case."

"I can't interfere," protested Collier.

He yielded rather reluctantly to the old manservant's insistence and followed him into the cheerful lamplit sitting-room where Miss Soper rose to receive him. Her broad, red face was tear stained and quivering with emotion.

"You know what they've done to my Tommy?"

"Yes."

"It's all wrong. He wouldn't hurt a fly. The young gentlemen worried his life out, but he wouldn't have harmed them. He's too soft-hearted. The vicar'll speak for him. He's known him from a baby. If you'd get Mr. Clare to say a good word for him, Inspector. That's what I wanted to ask. I'd go to the vicarage myself but I can't go out to-night with everything here at sixes and sevens. And Mr. Clare'd break it to his poor old mother."

"Very well," said Collier. "I'll ask him."

She was right, he thought. The vicar could probably throw more light on poor Tommy's mentality than anyone.

She blew her nose and sniffed pathetically. "And if you should see my poor boy, tell him Florrie'll stand by him. I'll draw my savings out of the Post Office for his defence."

"That may not be necessary," said Collier gently. "Cheer up." He shook hands with her. "I'm going on to the village now and I'll tell Mr. Clare what you say. I'm sure he'll do all he can."

The butler returned to the hall with him. Their footsteps sounded unnaturally loud in the silence that seemed to lie on the great house like a pall. Higgins glanced at his master's study door. To his relief it remained closed. Beyond the circle of light thrown on the steps by the lamp in the portico the darkness was profound. There was a clammy chill in the night air and Collier shivered involuntarily as he turned up his collar.

"Inspector"—Higgins lowered his voice to a husky whisper. "Will he be hanged?"

"What? Tommy? You go too fast. He's only being detained pending enquiries. But—in any case he wouldn't be. Arrested mental development. I thank God I haven't to judge these people," said Collier with unexpected bitterness. "I only help to catch them. Would you care to swop jobs with me, Higgins?"

"No, Inspector."

"Well then—good night."

CHAPTER XIX
THE DEAD HAND

COLLIER left his car by the roadside just past the vicarage gate. He glanced rather wistfully towards the lights twinkling through the darkness on the farther side of the green as he covered the radiator with a rug. Mrs. Fleming and Toby would be back from Durchester by now. Probably, he thought irritably, Mrs. Fleming was being quite unnecessarily nice to the young constable whose job it was to guard them during the night.

"It's just a bad habit of hers, being nice to people," he told himself as he trudged up the vicarage drive. "She ought to break herself of it."

As he stood waiting after having rung the doorbell he could hear the harsh dry sibilant whispering of the laurels in the over-grown shrubbery that screened the vicarage from the churchyard. After rather a long interval the door was opened a few inches and Mrs. Watkins peered out at him. Her anxious face brightened when she recognised him and she stood back to allow him to pass in.

"Can I see the vicar?"

"He's at the church."

"Is there an evening service? When will it be over?"

"There's no service. He spends hours there by himself, pray-ing. He can't get over poor Mr. Killick's death, and that's a fact. Praying's all very well in moderation, but a man of his age ought to take more care of himself, and not miss his meals and come in as he does at all hours, perished with cold and looking like a ghost."

"I'm sorry," said Collier, "I expect he needs a change. If he could get a locum."

The housekeeper shook her head. "He wouldn't leave the village, not after all these years. He's never missed a morning since his son died, putting a few flowers on his grave before he sits down to his breakfast. Saying good morning to Dicky he calls it. And keeps his medals, and the Victoria Cross in a little box on his bedside table."

"Well, I've got to see him now. Do you think he'd resent it if I went over to the church?"

"No need for that, sir. He told me to sound the old dinner gong if he was wanted. He can hear that. If you'll come into the study and wait. I keep a good fire there."

The vicar's study was shabby but it was a more friendly room, Collier thought, than the one he had lately left. He sank rather wearily into one of the big leather-covered armchairs and warmed his hands at the blaze. The booming of the gong sounded through the house. He rose as the vicar entered a few minutes later.

"Sorry to be troubling you again, sir."

"Not at all, not at all. Anything I can do?" The vicar lowered himself into his chair with a sigh, and fumbled for his pipe.

"You haven't heard of the trouble up at the Hall?" said Collier.

"At the Hall? No, no, no. What is it?"

"Sir Henry Webber's sons have died after a few hours' illness. The symptoms were those of arsenical poisoning. Tommy Yates has just been arrested."

The vicar's pipe dropped from his hand. He sat, with a very pale face and his mouth slightly open, gazing at the man from the Yard. "Tommy Yates. Impossible. The poor lad's weak in the head, but quite harmless."

"Unfortunately, padre, people of that sort do sometimes commit crimes. They don't realise the seriousness of what they are doing. I have just come from the Hall. Sir Henry told me his boys were in the habit of ragging Tommy and that he had to put a stop to it."

"Have they any evidence against him?"

"I am afraid so."

The vicar took the pipe that Collier had picked up for him and stared at it absently. "I can't believe it of Tommy. His poor mother will be heart-broken. Where have they taken him?"

"To Durchester."

"Should I be allowed to see him if I went?"

"I am sure of it. They want him to make a statement and apparently they can't get him to say anything. He knows you well and trusts you, sir. Perhaps you can induce him to give an explanation that will convince the authorities of his innocence. I've got my car outside if you'd care to come now."

Collier noticed that the vicar glanced, as if for reassurance at the young and smiling face that looked at them from the silver frame on the writing-table before he answered.

"Very well. If I can help. I won't fail him."

Half an hour later they were being shown into the superintendent's room at the Durchester police station. Captain Lowther was there with the superintendent and Inspector Brett. He shook hands with the vicar and nodded to Collier.

Clare, who had been silent during the drive, did not wait to be questioned but spoke with a firmness that surprised Collier.

"I hear you have detained Tommy Yates on suspicion of poisoning the Webber boy. There must be some mistake. I have known Tommy all his life. He's not very bright, but he certainly has no criminal tendencies. He has a most gentle and affectionate disposition. He is capable of a dog-like devotion to people who are kind to him."

"We aren't convinced of his guilt, Mr. Clare," said the Chief Constable. "If he can explain his actions—but he won't speak."

"The poor fellow's inarticulate at the best of times, but I may be able to get something out of him. What grounds have you for suspecting him of this fearful thing, Captain Lowther?"

"We have the evidence of the boy Toby Fleming who spent yesterday at the Hall with the Webbers. He says that there was a box of chocolates wrapped in brown paper on the table by the open window in the playroom. From what they said he gathered that neither of the Webber boys had seen it before. Harold took off the paper wrapping and they both ate several chocolates. He ate none himself as he was feeling sick."

"Toby?" said the vicar quickly. "He—he's all right, I hope. I—I'm fond of Toby."

"He seems to be a favourite of Inspector Collier's also," said the Chief Constable dryly. "I hope he justifies your good opinion, gentlemen. We're keeping an open mind about him here. Still, if we accept his statement about the chocolates it certainly tallies with the evidence of the postman who saw a similar parcel on the carrier of Tommy Yates' bicycle yesterday morning. He was on his way to his work at the Hall at the time. The postman saw him take the parcel and go down a path through the shrubberies that passes the playroom window. That's all we've got, Vicar, but I think you'll admit that it needs some explaining."

They all looked at the old clergyman. His lips moved for a moment before he spoke. "Yes," he said, "of course. But—poisoned chocolates! Surely some skill would be needed. . . . Poor Tommy is a clumsy creature. It is quite inconceivable that—" he stopped and it was evident to them all that he was facing a new and awful possibility.

"What is it, sir?" asked Captain Lowther, making no attempt to disguise his eagerness.

Clare made a gesture with his right hand as though so thrusting something away from him. "No, no," he muttered. "God forbid."

Captain Lowther said something to the superintendent who spoke to Brett, and Brett got up and left the room. The vicar sat motionless, with his white head bowed. They all waited in silence until Brett returned, bringing with him Florrie Soper's future husband. Tommy was in his working clothes. He had been digging in the Hall gardens all day and was earth-stained and dishevelled. His round and foolish face was red and swollen and stained with tears. He held his cap in both hands and fumbled with it as he stood forlornly by the door.

"Tommy," said Mr. Clare gently, "you mustn't be frightened."

He looked up at the sound of the familiar voice.

"Please, Mr. Clare, sir, I want to go home to Mother."

"All right, Tommy. You will soon. But you must answer a few questions first. Did you"—the vicar spoke slowly and carefully—"did you take a parcel to the Hall yesterday morning and leave it on a table by the playroom window?"

No answer.

The vicar, big and shapeless in his shabby clerical black, sat leaning forward, with his hands on his knees in an attitude that reminded Collier of a famous picture of Doctor Johnson. The superintendent had tilted the shade of the reading lamp so that the light fell on him, leaving the other four men in shadow.

"Do you know what was in the parcel, Tommy?"

"No, I never."

"I thought not. Somebody asked you to see that Master Kenneth had it without letting anyone in the house know. Wasn't that it?"

Tommy hung his head. "I-I swore I wouldn't tell," he mumbled. "See it wet, see it dry."

"And you've been a good boy and kept your promise, but now it's finished and you can tell me about it. If Florrie were here she would say the same."

There was a pause. Clare leaned forward in his chair. "I'm waiting, Tommy."

The half witted youth shuffled his feet uneasily. "He—he said there warn't no harm," he said at last.

"Who said that?"

"The master. Mr. Killick."

The vicar sighed. The others remained still.

"Mr. Killick gave you the parcel, Tommy? When was this?"

He spoke so quietly that Tommy was reassured.

"'Twarn't long before he was done in like. He told me to bide till Master Kenneth come home and then put the parcel in his way. 'Twas to be a surprise. So I kept he down in our shed at home, and when I heard Master Kenneth was expected I took he along and shoved un through the window, and that's all I know about it, and will you ask the police to let me go home now, sir? There was to be bloaters for tea, and I don't know what Mother'd say." He waited, twisting his dirty old tweed cap and gazing trustfully at Clare.

The vicar hesitated. "You felt you had to carry out Mr. Killick's wishes even though he was dead and gone?" he said.

"He—he was good to me," said Tommy, "I wanted to do all I could for him, see."

"Yes," said the vicar, "yes. I'm sure we all understand that. May Tommy go home now, Captain Lowther?"

The Chief Constable cleared his throat. "We'll see. Take him away now, Brett and come back as soon as possible."

Tommy turned very red and his underlip trembled. He was evidently on the verge of tears. "I wanna go home," he said pitifully. He looked anxiously at Clare. "Please, sir, you said—"

It was evident that he believed the vicar's powers to be unlimited even at the police headquarters. Clare responded to his appeal by rising from his chair and crossing the room to lay a kindly hand on the poor shambling creature's shoulder.

"It's all right, Tommy. You'll be going home presently, I promise you. You can trust me, can't you? Just be patient a little longer and do what they tell you here."

He turned back into the room as Tommy went out with Brett. "You see? He was only a tool."

"This is a very unexpected development, Mr. Clare," said the Chief Constable. "Will you sit down again? I am hoping you can throw some more light on the matter, I noticed that you did not seem very surprised when Killick's name was mentioned."

Brett had returned and resumed his place behind Captain Lowther's chair. The superintendent sat at his writing table taking notes. Collier, who had declined the offer of a chair, stood on the hearth rug. Clare, seated near the bookcase, faced them all. He looked tired and ill.

"You know that Mrs. Yates, Tommy's mother, worked for Killick? Tommy was given some of Killick's cast off suits. He did odd jobs for him now and again. Killick was sorry for the boy."

"Yes, yes," said the Chief Constable with a touch of impatience. "I can understand that; but are we to assume that Killick planned to murder these boys by sending them poisoned chocolates?"

Clare made an affirmative gesture. "I am afraid so."

"But—Good Heavens! What possible motive?"

"He wasn't quite sane. I realise that now," said the vicar sadly.

Collier spoke for the first time. "Do you know what reason he had to hate the Webbers, Mr. Clare?"

"I didn't know until lately. It was—connected with his dead son. He brooded over it until it became an obsession. He hated me, too, though I didn't realise it at the time."

"Can you tell us why, padre?" asked Collier gently.

"It was because of Richard, my boy. I fear I bore people by talking about him in season and out of season. He won the V.C. His colonel said he was a most promising young officer. I could show you his letter. I haven't it with me. In my desk at home. He won the V.C. I—I—God forgive me—perhaps I have been boastful—" his voice died away so that his last words were barely audible. He sat leaning forward in his former attitude, with his hands on his knees, staring at the ground. Nobody spoke for a moment. Then Captain Lowther said "I still don't see—"

Collier intervened. "I've got some information about Killick's son, sir. The Yard applied to the military authorities. They wouldn't say much. He was officially reported as killed in action, but—he was a very talented boy, but unusually sensitive and highly strung. I think his father learned what really happened from a sergeant in the same regiment who, in civil life had been his gardener. It was probably one of those pitiable breakdowns—"

"A coward," said Brett harshly.

Collier turned rather white. "If you care to use that word about boys who, through no fault of their own, were thrust into that pit of hell, I'd rather keep it for the people who make the wars."

Brett shrugged his shoulders. The superintendent, slightly shocked by this outburst, looked down his nose. Captain Lowther nodded.

"I'm inclined to agree with you. I mean—we all saw it—good stuff wasted. You couldn't blame his father for feeling bitter. It was a pity he ever came to know. But what is the connection with the Webbers?"

"I think I can tell you that," said Clare slowly. "Mind you, I didn't understand who he was talking of at the time. I didn't even know he had had a son killed in the war. I talked so much of mine, and he never said a word. But he told me once of an incident. He said he was walking in Kensington Gardens with a friend, a young fellow. A girl came towards them whom the boy knew-whom the boy quite evidently admired very much indeed. She came up to them, offered the young fellow a white feather, and walked on. The boy was left standing—holding it. Killick said he would never forget how the light that had been in his face went out of it. He said he felt he could have killed the girl. He didn't even know her name then, but he made it his business to find that out. The boy joined up, was sent to the front, and died. The girl's war work, after the white feather phase, consisted of giving officers home on short leave what was called a good time. She finally married a rich manufacturer who had been allowed to stay at home doing work of national importance. I remember that Killick said she had two sons growing up."

"Lady Webber? I see. An eye for an eye, a tooth for a tooth, a son for a son."

"After all these years?" said Captain Lowther in a shaken voice. "The motive seems to me inadequate. The white feather business at the beginning of the war was a mistaken form of patriotism. Those girls meant well."

"That's true," said Collier. "People who are by nature callous can inflict wounds that will never heal on others and remain blandly unaware of what they have done. I think that happened in this case."

The Chief Constable turned to him. "What do you know about this, Inspector?"

"I've found out a good deal about Killick's past history in the last few days, sir. I thought it might throw some light on the mystery of his end. Until 1918 he owned a factory manufacturing scents and cosmetics, the May Morning products. He used to work himself in the laboratory. It was at Stratford-on-Avon. I went up there yesterday—no, the day before—and talked to the manager, who knew nothing of Killick, and one who remembered him well. I also interviewed his former gardener, who was a sergeant in the same battalion as young Killick, and who is now a commission-aire at a local cinema. Killick was a kindly genial man and both liked and respected by his work people. The death of his son was a terrible blow to him, but the great change evidently coincided with the general demobilisation when his ex-gardener, Sergeant Collins, returned to Stratford. I couldn't get much out of Collins. He shut up like an oyster when he realised what I was trying to get at, but there's no doubt in my mind that he told the actual circumstances of his son's death, and that the unhappy father's brain gave way under the shock. He still derived the main part of his income from the May Morning factory but he ceased to take any active share in the business and he left Stratford. He bought a house in Croydon with a large garden and outbuildings and spent his time on some form chemical research work. The Webbers lived in Croydon. Sir Henry sold his place there and came to live at Brock Hall. A few months later Killick came to the Grange."

"I see," said Lowther. "It would be easy enough for a man of his experience to introduce poison into chocolates. We must see if we can trace the sale of the box in Durchester. And I think some-body ought to see Lady Webber about the white feather incident. Will you undertake that, Inspector Collier?"

"Very good, sir."

The vicar stood up. "It you don't need me any more, gentlemen, I'll be getting home. I take it that you are releasing Tommy Yates?"

The Chief Constable looked at the superintendent, who nodded. "I think so. But he must remain at Brock Green. We shall hold you responsible for his appearance whenever we may want him, Mr. Clare."

"That's all right. Tommy won't run away. I am much obliged to you for listening to me so patiently."

He shook hands with Captain Lowther and was turning to the door when Brett spoke.

"Just a moment, sir. There's one point that hasn't been cleared up. What became of the box of chocolates? Somebody removed it. You've been assuming that the actual murderer of the Webber boys was Killick, that the crime was planned by him and that Tommy Yates was his unconscious instrument. But doesn't the removal of the box prove a guilty knowledge?"

"You are not the only one who realises that there is a good deal of spade work to be done before we can be satisfied, Brett," said Captain Lowther in his chilliest tones. "But there is no need to detain the vicar any longer. My car is outside. Saunders shall drive you home, padre."

"And can I take Tommy along with me?"

"I see no objection."

"Thank you. I thank you all."

He faltered and Collier, who was nearest, went to him. "Take my arm, sir. I'll see you to Captain Lowther's car." He glanced back at the others. "I'll be back in a minute."

CHAPTER XX
THE WHITE FEATHER

"THE police again? I can't possibly see him. I know nothing. I can't help at all. Why must I be tortured? It's an outrage," said Lady Webber angrily. "You can take the tray away, Merton. I can't eat any more."

"Very good, my lady. But—he said he must see you. It's the detective who was sent down from Scotland Yard."

"Oh hell!" said Violet Webber. "If I must, I must. Show him up to my sitting-room when I ring. He'll have to wait until I'm ready. Just run my bath water."

She was too self-centred to realise that it might be a mistake to antagonise the man she was going to meet. Collier was kept chafing at the delay for over half an hour before he was taken up to her ladyship's own sitting-room on the first floor. His quick eyes noted the honey coloured Chinese carpet, the walls of dull gold, the easy chairs and the divan heaped with black silk cushions. The whole room had been designed as a frame for the portrait of Lady Webber, painted ten years earlier, in a black dress, with all the light concentrated on her mass of fair curls. He thought, cynically, that rampant and unashamed Narcissi could hardly be carried farther. He had been prepared to dislike her at the first encounter, and she evidently retained no very pleasant recollection of him for she frowned as she met his eyes, and she did not ask him to sit down but kept him standing at the foot of the divan on which she lay, wrapped in a grey satin cloak lined and edged with some dark fur that enhanced the dead white of her skin. She was, he noticed, very carefully made up. It was for this that she had kept him waiting. She was not, he knew, being called at the inquest that would be opened later in the day at the Durchester Town Hall.

"Well?" she said impatiently. "You insisted on seeing me."

"I am sorry," he said. "Recent developments oblige me to put some questions to you that may seem irrelevant. Were you in London in the autumn of 1914?"

"Yes. I was living with an aunt in Chelsea. Why?"

"Did you at that time offer white feathers to young men who seemed to you to be inclined to shirk joining the army?"

She looked surprised and then—he had expected that—amused."

"I certainly did. I used to carry a few in my handbag."

"Do you recall giving one to a young fellow called Killick?"

She shook her head. "No. Unless—wait—I believe that was Bunny's name. He was an art student and quite good at his job. I let him make a sketch of me. He had quite a pash for me. I met him at a party. Everyone called him Bunny. I never took him seriously, of course. I do remember meeting him months after he should have been in khaki and I showed the little slacker what I thought of him. How funny—" she was smiling to herself at the recollection. Collier watched her curiously. Her smile faded as she came back to a less agreeable present. "And you say his name was Killick? It may have been. Are you suggesting that he was the man who was murdered a fortnight ago down in the village?"

"No, Lady Webber. The object of your patriotic endeavours joined up and was killed in France. His father was with him when you made that presentation, and later he made it his business to keep you in view. You had a good time while the War lasted, and you married a man who made his fortune during those years that brought agony and ruin to others."

She stared at him. "I don't care for your manner, Inspector. It verges on the insolent. If you are not careful I shall complain to your superior in office," she said angrily.

"I am sorry, Lady Webber," said Collier woodenly, " I am simply stating the facts that have come to my notice. That's my job, to get at the facts. We have good reason to believe that Killick held you responsible for his son's death."

"How perfectly ridiculous. He must have been mad."

"On that point, certainly," said Collier, "it had become an obsession."

He was beginning to realise that she was not only self-centred but stupid. Even now she failed to see the drift of his questions.

"Dear me," she said impatiently, "you sound as if you'd been reading that awful man Freud or something. Do they teach you those things at the Police College? I can't imagine why you're wasting your time raking up things that happened more than twenty years ago. I should have thought your job was to find the brute who murdered my two poor darlings, but that's been done by the local police. They're more efficient than the Yard, after all. That dreadful half-witted man who worked in the gardens. Harold and Ken used to laugh at him. He should have been put away years ago. As it is I hope they won't send him to Broadmoor. I've heard they're quite comfortable there. He ought to be hanged. I'm going to insist on Sir Henry engaging the very best counsel to make sure he's punished as he deserves to be."

"The Crown undertakes the prosecution in criminal cases, Lady Webber," said Collier.

"That's what my husband said. Men always argue about things. Can I be left in peace now?"

He bowed and left her. He was glad to get out of that over-heated room with its scent of freesias. The raw November air outside was more wholesome. But he was not to leave the house yet. He found the old butler waiting for him in the hall when he went down. He was just closing the front door.

"Another of those newspaper men," he explained. "They're a perfect pest. Sir Henry won't see them, and that's flat, but they won't take no for an answer. We're all at sixes and sevens, Inspector. The cook, you know, sir, Florrie Soper that's going to marry the young chap they took up yesterday, she got more and more worked up after you left here last night. We tried to quieten her but it was no use. She wouldn't stay. I had to go to Sir Henry about it, and he said if she wanted to keep the young man's mother company he wouldn't stand in her way, and she was to be taken down to the village in his car."

"That was kind and considerate of Sir Henry," said Collier.

"Sir Henry's a good master. We wouldn't any of us have stayed as long as we have if it wasn't for him," said Higgins.

Collier looked at him. "I suppose the boys took after their mother?"

"That's about it, Inspector. And now will you come to the library? Sir Henry's finished his breakfast and he's in there attending to his correspondence, but he wanted a word with you."

Sir Henry was writing, but he laid down his pen as Collier entered and greeted the man from the Yard with a curt but not unfriendly nod.

"You've had some conversation with Lady Webber?"

"Yes, Sir Henry."

"Sit down, won't you. You'll find cigarettes in that box if you care to smoke. Are you in charge of this case now?"

Collier hesitated. "That's not clear at the moment. I am conducting the enquiry into the two murders that were committed in this neighbourhood two weeks ago. If they are connected with this business in any way this is my pigeon, too. It's an open question at present, and the local people and I are working together. If the two things prove to be separate my name won't come into this officially."

"I don't care who does the job so long as it is done," said Sir Henry gruffly. "Personally I fail to see any possible link. The Chief Constable rang me up late last night to say they had released the man who had been detained earlier in the evening. When I asked for further details the line went dead. That's very unsatisfactory. If the police try to keep me in the dark I shall have to take steps on my own account."

"I quite understand how you feel," said Collier, "but you must see that the police can't publish results until they have proved them to their own satisfaction. You'll hear some of the medical evidence at the inquest this afternoon. The analyst's results came through early this morning. Arsenic was the poison used. The housekeeper and the butler had the reversion of the dishes served in the dining-room and felt no ill effects. That does not remove Florrie Soper's name from our list of suspects, but it makes her guilt more unlikely. Then the paper bag that had contained acid drops belonging to Toby Fleming was subjected to the usual tests and showed no trace of arsenic. I was glad to hear that, Sir Henry. I've seen a good deal of that small boy in the last few days and I like him."

"I understand that he had considerable provocation," said Sir Henry grimly. "I dare say you know that my elder son was expelled from his school after his fag tried to commit suicide. I gather that young Fleming was ill-treated."

Nothing either in his face or his manner betrayed what it must have cost him to make such an admission, and Collier's voice was equally lacking in expression when he answered.

"We are aware of that, Sir Henry, and we faced the fact that even a normal boy might kill another on the impulse of the moment, if goaded to desperation. But this crime was premeditated, and from information received last night and confirmed just now by Lady Webber it seems certain that it was planned some time ago by somebody who had a grudge against her. Inspector Brett is visiting every confectioner and sweetshop in Durchester this morning trying to trace the sale of a box of chocolates to the person in question. If we could account for its disappearance—"

Sir Henry interrupted. "I found it myself not half an hour ago. I was going to ring up the Durchester police, but then I heard you were in the house interviewing my wife and I thought I would tell you. It's smaller than you suppose—a half pound size—and it was stuffed in the side pocket of Harold's leather motoring coat. He had ridden over from his crammer's, you know, on a motor cycle. Higgins tells me he was wearing the coat when the three boys left the playroom and went down to the woods together. Probably he leaned through the window to reach the box. Later when he came in he was already very ill and he pulled off his coat and left it lying on the floor in the hall. Higgins picked it up and hung it in the boot-room which is filled with coats and rainproofs, most of them belonging to me. Here it is," he added.

He pulled open a drawer and laid a somewhat stained and battered white cardboard box on his writing table. Collier moved forward.

172 | MORAY DALTON

"Thank you, Sir Henry. This is important. We must handle it as little as possible for the Bertillon system may help us here. The murderer may have worn gloves, but if he didn't and we get only one of his finger-prints our case will be proved up to the hilt." He lifted off the lid, holding very carefully by the edges. There were two rows of chocolates left in the bottom layer. He took a magnifying glass from his pocket and looked at them closely for a minute before he spoke again.

"Every one of these has been tampered with, cut in halves and joined up again. It's a very neat job. You'd never notice it if you weren't looking for it."

"A neat job, eh?" growled Sir Henry. "I hope they make a neat job of hanging him. Who is it? You haven't told me that yet. I'm waiting. Have you got him."

"No, Sir Henry, and we never shall. This case is unique in my experience. He's gone before a higher tribunal. He died before the murder he had planned was committed. Killick was the man. Tommy Yates merely carried out his instructions. He had no idea that there was any harm in what he did. He's weak in the upper storey, as you know, and capable of a dog-like devotion to people who are kind to him. A useful instrument."

Sir Henry drew a long breath. "This is a most extraordinary statement, Inspector. Killick—I read about him in the papers at the time of his murder but I had never so much as heard of him before. The Vicar of Brock Green has been up here two or three times for subscriptions to the parish funds, but we see nothing of the village people. You say he had a grudge against my wife. I should like to hear what it was."

"It goes back twenty-two years, Sir Henry." Collier retold, briefly, the tale of the white feather.

Sir Henry listened with close attention.

"And Lady Webber recalls the incident?"

"Yes. But she had never taken it seriously. She did not understand the trend of my questions. It may seem incredible to you that what some people would call a trifle could be magnified in a man's mind into a fearful wrong."

"Sir Henry held up his hand to stop him. "Not at all. You have made it clear. I understand. But my wife never will. I will leave it at that. Will all this come out at the inquest?"

"Eventually, but Captain Lowther wants an adjournment to-day after the evidence of the butler and the doctor. The enquiry is not complete. We have still to find out who killed Killick."

'You haven't cleared that up?"

"Not yet."

"Well, I wish you luck," said Webber in his toneless voice, "not that I care one way or the other." For a moment something looked out of his sunken eyes that turned the younger man cold. Collier realised that never before had he been actually face to face with despair. He got up quickly, muttering some word of thanks. Sir Henry nodded but he did not offer his hand.

Collier took the box of chocolates with him and asked Higgins, who was in the hall, for a piece of brown paper and string. Higgins took him into his pantry to do up the parcel.

"This is a bad business, Inspector. Sir Henry's taking it hard."

"I can see that. You must look after him, Higgins."

"Very good, sir."

Collier got through to the superintendent and told him that he was coming straight back to the Durchester police headquarters. The superintendent's voice came faintly over the wire. "Any news?"

"Yes. I'm coming."

He hung up the receiver and let himself out of the huge, silent house. It was good after the soft carpets and the scent of freesias to feel the ground hard under his feet and breathe the cold, moist air. He settled the little crumpled cushion at his back and pressed the self-starter. Twenty minutes later he was facing Brett across the superintendent's table. Brett had failed to trace the sale of a box of chocolates to anyone resembling Killick. This morning he chose to make it a grievance that he had been given this tedious routine job while Collier went over to Brock Hall.

"A blank, my lord," he said with mock humility. "I've failed in my humble task. I ought to be ashamed, oughtn't I? The sort of job that in the old days—before your time, Superintendent—

would have been given to one of the raw recruits. I shudder to think what our super sleuth from the Yard will think of me?"

Collier said nothing. The superintendent, anxious to avoid a scene, tried to smooth things over.

"You will have your joke, Brett, but this is hardly the time. Inspector Collier has something to tell us."

"All right, sir," said Brett doggedly, "but before we go into that I'd like to know whether this case is being handled by us or by the Yard? I'd like to know where I stand."

The superintendent lost patience. "Good lord, man, aren't you being rather petty? You should know as well as I do that Captain Lowther asked Inspector Collier to go to the Hall and interview Lady Webber about this white feather story because he thought it would be less unpleasant both for her and for us if it was tackled by a stranger. He did it simply to oblige us, and, speaking for myself, I'm grateful, and so may you be, Brett, when you go up to get your silver cup for the half-mile race from her ladyship at the police sports next summer."

He paused for breath, and Brett, abashed by this unexpected onslaught from his usually long suffering superior officer, looked so sheepish that Collier, weary as he was of these bickerings, had some difficulty in suppressing a smile. But he was not the man to let slip an opportunity to improve his relations with his colleague.

"I haven't meant to butt in, Brett," he said, "and I'm not going to. I've got my hands full as it is. It just happens that the two overlap. When I've reported the result of this morning's work to the superintendent and yourself, I'd be glad to return to my side of the problem."

Chapter XXI
THE BLANK WALL

COLLIER was beginning to feel that he had come up against a blank wall. That had happened before in other investigations, and a way had been found over an apparently insuperable obstacle.

"It's time for a bit of stock-taking," he told Duffield, and after the solid and satisfying meal provided by the Station Hotel at one o'clock they settled down together by the fire in their sitting-room. The sergeant filled his pipe and prepared to listen, and to intervene if anything occurred to his slower mind. Collier, his lean brown face anxious, sat turning over the leaves of his note book.

"We know from Alma Constantine that her brother came here on some kind of mission on the day of his death. He indicated that it would be financially profitable. Our people in London say that he was an agent for the importation of peasant embroideries and handicrafts from several Balkan countries. They suspect political activities but have no proofs. He had never been in trouble with the police, and, so far as is known he always travelled under his own name. He had a bed-sitting-room in a house in Guilford Street. His landlady, an Englishwoman, spoke well of him. He was often away, of course. The room has been searched and no papers were found. No papers were found on the body. What do we know about the killers, Duffield?"

Duffield removed his pipe from his mouth. "Constantine was on foot. He told his sister he had come down by train. The killers must have had a car. He hid a paper under the church brass before he met them. Perhaps he was afraid they might take it from him by force if he didn't agree to their price and thought he would be in a stronger position if he had not got it on him. When they had shot him they went through his clothing and took his shoes away with them, thinking it might be hidden in one of the soles. They beat it when they saw the boy Fleming but they were near enough to see that Constantine spoke to him before he passed out. That's why they took the risk of coming back and breaking into the Flemings' cottage. There were two of them, and they knew enough about the neighbourhood to guess what was meant by the kneeling woman."

"You remember that Toby was knocked off his bicycle by a speeding car just by the A.A. box at the cross roads as he was going for the police? They may have been in that very car. I wouldn't be surprised. But that doesn't help us much for the A.A. man didn't get the number, and he didn't ring up about it as the car hadn't actually touched the boy. It was Toby's own fault, apparently, for turning too quickly out of a side road. They didn't leave the country at once since they were here three nights ago. They may try to go now that they're got the paper they wanted so badly. All ports are being watched. We've got a list of all the people who were known to be acquainted with Constantine, but if it's political it will be transferred to its destination by somebody else. These people are well organised."

"You haven't mentioned Killick yet," said Duffield. "Where does he come in—or doesn't he come in all?"

"He was killed some hours later, some time after seven that night, to be exact. The papers were turned out of his bureau and some if not all of them were burnt. We have the evidence of the empty drawers and the white ash found on the hearth. Isn't it obvious that the murderers, having failed to find the paper they were after on Constantine, decided that it must be still in Killick's possession, and killed him when he either denied having it or, alternatively, refused to give it up to them? We can't fit the two murders into the time table in any other way to make sense."

Duffield grunted. "Yes. That makes it all neat and ship-shape."

But Collier was quick to see that he still appeared dissatisfied. "All right," he said. "Where's the snag? Don't spare my feelings."

"No snag exactly," said Duffield mildly. "I was just thinking they were taking a big risk. The boy had found the dying man in Hammerpot wood. They must have known he would raise the alarm. Yet, according to your theory, they stayed within four miles of the spot for over three hours. And, if they did, they couldn't have been in that car that nearly ran the kid down at the cross roads."

"You've got me there. That was just an idea. There are plenty of places between Hammerpot and the village where they could have left the car and waited themselves until it suited them to call on Killick. It was dark before the police arrived at the scene of the murder. They didn't attempt to make a thorough search of the woods until the following day."

He leaned forward to poke the fire, and neither of them spoke for a minute. Then Duffield said, "Isn't it possible that Killick was with the others when they shot Constantine and that they went back with him to the Grange and were actually hidden in the house when the vicar called? A quarrel may have developed later and ended as we know. After all we have the proof that Killick was capable of committing murder."

"Yes. But you've got to consider Killick's character. That's of tremendous importance to this problem, Duffield. He had planned the death of the Webber boys deliberately to avenge the death of his son. I fancy that in his warped mind that crime wasn't merely justified, it had become a sacred duty. This business involving Constantine may have only affected the surface of his consciousness, and he must have been sane superficially or he wouldn't have been at large. Killick wasn't a crook, Duffield, he wasn't a naturally wicked or cruel man. He was liked and respected by his work people and his servants. He's a murderer, but—well, you know how it is. Sometimes, in spite of what they've done one can't help liking them"—he got up and walked about the room. "The thing he planned was monstrous—but so was the war that turned his brain."

Duffield relit his pipe. "Are you a pacifist, Inspector? I've sometimes wondered from the things you say—"

"I've a right to be, haven't I, after three years of hell? You were in it, too. What do you say?"

"Nothing. What's the good? Once I started I might not be able to stop."

"You're right. What the soldier said isn't evidence. The question is are we doing any good by remaining on here? We mustn't waste the ratepayers' money. But I think I'll pay a round of farewell visits to our local doubtfuls." He sat down again and reopened his note book. "Old Constantine and his daughter. I really think we can cross them out. The old man's physically too frail to climb through windows and all the rest of it, and I believe the girl is straight. She was fond of her brother. She's told us all she knows. Contarini, the organ grinder, had an alibi for Wednesday afternoon. We agreed that he couldn't be playing his organ in Park Crescent and shooting a man in Hammerpot woods six miles away at one and the same time. The violinist was in hospital after an operation. But there's the Swiss, Muller. He's all over the place on his motor cycle. What do you think of him, Duffield?"

"I've never actually seen him. He's always out giving lessons when I call."

"Then you'd better go round to his lodgings now, and, if he's not there, wait until he returns. Take one of the local plain clothes men with you and find out all you can. How long he's been in England, why he left Switzerland, if he knew Constantine, if he takes brass rubbings. You may be able to get something from his reactions."

Duffield rose obediently. "Very good, Inspector." He glanced at the clock. "You're not going to the inquest? It will be opening in ten minutes. You'd just have time to get to the Town Hall."

"No. Let 'em stew in their own juice. I practically gave my word to stay away. Brett was up in the air again this morning, and if one of the local pressmen saw me in Court and put some reference to the Yard in his account, things might be uncomfortable all round. It isn't Captain Lowther or the super, it's only Brett. The poor devil can't help his jealous temper, and they all tell me he's a hard working, capable chap apart from that. So let us be wise as serpents, Sergeant. I shall go over to Brock Green. I want a little talk with Mr. Clare. The vicar is a dear old thing, Duffield, but he's the world's worst witness. Why didn't he tell me before about Killick's queer mental state? He's just the sort of person who might hold a clue of the utmost importance and never realise it."

Collier took the lower road through the woods. The A.A. man was at the cross roads, a cheerful note of colour in his yellow oilskins in the gathering dusk of the wintry afternoon. Collier pulled up to speak to him.

"I say, Metcalfe, I want you to go back to the afternoon of the first two murders. Did you patrol the upper road at all?"

"Once, before noon; but it's a by-road, you know, Inspector. We get very little motor traffic that way."

"I want to know if a car could have been parked along that road from dusk until—say—midnight, unnoticed."

"Oh lord, yes. Sir Henry has had his part of the woods fenced in, but there's a strip farther on that's been up for sale a long time.

Picnic parties use it in the summer. There's lots of undergrowth. The police went all over it the next day."

Collier nodded. "I know. Unfortunately a lot of enthusiastic amateur sleuths and sensation mongers came from all about, some on cycles and some in cars and made any search for tyre marks or oil droppings hopeless."

"How is it you're not at the inquest, Inspector? I heard it was to be at the Town Hall this afternoon? Or is it over?"

Collier glanced at the clock on his dashboard. "It should be by now. It will be adjourned, I fancy, They were only taking the formal identification and medical evidence, I believe, but I know nothing for certain. It's not my case. Good-bye."

Metcalfe saluted smartly and stepped back, and Collier drove on. He would have to write out his report for his superiors at the Yard that evening. It would be considered and he felt fairly sure that as a result, he and Sergeant Duffield would be recalled to London. The newspapers would refer to the case as another unsolved mystery, Collier and his colleagues would go on working on it though it would no longer be a whole time job, and they might in time identify the murderers of Michael Constantine and Mr. Killick, but it was very unlikely now that they would obtain sufficient evidence to justify an arrest. One of his failures, thought Collier bitterly. But, looking back on the work he had done, he could not see that he had made any bloomers. It was the irony of fate that most of his investigations should have served to have cleared up the riddle of the Webber boys' deaths for Inspector Brett, while leaving his own problem very much as he found it. Only the vicar, who was the only person who might be described as a friend of Killick, might still throw some fresh light on that enigmatic personality.

Collier was on his way to the vicarage, but the warm glow of firelight in the sitting-room window of the old Forge Cottage tempted him. After all, he told himself, he might be leaving the neighbourhood to-morrow, and it would be only civil to drop in for a few minutes to say good-bye.

Sandra Fleming answered the door. She was looking very young, he thought. Her blue overall matched her eyes and her brown hair shone in the lamp-light.

"Oh—do come in"—her voice was warm and friendly. "We were talking about you. Tea's just ready."

He smiled down at her, for the moment forgetting his anxieties. "I thought it might be. There's a gorgeous smell of buttered toast."

"Toby's made a mound of it. I'm so glad you've come to help us eat it."

He hung up his coat and hat in the tiny passage and followed her into the front room. Toby was kneeling on the hearth rug, very red in the face after his exertions. Mr. Clare was sitting in one of the well cushioned wicker chairs, smoking placidly, with his eyes on the fire. He looked round as Collier entered and the latter gained the impression that to the old man his arrival was not altogether welcome. He reflected, ruefully, that he could hardly expect anything else. He must be associated in the minds of these people, with the painful experiences of the past fortnight. He could hardly hope to live down the fact that he was the detective sent down by Scotland Yard to hunt for a murderer or two. That might add to his interest in Toby's eyes—he was quite aware of Toby's hero worship—but he felt that with the others it might well be a handicap. He moved forward, therefore, since this visit was not official, with something less than his usual self-possession.

Toby had scrambled to his feet. "Have you come to tea? Oh, good egg!"

Mr. Clare greeted him with his usual deliberate courtesy. "You find me enjoying the hospitality of my young friend Toby and his dear mother. My housekeeper, the worthy Mrs. Watkins, can't make toast, it is always either flabby or burnt to a chip"—he took his cup rather shakily from Mrs. Fleming. Collier noticed that his big hands were thickened at the joints with arthritis. He turned with a smile to Toby, who had fetched a little table and set it down by his side. "Thank you, my dear boy. I'm not used to being waited on. It's very pleasant. I remember people used to say my son Dick had good manners. He was generally liked"—his tired old voice faded away into silence as he sat stirring his tea, his thoughts far away in a distant past.

Collier, reassured by Sandra's welcome, was enjoying his tea. He was glad to see that Toby seemed to have recovered his usual spirits though his small freckled face still looked rather pale and drawn. "Where are the dogs?" he asked, noticing the empty basket.

Toby lowered his voice though there was no need for the vicar obviously did not hear a word they were saying. "I took them down to the shed at the bottom of the garden and gave them a bone each when Mr. Clare came. They're apt to bark and Mother thought they might worry him. Was it you who arranged that the policeman wasn't to come up here at night any more?"

"Yes." He turned to Mrs. Fleming. "I don't think there's the slightest chance of any more trouble here," he said earnestly. "The police on this beat will keep an eye on your place, but those men got what they wanted and you may be sure they'll keep well away after this."

"I should think so, too," said Sandra. "We were pleased to have that very nice boy these last few nights and he was quite good at Ludo, wasn't he, Toby, but it really can't be necessary to keep on guarding us as if we were Crown jewels or something. They got what they wanted from Toby—"

"It was rotten of me to tell them."

"Rubbish, darling. You had to," said his mother firmly. She hesitated a moment. "Have you got them yet—or shouldn't I ask?"

"You can ask," said Collier. "We may get them, but at the moment I think it unlikely. We're very short of clues. If they were crooks we might hope to get them eventually through some friend giving them away—there isn't much honour among thieves, Mrs. Fleming; but I don't fancy these were crooks in the usual sense."

"You mean—"

"Politics. The sort of stuff that's always boiling up in the mid-European cauldron. The man they shot, Michael Constantine, was English born, but the Constantines came originally from Jugo-slavia. Oh, I forgot—you didn't know we'd discovered the identity of the first victim. We kept it dark, but it will be in all the papers to-morrow. And, after that, I expect the talk will die down."

Sandra Fleming sighed. "I hope so. They let poor Tommy come home to his mother's cottage last night. It was all over the village that he'd been charged with the murder of Harold and Kenneth Webber. They can't do anything to him, can they?"

"I don't think you need worry about him," said Collier. "I'm talking more than I should perhaps, but"—he turned rather red—"I hope you won't think it cheek, Mrs. Fleming, if I say that I can't help looking on you and Toby as friends."

Blushing is apt to be catching and Sandra's cheeks were rather pink as she answered with a fervour for which she blamed herself when she woke up in the night and thought it over. "Of course not. It's been so nice—I mean you have—I mean other things were so horrible it was such a relief to have somebody decent whom we could trust—wasn't it, Toby?"

"Rather," said Toby with conviction, and then, "does that mean you're going away, Inspector?"

"I'm afraid it does, Toby. There's nothing more I can do here and I'm almost certain to be recalled to London to-morrow."

"How putrid," said Toby, "we shall miss him, shan't we, Mother?"

"Yes."

There was a pause that threatened to prove awkward. It was a relief to both his elders when Toby resumed. "Do you think I shall be allowed to keep the dogs, Inspector? I want to awfully."

"I should think so. They've found no will, and we haven't discovered any next of kin. It looks as if what he had will go to the Crown. You're fond of animals, Toby?"

"Yes."

"If ever you're up in London I'd like to take you to the Zoo. One of the keepers is a friend of mine. He'd give you a peep behind the scenes."

Toby beamed. An inspector at Scotland Yard and a keeper at the Zoo. He would be envied by every other boy in the school.

"Beefy!" he murmured. "You won't forget?"

"No, I shan't forget. Just let me know a day or two before and if it's humanly possible I'll get an afternoon off." Collier turned again to Sandra. "I'd feel happier about you, Mrs. Fleming, if you were on the telephone. You're rather isolated here with nothing nearer than those cottages down the lane."

"I'm inclined to agree with you," she said. "I thought I'd write to the post office next week."

"Good," he said.

The vicar, who had been dozing, lulled by the murmur of voices and the warmth of the fire, woke up with a start.

"My dear boy," he said eagerly, and then, with evident disappointment, "I thought Dick was here. I must have been dreaming. I must have dropped off—unpardonable bad manners—the fact is I don't sleep so well at night. But Dick has come closer to me lately. He's often here, often here." He gripped the arms of his chair to help himself up. "I must be going."

"I'll take you back to the vicarage in my car if you like, padre," said Collier. "I was coming along to see you."

"Really? Well, I shall be glad of a lift."

Toby and his mother accompanied them into the tiny passage where Sandra helped the old man on with his Inverness cape and wound a black woollen muffler that had gone green with age round his neck.

"Thank you, my dear, thank you. You're too good to me." The tired voice shook a little. "Toby, you shall lead me to the gate. It's too cold and damp for your mother to come out."

Sandra, who went out in all weathers, was about to protest, but Collier, whether consciously or not, was blocking up the doorway. She let the vicar and Toby go down the path together.

Collier, looking at her very hard, saw that her eyes had filled with tears. "Poor old thing. He's so lonely—and so pathetic with his visions of his dead son."

"Yes. But—" He took her proffered hand and gripped it so fiercely that she could hardly repress a cry. "Good-bye," he said, and bent over her, and was gone.

Sandra stood leaning against the wall, staring out into the misty darkness of the November night that had swallowed all three of them. Her hand stole up to her cheek. Her heart was thudding under the blue overall that made her look so absurdly young. That hasty kiss had taken her by surprise. Or perhaps—she tried to be honest with herself—not altogether.

She heard the click of the gate. The car had started and Toby was running back up the path, "I'm going to fetch the dogs, Mother."

"Very well, darling."

She was glad to have a little breathing space. Toby had the extreme tactlessness of youth. And she had got to be sensible. It was the end really—if a thing can be said to have ended that has hardly begun.

"I must wash up the tea things," she said aloud. Toby, when he came in with Mac and Sandy snuffling excitedly at his heels, found her busy at the scullery sink. Her employment was prosaic, but there was still a faint red mark on her left cheek and when they went back to the sitting-room she was a little absent in her manner.

"I believe you've got a headache, Mother?"

"No—not exactly."

Inwardly she was saying, "I didn't know one could be such an idiot—at thirty-three."

Chapter XXII
THE TWO VOICES

Mrs. Watkins had only been waiting for her employer's return to go down to the village to see her married niece. Collier had already remarked that as a housekeeper she was well meaning but inefficient, and it was characteristic of her that the fire in the study was nearly out. The contrast between that room and the one they had just left was not cheering.

"I'm sorry I've so little to offer," said the vicar ruefully. "There's tobacco in that jar."

"Thanks. I won't smoke just now."

"As you like."

The vicar sank into his roomy old chair and went through the familiar motions of fumbling for and filling his pipe, with his eyes fixed on the picture in the silver frame that was the one bright and polished thing on his littered and dusty writing table.

"Did I hear you telling the Flemings that you were returning to London?"

"Yes."

"Does that mean that you're giving up?"

"We never give up, but I'll admit I don't feel sanguine of success now. I wish they'd called us in earlier. The scent was cold. But apart I'm not very happy about the way I've tackled the job, padre. I've missed something, and I've a notion that it's been sticking up right in front of me all time and that I may have to look back and say to myself, Gosh! What a fool, what a mutt, what a nit-wit you were!"

Clare smiled faintly at the younger man's vehemence but said nothing.

Collier looked at him. "You know you might have helped us more than you have done, Mr. Clare."

The fire was not going out after all. A little flame flickered among the cinders. The vicar reached for the tongs and placed some lumps of coal where they would be most likely to burn, before he answered, "What makes you say that?"

"Well—that obsession of Killick's about the Webbers. You knew of that but you never mentioned it until last night."

"He was a strange man, eccentric. It seemed to have nothing to do with the case. I never dreamed that he could strike at them after he was dead. I have been troubled about that since," said the vicar anxiously. "I lay awake last night, worrying. But if you had known he hated Lady Webber you could not have prevented the tragedy at the Hall."

"That's true," acknowledged Collier. "I should have assumed that all danger from that quarter was at an end. Don't blame yourself about that. But I was just wondering if there wasn't some other thing about him that might help us. You saw more of him than anyone since he settled in Brock Green. For instance, we've found out that after he retired from business and was living in Croydon he spent a good deal of his time in a sort of laboratory making some kind of experiments. Apparently he didn't do anything of that sort here. Did he ever tell you why he gave it up?"

The vicar thought a moment. "I should say he gave it up when he had gained his end."

"Gained his end? What would that be?"

"I believe it was some very destructive form of poison gas."

Collier whistled. "So that was it. Why on earth—" he checked himself. "I beg your pardon, sir. I'm sure you don't realise that you've been withholding important information. A formula for poison gas, eh? I thought it might be something of the kind. Constantine and the others were after it. Constantine got it, and knowing the others were after him, hid it under the church brass. Failing to find the paper on his body after they had shot him they went back to the Grange to get the formula from Killick. He refused, and they killed him. The pieces fit"—his excitement died down. "But actually we're no farther forward. Did he talk to you much about this gas, Mr. Clare?"

"He only mentioned it once, a few days before his death. On the Monday evening, to be exact. I had gone over to play chess. He told me that he had been trying to find a gas that would wipe out whole populations. He said that after years of experiment he had found it almost by accident. It would be easy to make once the secret was known. He showed me what was left of a rabbit after one drop of essence diluted in an incredible quantity of water had been vaporised. Is that the right expression?—I'm no chemist—but you know what I mean. It was horrible to look at. I still dream of it."

"Was it mummified, or what?"

"It was preserved in spirit in a glass jar."

"Funny we haven't come across it. Brett had the house and the outbuildings searched. Did he tell you if he had offered his formula to the War Office, Mr. Clare?"

"I asked him. He said that he had not."

Collier pondered. "Those fellows who came were foreign agents." His face hardened. "A traitor to his own country."

The vicar was silent for a moment. Then he said, "I want you to do him justice. He's dead, silent in his grave, he can't put his case to you as he saw it. But I can, and it's the least I can do. To him war was mass murder, a devilish machine that caught up in its workings a fine and gentle soul like that of his son and ground it slowly—slowly, mark you—out of existence. He thought that if men were determined on destruction it had better be done quickly. And he meant to place the lethal weapon in some other hands than England's because he had not forgiven those in authority for what they did to his son. He would have suffered as much or more in any other army—but that was part of his hate obsession. They're resolved to smash up civilization—I'll give them the means to do it quickly. That was his argument. I tried to combat it, to convince him that if people are given a little more time we may see a change of heart. He only laughed at me."

"I see. And this discussion took place on Monday evening?"

"Yes. It upset me very much. I think—I am afraid he enjoyed my distress. He—I realise now that I must have irritated him when I talked about Dick. My son—I think I told you he won the V C. I had no idea then that Killick had a boy of his own. He had never mentioned him."

"Did he tell you he was going to sell the formula?"

"Yes. He said he was expecting visitors on Thursday."

"You mean Wednesday, don't you?"

"No. He said Thursday."

"Did you refer to the matter again when you called to return the book you had borrowed on Wednesday evening?"

"I had begged him to reconsider. I asked him if he had done so. He said his mind was made up."

"I wonder if those two were in the house then, or if they came after you had gone back to the vicarage. The body of the man they shot in Hammerpot woods had been taken to the mortuary by that time, and the police all over the country had been warned to stop all cars within a thirty mile radius. They probably didn't get away from the Grange until nine at the earliest. It's astonishing how they slipped through the net. If they'd beat it directly after the shooting it would have been easy enough."

"You are just guessing at the approximate time, I suppose?" said the vicar.

"Not altogether. We have your evidence and that of your house-keeper. You left the Grange at about five minutes to seven and came back home by the short cut across the churchyard. The church clock was striking as Tommy Yates and his intended arrived to ask you to put up their banns."

"But you said nine."

"I said nine at the earliest. We have evidence that Killick was alive at a quarter past eight."

The vicar's pipe dropped from his hand and he stooped to retrieve it. "Dear me. I hadn't heard that"—he hitched his chair a little nearer to the fire. "It's really very cold to-night," he complained.

"The cobbler they call Uncle Daniel took back a pair of shoes that he had mended for Killick. He went to the front door but did not gain admittance. Killick called out that he was busy. So the cobbler went on to the Red Lion. He's quite sure about the time—" he broke off. "There's someone at your front door now."

"You will excuse me? It will be one of my parishioners."

Left to himself Collier got up and wandered restlessly about the room. Through the uncurtained window he could see the dark mass of the shrubbery and the church tower beyond. He paused for a moment to look at the cheerful, candid face of the late Second Lieutenant Richard Clare, V.C., smiling up at him from the silver frame. After all, he thought, of those three fathers the vicar had been the luckiest. He could still be proud of his boy. As he moved round by the bookcase his sleeve brushed against the green baize cover of the parrot's cage and it slipped to the floor. He stooped to recover it but did not replace it immediately. The parrot was awake and had fixed its beady eye on him. It was sidling towards him along its perch. Its grey feathers were rumpled and there was a bald patch on its head.

"I wonder how old you are, Pollie," said Collier. "You're fear-fully ugly."

To his surprise the bird responded with a raucous chuckle. It left its perch and began to climb up the side of the cage. And then, with a shattering effect, it spoke, very distinctly, and with a kind of controlled impatience.

"Go away. I'm busy."

A new and dreadful light broke on Collier. He turned quickly and saw that the vicar had just come in and was facing him across the writing table. There was complete silence for a moment. Collier's mouth had gone dry. He could not have uttered at that moment if his life had depended on it. Clare, meanwhile, made a visible effort to pull himself together. Collier saw his knuckles whiten as he clutched the door knob. When, at last, he broke that stricken silence his voice was as gentle as ever.

"So the parrot has destroyed my alibi? Yes, I see that he has. You startled me just now when you told me that Uncle Daniel had been answered, because, of course, I knew that Killick had been dead for nearly two hours. For the moment, I had forgotten the bird. He was found, you know, flying about the hall the next morning."

Collier moistened his lips. "You—you—"

The vicar shut the door and went back to his chair by the fire.

"You look quite upset," he said. "Come and sit down, Inspector. It is nice of you to mind so much. Perhaps you blame yourself for discovering the truth. You will forgive an old man, I am sure, for being personal—your attention has been distracted, hasn't it? You have been thinking more of Mrs. Fleming."

Collier sat down. "Look here, sir," he said, "I gather you're trying to shield somebody. Are you telling me that Killick was dead when you called at the Grange—that you found his body?"

Chapter XXIII
THE MOTIVE

THE old clergyman's child-like blue eyes met Collier's steadily. In their former interviews he had always shown a tendency to become dazed and flurried and to wander off the point. He spoke with a firmness that was new to his interlocutor.

"I have tried to avoid this disclosure—for Dick's sake more than my own—but in a way it is a relief. You asked me just now if I found Killick's body. No. He was alive when I went to his house—"

Collier interrupted him. "Just a minute, sir. It's my duty to warn you that anything you may say to me now might be used in evidence against you."

Clare smiled. "Quite, quite. I understand. And I realise that I shall have to make a more formal statement later on. But—I like you. Collier. I may not have many more opportunities of talking to you, or to anyone as man to man. I can go with you to Durchester now if you insist, but I should be grateful if you would spare me half an hour longer for a last chat with—dare I still say a friend?—by my study fire?"

"If you wish it. But I'll have to make use of any information you give me. I can't regard anything you tell me as confidential. I have my duty, Mr. Clare," said Collier.

The vicar filled his pipe and lit it. "I shall miss this where I am going," he remarked. "Smoking isn't allowed, I have heard, and I can scarcely expect special privileges."

"Mr. Clare," said Collier, "if you're trying to shield someone—"

"My dear boy," said the vicar, "you made that suggestion before. It is quite unfounded. I killed poor Killick myself, for what I regarded as a sufficiently good reason."

"My God!"

"I am distressing you. I am sorry for that. I have already related what passed between Killick and me on the Monday. He told me he was going to sell the formula of his poison gas, and that he expected some offers on the Thursday. I gathered that he had been in communication with the agents of more than one foreign power, and that his hellish invention was to go to the highest bidder. I implored him, in the name of humanity, to reconsider his decision. He only laughed at me. During the two ensuing days the thing was never out of my mind. My son was gassed, you know, Inspector. A lingering death. The end came three months after the armistice—"

He passed his hand across his eyes. "Eighteen years ago—and even now I sometimes wake in the night fancying I hear him coughing in his room across the passage, his poor racked body trying to rid itself of the stuff that was eating away his lungs."

Collier nodded. "I know." He had been in a dressing station when the Canadians were brought in after the first gas attack. It was not a scene he was ever likely to forget.

"On Wednesday afternoon I was working in my garden, patching up the trellis. I decided to go over to the Grange during the evening and make a last appeal to his better nature. I wasn't hopeful, for I had realised that on that point he wasn't sane. I knew that I must prevent him selling his formula at all costs. I had nailed up the trellis. I slipped the hammer into my coat pocket. After tea I sat here and thought about it. At six o'clock I went over, taking the short cut through the churchyard. I knocked at the side door. I could hear the dogs upstairs. They had begun to bark. Killick came down to admit me. He said, 'Oh, it's you. I might have let the dogs out if I'd known. They make such a row when strangers come to the house. Come along.' I followed him into his sitting-room. I told him I couldn't stay—I was expecting a couple who wanted to have their banns put up—but I had brought back the book he had lent me. Then I said 'Killick—that stuff you told me about—I ask you most solemnly, in the name of the God who made us all, to destroy the formula here and now. For the last time.' He said 'Nothing doing. They didn't spare my son. I won't spare theirs— or any living thing.' I said 'Is that final?' and he said, 'Yes.' I said, 'Then I'll be going.' He said, 'I'll see you out,' and preceded me down the little lobby to the garden door. I took the hammer out of my pocket and put every atom of strength I had into the blow. I—I didn't have to strike more than once. I left him lying there. The dogs, shut up in his room upstairs, were yelping and whining and scrabbling at the door. I went back to the sitting-room. I had brought an old pair of gloves with me because I knew I must not leave finger-prints. I hoped to find the formula and burn it. I turned out all the papers in his bureau. I imagined it would look something like a doctor's prescription. But I was very agitated and there wasn't much time. I thought it best to pile the contents of all the drawers on the hearth and burn them. I knew he might keep it in his bedroom but I could not go in there because of the dogs. Besides I—I'd reached the limit of endurance. As it was I had to step over him on my way out. It was quite dark in the lobby. I struck a match, I had to be careful where I trod not to get blood on my shoes. I took away the jar with the remains of the rabbit— one of his damnable experiments—and destroyed it the next day on the bonfire of weeds in my garden. Meanwhile I had scarcely got back here when Tommy Yates and Florrie Soper arrived. After they had gone I had my supper. Mrs. Watkins had come in. I told her I felt unwell and she brought me up a hot water bottle and made me drink a little brandy and water. It wasn't until two or three days later that I realised that he had tricked me. When I delivered that ultimatum it was already too late. He had sold the formula that afternoon. If he had only told me that—"

"You mean—you had killed him—and it was no use—"

"Yes. Knowing what I did I guessed that the formula had not been among the papers I burnt. The man who was shot in Hammerpot woods had it. The men who killed him searched his body—but had they found it? I—I suffered, Collier. If my hair hadn't been white already, I think it would have turned white then. Killick was buried—and I had read the burial service. Then Toby Fleming came to me with his story of the men who had broken into the cottage and forced him to repeat the dying man's last words. I advised him to tell you the next day. I was greatly excited for it seemed to me very unlikely that they would understand what he had meant. I had told Toby that I was visiting one of my parishioners in that direction and that I would lock the church. I got out my bicycle and went there at once. I lifted the brass and found the paper underneath. I brought it back here and burnt it in this fire. The next morning I accompanied you and Toby and professed to have forgotten to lock up the church. You did not suspect me then, did you?"

"No."

"I hoped that would be the end. I was almost happy. For, after all, I had accomplished what I set out to do. Looking back—and I can assure you that I have lived through the last fortnight over and over again—I do not see that I could have acted otherwise. That is all I have to say."

He had been looking at the fire, which was now blazing brightly. He glanced round at Collier's rigid face. "You'll want me to come with you? I suppose I must take a few things. I ought to pack a bag."

He rose and Collier stood up too. "I'll have to come up with you.

"Very well." Clare had gone over to the table. He put aside the pages of a sermon never to be finished and picked up the photograph in the silver frame. "I may take this one with me?"

"What you want," said Collier, "is a leather case for it so that you can carry it about in your pocket. I'll get you one to-morrow if you like."

"That's very good of you, my dear fellow. And you've listened to me very patiently. I'm grateful."

"Don't say that, sir," said Collier in a voice that he strove to keep calm and self-possessed. "I've got to take you to Durchester and charge you—"

"I know." Clare was much less moved than the younger man at that moment. He even laid a reassuring hand on the inspector's arm. "Don't take it so much to heart. I took the law into my own hands. I am prepared to pay the penalty."

But Collier knew better than he did what lay before him. "If only you had wrung that bird's neck," he said regretfully.

Clare shook his head. "No. It is better as it is. I was living a lie. I couldn't have gone on."

They left the homely, firelit room together. The parrot heard them moving about in the room above, and then, after a short interval, the closing of the front door. The house was very quiet after that. The parrot, pleased that the baize cover had not been replaced on his cage, was sidling to and fro on his perch. Now and again he made a sound, uncanny in that empty room, of a man clearing his throat.

Chapter XXIV
THE TRIAL

ON THE day before the opening of the Durchester Assizes, Violet Webber was photographed walking with the young Russian who was her favourite dancing partner on the terrace at Monte Carlo. She was wearing a white sports suit of superlative cut. Her black gloves and a black velvet beret clinging precariously to one side of her golden head indicated that she was in mourning. Sir Henry had gone back to England on business. It had not occurred to her that he meant to attend the trial of the Reverend John Clare. Lady Webber's attitude to life was summed up in one sentence. "It's no use being morbid." Sir Henry, yielding to her insistence, had bought a villa at Cap Martin. Brock Hall was in the market.

The vicarage at Brock Green was standing empty. Mrs. Watkins went in once a week to light fires and open windows. No one had asked her to do so, It was her own idea. "I wouldn't like it to be damp when he comes home," she said. And the flowers on the War Memorial and on Richard Clare's grave were not left to fade. Sandra Fleming saw to that. She was alone now but for the dogs. Toby had gone back to school after giving his evidence at the inquest on the Webber boys. The coroner's jury had brought in a verdict of wilful murder against Simon Killick. A curate from a neighbouring village came over to take the Sunday services.

Sandra had had one letter from Inspector Collier expressing a hope that she would lunch with him next time she came up to Town. She was not to know that he had wasted an evening making rough copies and tearing them up. The letter he sent in the end was stiffly and clumsily worded. It did nothing to remove the unfortunate impression made on Sandra by the published accounts of the vicar's arrest. She yielded to the impulse to tell him what she thought of him. " I can't forget that you gained his confidence and pretended to be sympathetic. That may be good detection, but I think it's horrible. The sight of you would remind me of things I hope to forget, so I must decline your kind invitation."

For some days after she sent off her reply her heart beat faster whenever she saw the postman get off his red painted bicycle at her gate and come lumbering up the path, but Collier made no attempt to defend himself. Her mood changed and she began to wonder uneasily if she had not been unfair as well as rude. But she had made the break. It was no use regretting it now.

Collier took his rebuff as he had taken other knocks in the past, quietly. Only Superintendent Cardew, who was fond of the younger man, noticed that he looked tired and that he was working even harder than usual. He sent for him the day before he was due to go down to Durchester to give his evidence in the case of Rex *v.* John Clare, and waved him to a chair. The Superintendent's room as usual was full of smoke from his foul briar pipe mingled with the smell of the moth balls with which Mrs. Cardew, a careful housewife, preserved her husband's winter overcoat.

"I suppose the verdict's almost a foregone conclusion?" he said.

"It's never safe to say that. We don't know what line the defence is taking."

"They'll have a job to prove insanity," said Cardew. "The A.C. was talking to me about it yesterday. Clare's spent most of his time on remand in the prison infirmary. His heart's very dicky, it seems. He talks to the doctor, the chaplain, the nurses. They all like him, and they all agree that he's calm and collected, as sane as you or I."

"Yes," said Collier slowly. "He did what he thought was the right thing. It happened to be murder. And that's that."

"The A.C. was saying he'd been talking to Professor Pallant—you know—the chemistry man. He seemed to think it very unlikely that Killick really discovered a new and more deadly gas. He said Killick, working alone in a makeshift laboratory, would be quite unable to make all the necessary tests. He didn't doubt Killick's good faith, but he said it wouldn't surprise him if the formula wasn't something you can buy at any chemist's if you happen to collect butterflies. Of course that can never be proved as Clare found the paper and destroyed it."

"But Killick knew his job," argued Collier. "He was pretty useful to the Morning Products."

"Yes. But you've got to remember he was mad. We shall never know if he had stumbled on something particularly lethal—or only fancied that he had."

"What an irony if the formula was really valueless," said Collier. "I suppose there's no likelihood of our clearing up that end of the case, sir? I mean—the man who shot Constantine?"

"Not an earthly. Our fellows did their best to trace them. They kept a watch on the ports and combed out the West End. But if they were agents of some foreign Power they will have had a pretty useful organisation behind them. There's only one comfort, Collier. Thanks to that small boy and to the parson they didn't get the formula—and if its inventor was right about it that really is something to be thankful for."

He knocked the dottle out of his pipe and glanced shrewdly at the younger man's worried face.

"No one pulls it off every time, lad. You ask a bit too much of life. I'll try and wangle a few days' leave for you when this is over."

It was not until late the following afternoon that Collier entered the witness box. His evidence dealt mainly with his last fateful interview with Mr. Clare at the vicarage.

"You did not at that time suspect the accused although you knew he was the last person to have seen the deceased alive?"

"That is so."

"You thought he had a good alibi?"

"Yes. The village cobbler had called at the Grange at a quarter past eight, and Mr. Killick called to him to go away because he was busy. I accepted that. According to the vicar's housekeeper Mr. Clare was then in his room. He was unwell and she took him up a hot water bottle."

"Quite. He had an alibi founded on the assumed fact that Killick was still alive at a quarter past eight?"

"Yes."

"What happened during your visit to the vicarage to cause you to change your opinion?"

"Killick had a parrot which was allowed to come out of its cage. It was found in the hall of the Grange when the police searched the house after the finding of the body. The vicar had taken charge of the bird and it was then in his study. While Mr. Clare was out of the room I accidentally knocked the cover off the cage. The bird said 'Go away. I'm busy.' I—I realised what that might imply. At that moment the vicar returned. I suppose he saw by my face—"

"Just so. And he then made the statement which we went through just now. Did you warn him that anything he said might be used against him?"

"Yes."

"Later that same evening he repeated and enlarged upon that statement at the police station in the presence of the Chief Constable and two other officers besides yourself?"

"Yes."

"He described exactly the position of the body?"

"Yes."

"Was this description accurate? *The left arm flung out and the right arm doubled under him.* Could the vicar have heard that from the woman who found the body or from any of the police?"

"I don't think so."

"As a matter of fact you know that every single person who was in a position to know these details has been questioned and that they are all prepared to go into the witness box if necessary and swear that they did not pass on this information?"

"Yes."

"Thank you. That will be all, Inspector."

The counsel for the defence, who was tall and thin, with a deceptive air of languor, stood up. "My learned friend has been flogging a dead horse. We shall not dispute the fact that my client saw Killick's body lying in the lobby. I have no questions to ask this witness on that point. Inspector Collier—"

"Yes, sir."

"Until the vicar made his statement you had no doubt in your own mind that Killick had been murdered by the people who shot a man named Michael Constantine in Hammerpot woods a few hours previously?"

"I was fairly certain. Yes."

"The evidence for that was circumstantial but fairly convincing to your mind."

"Well, I needed a bit more evidence."

"Are the men who shot Constantine still at large?"

"Yes."

"Have you any proof, beyond Mr. Clare's admissions, that they were not responsible for the death of Simon Killick?"

"No."

"Thank you, Inspector."

The court was rising for the day. Collier found himself jammed in a corner under the public gallery with the police surgeon as the crowds that had filled the place to suffocation were streaming out by every exit into the murky gloom of a February evening.

"The very man," said the doctor hurriedly. "I've a message for you, Inspector, from the prisoner. I'll give it you word for word. 'I'd like Toby's mother to be where I can see her. Ask Collier to bring her.' I promised to tell you."

"All right," said Collier. "I'm sure she'll come if she knows he wants her. How is he standing the strain?"

"Pretty well, considering. Better than most men would in his place. You see, he isn't hoping for an acquittal. One of the warders sitting with him told me just now he was dozing part of the time."

Collier bit his lip. "Was he? The fact is I've funked looking his way. Tell him to look out for Mrs. Fleming in court to-morrow."

He elbowed his way through the jostling throng that filled the market square to his car, drove carefully until he reached the outskirts of the town and watched the needle of his speedometer jump up as he swung on to the well remembered lower road through the woods. He heard the dogs barking as he went up the brick path. They knew him and leapt up trying to lick his hands when Sandra opened the door. She looked at him with a sort of shrinking that hurt him more than he would have cared to admit.

"What is it?"

"May I come in, just for a moment?"

She led the way into the cosy lamp-lit room. He glanced involuntarily at the armchair in which Clare had been sitting the last time he crossed that threshold.

"What do you want?" Her voice was icy. He saw that she had been crying.

"I know you can't forgive me for arresting him," he said. "I had to do it. I hated the necessity."

"You needn't have pretended to be his friend. We all liked you and hated Inspector Brett. But he was more honest. He didn't pretend."

"I wasn't pretending I—I got fond of him. I am still. And he understands. He's more generous than you are, Mrs. Fleming."

"He may forgive you. That doesn't make you any better—"

"All right," he said fiercely, "if it gives you any satisfaction to be damnably unjust and unfair. Think what you choose about me. I've come from him now."

"What?"

"His trial opened to-day. You know that, I suppose? He got through a message to me. He'd like you to be in court where he can see you. I can arrange that for you and send a car to fetch you in the morning if you agree. It will be a painful ordeal for you, but if it gives him any pleasure—"

"I'll come, of course," she said.

"Thank you."

He left her then without another word. She heard the front door close and the click of the garden gate. "He's much too bossy," she said to Mac who had scrambled on to her lap as soon as she sat down, but she was ready when the car Collier had hired for her came the next morning, and he had been busy on her behalf for a young constable came forward as the battered Ford was stopped at the entrance to the market square.

"Mrs. Fleming? This way, madam. The square has been closed to motor traffic since yesterday's block."

He took her past the long queue of people waiting to be admitted to the public gallery and down a narrow alley to the back of the Town Hall, and then through a small door along a white-washed passage hung with fire buckets and another and darker passage smelling of mice. "You'll find your seat just on the left as you go in," he said as he unlocked the door. "You'll have a first-class view of the dock. And the Inspector said I was to give you this. It's just some biscuits and a Thermos of coffee. It'll be a bit of a job getting anything to eat in the town with this crowd and he thought you'd rather stay here quietly in the lunch interval. It's no trouble, madam. Proud to do anything for any friend of the Inspector."

Sandra, who was used to fending for herself, was touched by this forethought. She had done nothing to deserve so much consideration for her comfort. She murmured her thanks and moved forward, finding herself in the well of the court and under the gallery. There was one vacant space on the long bench against the wall on her left. She sat down and began to look about her. She was facing a railed enclosure raised several feet above the level of the floor which she guessed must be the dock. The judge's dais and the jury box were on her left. The well of the court was filled with a restless crowd of men, some wearing wigs and gowns. There was a murmur of voices and a trampling of feet from the gallery which was filling up rapidly since the doors had been opened. Sandra's neighbour, a stout man with a self-satisfied manner, turned to her.

"You weren't here yesterday."

"No."

"A pity. You missed Mr. Cordell's opening of the case for the prosecution. He's got a walk over before him. the issue isn't in doubt. Here comes the judge. You'll have to stand up."

Sandra stood with everyone else and sat down again. The jury, nine men and three women, were in their places. Her neighbour pointed out a tall man, who seemed to be half asleep.

"That's Sir James Milsom. He's for the defence. What do you think of the judge?"

He looked remote and inhuman, she thought, in his scarlet robes. The face, framed by the white wig, was brown and wrinkled and curiously still. There was something reptilian about that impassivity. Something, when he turned his head slowly, that reminded Sandra of a tortoise. He was speaking to the prisoner who had just been brought into the dock.

"You may remain seated."

"Thank you, my lord."

Mrs. Watkins was in the witness box. She had been down the village the evening of the murder. She returned to the vicarage about ten minutes past seven. Tommy Yates and Florrie Soper were in the study with the vicar. They left about ten minutes later and she took up the supper tray.

"Did he eat his supper?"

"Well, no, he didn't. When I went up to fetch the tray he hadn't touched it. I said 'What's the matter, sir? Don't you feel well?' I thought he looked queer. He said he felt unwell and would go up to bed. I got him a drop of brandy and took up his hot water bottle. He was in bed then. I told him out if he wanted anything and I left his door ajar so I could hear. My room's just across the landing."

"Could he have left his room and gone downstairs during the night without your knowledge?"

"I should have heard him. I'm a light sleeper."

"Were you worried about him?"

"Yes. I'd never seen him look so queer."

"Did he appear to be suffering from shock?"

"Yes. He was all of a tremble and his eyes staring."

"Would it be accurate to say that you noticed a change in him dating from that night?"

"Yes. He took to walking about his room in the night and talking to himself, or it might have been praying."

She was cross-examined by Sir James Milsom. "You have been housekeeper at the vicarage for twelve years?"

"Yes."

"Was the vicar a man of violent temper?"

"Him? Oh, no, sir. I've never heard a cross word from him. Like a lamb he was, poor gentleman."

"Would you describe him as absent-minded? I mean, was he apt to forget things?"

"Yes, he was that, sir. Sort of rambling like from reading so many books. He didn't trust his memory. Anything like a christening or a sick person to visit he'd put down in his diary. If he hadn't put it down he might remember or he might not. Only last September he kept a wedding party waiting an hour and a half."

"Just so. And did he ever do a thing and forget that he'd done it?"

Sir James leaned forward, swinging his eyeglasses from their cord. It was evident that he attached considerable importance to her answer.

Mrs. Watkins hesitated. It was obvious that she was anxious not to say anything that might incriminate her employer. Sir James encouraged her. "Don't be afraid. Remember you are on oath."

"Well, he did then. In little things, about taking his digestive tablets after meals, for instance. He spoke to me about it. He said 'Mrs. Watkins. This box should have lasted me three weeks, but they're all gone in nine days.' I knew how it was. He'd take one and then after a few minutes he'd think to himself, 'That tablet!' and take another. There was other little things. There was Sallie Bates' churching. He came in one day and complained to me, 'I've been waiting the whole morning in the church for a young woman to come to be churched, and she never turned up,' he said. I said, 'You don't mean Sallie Bates, sir?' And he said, 'Yes. The cowman's wife from Poynter's Farm.' And I said 'Why, you did her yesterday. Don't you remember? You gave her half a crown to buy the baby a bonnet, and she come into my kitchen after for a cup of tea.' I was bound to laugh, and after a bit he did, too, but I could see that even then he didn't really call it to mind. He just took my word for it."

"Thank you, Mrs. Watkins. One more question. Can you recall any instance of the vicar fancying he had carried out some duty which, in fact, had slipped his memory?"

Mrs. Watkins looked rather bewildered. "I don't know as I follow—"

"I'll try to put more clearly. Did he ever go out before you had served a meal under the impression that he had had it, or, when you reminded him of some visit to be paid to a parishioner, did he assure you that he had already been?"

"Yes. I see what you mean now, sir. That's right. No so often as the other way round, but it did happen, and when I'd tell him of it he'd say 'I must have dreamt it. I dream such a lot,' he'd say."

"Thank you. That's very interesting and I hope to show presently that you have thrown a good deal of light on this strange case. That will be all, Mrs. Watkins."

The Court was rising for the lunch hour. Everybody stood up as the judge passed out through a door at the back of the dais, followed by his attendants. The jury had filed out of their box, and the well of the court was deserted. The prisoner and his warders had disappeared from the dock.

You're staying?" said Sandra's neighbour. "So am I. The wife put me up some sandwiches. My brother-in-law's in the Town Clerk's office. That's how I got such a good place. The jury don't look any too happy, do they? Well, I mean to say, there's nothing against this fellow Clare except for the fact, which he admits, that he did this fellow Killick in, and Killick himself was a homicidal maniac and better out of the way. You know about the case, I suppose? He sent a box of poisoned chocolates—"

Sandra did not want to hear but there seemed no way of stopping him. She tried to eat her biscuits but they seemed to turn to sand in her mouth. After a while, to her relief, her neighbour produced a crumpled newspaper from the pocket of his shabby over-coat and became absorbed in the football results.

The jury were returning. Sandra, watching them settling down in their places, missed the return of the accused to the dock. The counsel for the prosecution was speaking.

"That is the case for the Crown, my lord, and members of the jury."

He sat down and Sir James Milsom stood up. "My first witness for the defence, my lord, is the prisoner himself. I call John Clare."

There was a kind of murmur and rustling in the crowded court as if a wind had come up and died down again. The ushers called for silence, but there was no need; the stillness as Clare left the dock and crossed the floor to the witness box, was so absolute that Sandra could hear the beating of her own heart and the ticking of the watch on her wrist. The vicar moved slowly and feebly, leaning on the arm of one of his warders.

The judge's dry deliberate voice broke the silence. "Let him have a chair."

"Thank you, my lord. That is kind. But I will stand as long as I am able. I have the support of the rail."

He repeated the tremendous words of the oath in a voice
that was startling to ears accustomed to a gabbled monotone,
and waited.

Sandra saw that he had grown much thinner, and his clothes
hung loosely on his large frame.

Sir James was swinging his eyeglasses on their cord. "You
went twice a week to the Grange to play chess with Mr. Killick,
didn't you?"

"Yes."

"To please yourself?"

"Certainly. I am fond of chess—but I also felt it to be my duty.
Killick was a lonely man. He had a most unhappy disposition. I
hoped—"

"Will you tell the court what passed between you on the
Monday evening two days before his death?"

"He told me he was expecting visitors on the following Thursday. I said I was glad to hear it. He laughed, and said they were
not friends of his. He told me that he had discovered a gas that
would be far more destructive than anything that had been used
hitherto. From what he said, or rather hinted, I gathered that the
agents of more than one foreign Power had become interested,
and that he meant to sell to the highest bidder."

"Did you ask him if he had offered the formula of his discovery to our War Office?"

"Yes. He said that he had not. I learned later the reason for
his hatred of our own military authorities. He thought his son
should never have been accepted for service in the Great War
I—I believe the boy went mad before he died. His father never got
over the tragedy. But I would like to say that if he had been trying
to sell his formula to the English War Office, I should have felt it
just as much my duty to stop him. My God is not a tribal God."

Sir James cleared his throat. "Just so," he said hurriedly. He
was wishing his difficult client had not said that. It might create a
prejudice against him. "You begged him to reconsider the matter?"

"Yes. I begged him."

"You were greatly worried and distressed?"

"Yes."

"Did you sleep well that night or the next?"

"Hardly at all. I realised that the responsibility was mine. It was in my power to avert a hideous calamity, death in its most ghastly form."

"Did you dream about it?"

"Yes. Yes. I dreamed—"

"You were trying to decide on a course of action?"

"Yes. The whole thing was a nightmare."

"Had you any personal animus against Killick?"

"No."

"You did not dislike him?"

"No. I was—I had always been—sorry for him. I was sometimes in doubt of his feeling for me. He liked me to come, but there were times when he almost seemed to enjoy hurting me. He would deliberately say things to shock and to wound. I realise now that I brought that on myself. I was apt to be foolishly boastful about my son Richard."

They could all see the effort he had to make to remain standing. The old veined hands, swollen with arthritis, gripped the rail. The warder standing at the foot of the steps leading to the witness box was watching him anxiously.

"Thank you," said Sir James, and paused before dropping his bombshell. "That is all I wish to ask, Mr. Clare."

He sat down. There was an irrepressible excited buzz of comment in the court. Sandra's talkative neighbour expressed the general feeling. "Gosh! He's thrown up the case. But—why? It's incredible." Fellow members of the Bar, who knew Sir James better, were not inclined to accept this solution, but even they were staggered. The trial was taking a turn they had not foreseen. The judge raised his eyes from his notes. Again the old wrinkled head moved like that of a tortoise emerging from its carapace. "Are you feeling unwell, Sir James?"

"No, my lord."

"Oh. I thought perhaps you felt yourself unable to go on."

"Thank you, my lord. I have asked all the questions that appear to me to be relevant."

"Well, I will assume that you know best. Mr. Cordell?"

The counsel for the crown stood up. "My lord, members of the jury, it would be inhuman to cross-examine this witness. You can leave the box now, Mr. Clare."

Clare had been looking from one to the other doubtfully as if he hardly understood what was going on. The warder mounted the steps and touched him on the arm.

"No." Clare turned towards the judge and appealed to him with unexpected vigour. "I don't know what this means, my lord. Sir James did not want me to give evidence. I insisted, and, in the end, he gave in. I want the truth, the whole truth, to be known. I am here to tell you how I killed that man."

"Sir James is doing his best for you, Mr. Clare," said the judge slowly. "You have chosen to disregard his advice. I do not think that in law you can be prevented from making a statement. Mr. Cordell has declined to cross-examine you, but I will question you myself if you are determined."

"Thank you, my lord. I—I will sit down if I may"—he sank heavily into the chair that had been provided.

No one in the court moved.

"Well," the judge resumed. " Will you tell me and the jury what happened on the Wednesday evening?"

"I had a book he had lent me to return. I thought the would-be purchasers of the formula were coming on Thursday and that there was still time to make a final appeal"—he went on to repeat, almost word for word, the story he had told Collier before his arrest.

"That is all," he said at last. "I thank you all for listening so patiently."

There was a profound silence as he crossed the court from the witness stand to the dock. He leaned heavily on the warder's arm. It was apparent that he was exhausted. Before he entered the dock he spoke to his counsel, who had risen as he approached.

"I'm sorry, Sir James. I hope you're not angry with me. I had to do it."

Sir James' face had been quite expressionless throughout. He smiled slightly now as he shook his head. "It wouldn't do as a general thing, Mr. Clare, but, as it happens, your burst of candour hasn't worried me at all. I shan't have to alter a word of my speech in your defence."

Two witnesses to character followed, one of them being no less a person than the bishop of the diocese, and the other a farmer who had acted for fifteen years as the vicar's churchwarden. Their evidence was brief and emphatic. The Reverend John Clare was a man of unblemished character who carried out his duties as a parish priest efficiently. The farmer admitted that of late his memory seemed to be failing, but not to an extent that interfered with his work. He was known to be very kind-hearted and to detest cruelty and violence in any form. He was always trying to stop the boys from birds' nesting. Neither of these witnesses was cross-examined.

Sir James intimated that he did not propose to call any further witnesses, and the counsel for the Crown rose to sum up the case for the prosecution.

Sandra listened to him with strained attention from his opening words.

"This, my lord and members of the jury, is a painful case, one of the most painful in which it has been my duty to point out that, whatever our natural feelings of pity and even of sympathy with a person accused of a capital crime, justice must be done. The facts are hardly in dispute. You have heard the evidence of the police and of other witnesses who knew both the murdered man and the accused, and you have heard Mr. Clare's own statement. There was another murder committed that same day within a few miles of the village. There is no evidence that either Killick or the accused committed that crime. The perpetrators are still at large and the police still making enquiries which may sooner or later lead to more than one arrest. But we may dismiss that case from our minds except in so far that it affords corroborative evidence of the motive alleged by the prosecution and admitted by the defence. You have just heard from Mr. Clare's own lips the poignant, the terrible description of how the murder was committed. I say murder. I have to say it. There is no question here of a blow struck in hot blood or in self-defence. He brought the hammer with him. He struck—with all his might—when his victim's back was turned. Subsequent events—I refer to the tragedy, known to all of you, that bereaved Sir Henry and Lady Webber of both their sons— has proved that Killick was a homicidal maniac. He had passed the border line of sanity and could have been put under restraint, but no one knew it. The accused—let us admit so much—had as good a motive as can be imagined for his deed. But are we to admit the right to kill? Suppose—it may be unlikely, but it is not beyond the bounds of possibility—there had been no truth in Killick's story of his invention. He might have invented the whole thing to see what the other's reactions would be. Is he to die for that? And—whatever we may think—in proposing to sell the formula of some chemical combination Killick was not contravening any law. He was within his rights. Whatever respect we may feel for the character of the accused and for his motives we must not allow ourselves to be swayed by sentiment. If once we admit that if a killer's motive is good enough he may be excused, we open the door to a very sinister personage whom I, for one, should be very sorry to see established in this country—I refer to Mr. Justice Lynch. My lord, members of the jury, it is not for a private individual to arrogate to himself the powers that are vested in the law. I do not wish to press too hardly on a most unhappy man, but I cannot—and you cannot—shut your eyes to the facts. We have to do our duty as citizens—law-abiding citizens—however painful it may be. That is all I have to say."

The echoes of his resonant voice died away. Sandra, glancing at the jury, thought that they all, and especially the women, were beginning to look physically ill. Their strained faces affected her unpleasantly and she felt thankful that she was not among them, and yet, if she had been, might she not have done something to help her old friend? She shivered involuntarily in spite of the close heat of the court. Her neighbour had turned to her, but he checked himself. Sir James Milsom had risen to make his speech for the defence.

"This, my lord and members of the jury, is a most unusual, I might even say an unprecedented case, and for more than one reason. There has been no conflict of evidence. We accept the narrative outlined by my learned friend and substantiated by his witnesses of the events leading up to the death of Simon Killick. We cast no doubt on that. You have heard the story, the tragedy of a warped mind, that began nearly twenty years ago; the story of Simon Killick's grudge against the civilization that prostitutes science in the manufacture of engines of death, the civilization that destroyed his son. Some crimes are committed for gain and some are the result of the passions aroused by our animal nature. We are faced here with something more complex and more difficult. This case does not stand alone. The counsel for the Crown when opening his case referred rather briefly to the death of Michael Constantine, who was shot in Hammerpot woods a few hours before the body of Killick was found in the lobby of his house a few miles away. It is known that two men were involved in this crime, but so far they have escaped arrest. My learned friend asked you to dismiss this affair from your minds and to concentrate on the issue as between Killick and the accused whom you see in the dock. It has been admitted that until my client made his statement to the police they were working on the supposition that the men who shot Constantine, failing to find the formula in his possession, returned to the Grange to obtain it from the inventor, and killed him when he declined to give it to them. You may ask why he should decline? The answer is that Killick was, according to his own strange lights, an honest man. He had sold the formula to Constantine, and he would not sell it to another. This was their theory and it was supported by circumstantial evidence. If it had been put before you it would have involved the calling of several witnesses who have not been called, including the boy who found Constantine in the wood. But the police changed their minds when Mr. Clare made his statement, which was practically a confession of his guilt, and you have been asked to dismiss any thought of a possible alternative from yours. Why?"

Sir James paused to allow that query and all that it implied to sink into the minds of his audience.

"I have seen prisoners who have betrayed themselves unconsciously in the witness box, who under the ordeal of cross-examination have revealed their falsity, have contradicted themselves, have shown the callousness, the insensitive egoism

210 | MORAY DALTON

that is the stamp and hall mark of the murderer, the man who regards his own safety, or perhaps only his comfort and his convenience as of more value than the life of a fellow creature, but I have never heard anything that even remotely resembled the evidence given by Mr. Clare. I don't know what effect it made on you but to me it was infinitely touching in its simplicity. But—now I want to stress a point that was not made by the prosecution. Mr. Clare's evidence is unsupported. We have his word for it, and nothing else. How far can we rely on that word? I am now about to suggest to you, my lord and members of the jury, what I believe actually happened on that Wednesday evening. I accept all that the accused has said of his state of mind as the result of that most disturbing conversation with Killick on the Monday, his sleepless nights, his increasing agitation. I am prepared to admit that he actually did take a hammer with him in his coat pocket. I think I am right in saying that the only hammer at the vicarage was examined and that no trace of human blood was found on it—"

Mr. Cordell stood up. "That is so, my lord. The accused informed the police that he washed the hammer."

"Thank you," said Sir James. "That does not affect my contention. Mr. Clare went over to the Grange to return a book. He meant to make a final appeal to Killick, and if that failed it was in his mind that he might resort to violence. He opened the door of the lobby and almost fell headlong over some obstruction just inside the passage. He struck a match and saw the body of Killick, the head lying in a pool of blood. The shock was terrific. He may have lost consciousness. When he recovered a little he was still too dazed to have the full possession of his faculties. A terrible doubt assailed him. Had he just discovered the body, or was he suffering from some lapse of memory? Was this his work? Had he actually carried out what he had planned? He listened and heard the barking of the dogs upstairs. He stumbled into the living-room and found a charred mass of burnt papers on the hearth, and the bureau drawers empty. You must remember that at that time he had no idea that Killick's visitors had already come and gone. Killick had told him he expected them on Thursday. It must have seemed to him that nobody but himself could have committed the crime. He had done it. He must have done it. There was no loophole. He left the dead man lying where he had found him, and crept back to the vicarage to carry on as best he could the routine of his normal life. Later when he heard of Constantine and of the men who had shot him it still did not occur to him to doubt his own guilt. That delusion was now fixed in his tormented mind. What troubled him now was the fate of the formula. When he learned that it might have been hidden under a brass in Botolph's church he went there, found it, and destroyed it. He had at that time what appeared to be an unshakable alibi. His housekeeper could prove that he had not left his room at the vicarage after about half past seven when he complained of feeling queer and went up to bed, and, according to the village cobbler, Killick had answered him when he knocked at the front door of the Grange at some time between eight and half past. That alibi crashed when the words supposed to have been uttered by Killick proved to be part of the repertory of the dead man's grey African parrot. Mr. Clare, oppressed by the burden of his imagined crime was only too ready to give himself up. That, my lord and members of the jury, is what, on my soul and honour, I believe to be the truth, and I would ask you to consider it very carefully. I would ask you to remember all you have heard of the accused from the woman who has lived under his roof and seen him from day to day, and to remember that the evidence that his was the hand that struck Simon Killick down is his own uncorroborated word. Apart from what he himself has admitted there isn't an atom, not a vestige of proof. Did he do it? I have shown you the torturing doubt at work in that noble mind, perplexed, as was Othello's, in the extreme. But there should be no doubt in ours. This man is innocent. Innocent, you may say, when he took the hammer and made his plans? He admits that, and I admit it on his behalf. But you are not here to try a man for what he was tempted to do, but for what he did. I say to you that, whatever he may have thought, John Clare, when it came to the point, could never have struck that blow, and that when the police arrest the men who shot Constantine they will be laying their hands, at the same time, on the murderers of Simon Killick. I need not say that one should not even think of, much less get so far as to plan the death of a fellow creature. I am not trying to find excuses for my client's moral lapse, but I would remind you of the horrible nature of the disaster he believed he might avert by preventing, by any means, the sale of Killick's formula. He, too, had a son, and his son had died—slowly—of the effects of poison gas.

"In conclusion I must say this. I am not suggesting to you that my client is of unsound mind. He has been under observation while awaiting trial. The prison doctor was convinced of his sanity. All who have come in contact with him since his arrest, myself included, share that conviction. You may, if you like, say that he has one delusion. I have explained to you how that arose. You have seen with what dignity he has shouldered his imagined guilt and resigned himself to face its consequences. I will say no more. The fate of John Clare is in your hands."

CHAPTER XXV
THE LAST WORD

THE court had risen at the close of Sir James Milsom's speech and Sandra passed out with the crowd. She had seen nothing of Collier, but the man who was waiting to drive her home told her that he had orders to fetch her the following morning. He had to make a detour to avoid the dense mass of people that filled the market place and overflowed into the High Street.

"They say there isn't a bed to be had in the town for love or money," he informed her. "There'll be an all night queue to get in I shouldn't wonder. They're bringing down extra police from all over the county in case there's trouble."

"Why should there be trouble?"

"Well, they've got to keep the way clear."

Sandra let that pass without comment. Her head ached. Though she had not realised it at the time she had sat during the greater part of Sir James' speech with tears running down her cheeks. When she reached the cottage she was greeted with rapture by the dogs, who had been shut up all day in the run Toby had made for them before he went back to school. She gave them their supper, made herself some tea, and went to bed.

The young constable who had taken her round the back of the building on the previous day was waiting for her when she arrived at the Town Hall. The square was already blocked and the police were having some difficulty in keeping clear a roped off space between the Red Lion Hotel where the judge had his lodgings and the entrance to the court. All the posters displayed outside the newsagents' referred to the trial. AMAZING DEVELOPMENT IN POISON GAS CASE. VICAR IN MURDER TRIAL. COUNSEL'S ELOQUENT PLEA. SENSATIONAL TURN IN BROCK GREEN MYSTERY. SIR JAMES MILSOM'S DEFENCE. GREATEST SPEECH OF HIS CAREER.

Again there was no sign of Collier, but Sandra's guide, just before he left her in the whitewashed passage with the fire buckets and the brooms, produced a crumpled envelope addressed to her.

"You know your way. Through that door. Same place as yesterday. You'll excuse me. We're pretty busy."

He hurried off, leaving her to read her letter before she went into the court room.

"It is almost certain to be decided one way or the other to-day. Will you wait in your place until I come to you? I shall be able to get leave for you to visit him in any case. He wants to see you. The defence was a stroke of genius. It almost if not quite persuaded me that I had made the most terrible gaffe of my life. But don't be too hopeful. There's still the judge's summing up.—H.C."

Sandra placed her letter in her handbag, opened the little door under the gallery and slipped unnoticed into her place. Unnoticed, that is, except by her neighbour of the previous day who greeted her familiarly. "Run it pretty fine, haven't you? Here they come now."

The curtain was rising on the last act of the drama, the principal actors were taking their places. The judge, his withered face looking browner and more like a mummy's than ever in the morning light; the jury, cheered by a night's rest and a hearty breakfast at their hotel, the prisoner in the dock, struggling to his feet to bow to the judge and sinking back again with a sigh that was almost a groan.

"They say," whispered Sandra's neighbour, "they had to give him oxygen last night. He was completely exhausted after the effort he made. He's looking this way. Do you know him?"

"Yes. He's a very dear friend—"

The ushers were calling for silence. The judge was about to sum up. Sandra realised after a minute that he was going over the whole story again carefully, patiently, breaking off his narrative now and again to elucidate some point. Sandra found her attention wandering. She felt that she knew it all by now almost by heart. She watched the nine men and the three women in the jury box, wondering uneasily if this studiously unemotional catalogue of facts would undo the effect of Sir James' passionate pleading. She looked at the man whose life or death depended on their reactions. He sat motionless between his warders, his white head silhouetted between the dark panelling behind him. His eyes seemed to be closed. She wondered if he had actually dozed off as he sometimes did at home when people were talking. The jury, she supposed, were taking it all in. The judge's precise voice went on and on. He had been speaking now for over an hour.

"You have heard the very ingenious theory put forward by the defence. It had, as you will have remarked, no backing of medical experts giving evidence on oath and citing parallel cases. I have the greatest respect for medical evidence," said the judge very drily indeed. "I have heard a good deal of it and when experts are called by both sides it has cancelled out in a remarkable manner. In this case neither the prosecution nor the defence have seen fit to call upon the denizens of Harley or Wimpole Street to assist them. To be quite candid I doubt if they could have helped us much. Sir James, greatly daring, has assured us that the accused is quite sane. At the same time he would have us believe that as a result of a shock—the shock of finding Simon Killick's body—he suffered a moment of anaesthesia and of mental confusion that left him believing that he had committed the crime. Is this possible? Speaking for myself I am inclined to think that it is, but that is for you to decide. It is certainly possible that the men who shot Constantine came back to the Grange and murdered Killick. I would even suggest another theory which has not been put forward by the defence. Killick may have been killed first. Against that there is the evidence of the doctor, who put the time somewhere between six and ten. If you accept John Clare's statement that he struck the blow we know the time was about half past six. The point is interesting, but it is not likely to be cleared up now and you can dismiss these details from your minds as irrelevant. The question before you is relatively a simple one. Did John Clare kill Simon Killick by striking him on the head with a hammer? We have all heard him In the witness box and we cannot doubt his sincerity. He thinks he did —but did he? I would have you consider Sir James' arguments very carefully before you decide. You can, of course, call upon me, if you require any further advice or assistance. You will now retire to consider your verdict."

The jury passed out through the door at the back of their box. They looked awkward and self-conscious. The judge had gone to his room, and the prisoner had been removed from the dock.

"They'll give the poor bloke a cigarette, or maybe a cup of tea to help pass the time," said Sandra's neighbour. He seemed to know everything that went on behind the scenes, on the strength of having a brother-in-law who was usher at the New Bailey, but she could not feel sure that his information was accurate.

"How long will the jury be?" she asked, and felt as she asked it how futile such a question was.

"Hard to say. Get one pig-headed contrary chap and he'll hold them up for hours, or a woman. The women are often the worst. In this case I wouldn't be surprised if they fail to agree."

"What does that mean?"

"Another trial. More expenses to the taxpayers and money in the lawyers' pockets, to say nothing of the wear and tear to the feelings of the poor chap who's got to fight for his life all over again. Not that that applies in this case. Fighting for his life, I mean. Why, he's as good as asked to be convicted. It's a new one on me that is."

Sandra was watching the white-faced clock on the wall. Twelve minutes.

"I'll tell you who's here. Got a privileged place like you and me but the other side of the court. See that big man in a dark suit next to the pillar? Perhaps you know him, though?"

"No. Who is it?"

"That's Sir Henry Webber. He went to the South of France with Lady Webber directly after their sons' funeral. It's said he's bought a villa that used to belong to a Russian Grand Duke at a place called Cap Martin. But he's come back for this. They were talking in the saloon bar of the Station Hotel last night about it. Some say he offered to pay all the expenses of the defence, but the vicar wouldn't have his help."

"Why should he offer?" asked Sandra. "He hardly knew Mr Clare."

"That may be, but you've heard what came out at the inquest on his boys. That was Killick's doing."

"You mean he—he would be grateful to Mr. Clare for—"

He beamed at her. "That's right. Mind you, it's only a rumour. But anyway, that's him. Stop talking now. Here's the judge—"

But the door that had been opened was shut again and the subdued murmur of conversation that had ceased for a moment in the crowded court, was resumed. Seventeen minutes. Was it a bad sign that they were taking so long?

"False alarm." Sandra's neighbour, hearty, insensitive, had been eyeing her approvingly. Youngish, prettyish, a bit on the quiet side, but a nice little thing. "Can't be much longer now. What about a cup of tea and etcetera with yours truly after it's over? There's a posh café just round the corner. Do us both good."

"Thank you. But I have to wait here for a friend."

"Oh, I see. Sorry I spoke," he said in a tone that showed that he had taken offence. "I'm never one to intrude where I'm not wanted. May I ask if your friend is a policeman?"

"Yes, he is."

"You ought to be praying for a conviction then. He's for it if Clare's let off. I wouldn't be in his shoes."

He was a common pushing little man and Sandra knew it would be better to say nothing, but she was goaded into attempting a reply.

"But surely—" she broke off as the judge came out, shuffling rather wearily in his trailing crimson draperies, and resumed his seat. The light from the ceiling fell on him, but the dark figures ranged behind him were in shadow. Sandra remembered hearing that the black cap was not a cap but a square of cloth.

The jury were returning. They remained standing. The judge's head turned slowly on the withered neck.

"Do you find the prisoner at the bar guilty or not guilty?"

"Not guilty, my lord."

An outburst followed from the public galleries that drowned the voice of the judge. The ushers tried in vain to restore order. After a moment, as the news that the trial had ended became known outside, there was a roar of applause from the crowds waiting in the square.

Sandra sat still, shut her eyes, and let the waves of sound flow over her. The court had risen and the people were making for the exits. Her talkative acquaintance had hurried away without a word of farewell to have a cup of tea at his posh cafe without her—or, more probably, to wait for the bars to open. She was quite alone now, the last person left in court. An usher, going round closing the doors, eyed her doubtfully, but before he could approach Collier hurried in.

"Mrs. Fleming—"

She opened her eyes and looked at him as he stood before her, paler than usual and unsmiling. Her heart sank. Had that horrible little man been right? Was he sorry that the vicar had been acquitted! His first words reassured her.

"Sir James pulled it off. A magnificent effort. He saw you. He was pleased."

"Where is he?"

"He has been taken in an ambulance to a nursing home. It was all arranged. Come along. There's no time to lose. I'll take you in my car."

In the square the crowds were still cheering. Some were singing "For he's a jolly good fellow!" Collier's lips twitched.

"I believe they wanted to chair Sir James across to his hotel. We had to make way for him. He laps it up. But he deserves it." He edged his car out of the yard where he had left it into the deserted side street. "We haven't far to go, but keep that rug over your knees."

"It's splendid," she said. "But—will you be blamed for having arrested him?"

"You think it will serve me right?"

"No. I—I realise that I was unreasonable," she said in a low voice. He made no answer and she was not sure that he had heard her.

The nursing home was in a new road on the out-skirts of the town. They were kept waiting for a few minutes and then a fresh-faced young nurse took them up to a pleasant room on the first floor, bright with flowered chintz and white paint, where John Clare lay, propped with pillows, with the gnarled tremulous old hands that had clutched at the rail of the dock for support quietly folded on the counterpane. He turned his eyes but not his head as they entered, and smiled.

"They got me into bed in record time," he said weakly, "and now you're going to have tea with me. Everybody—so kind." The nurse reappeared wheeling in the tea waggon. "Perhaps you will pour out," she said to Sandra. "He may have anything he fancies, but don't let him sit up or exert himself. I shall be just outside if you want me."

"Isn't this jolly," said Collier, "will you have bread and butter sir, or cake? I'll put your cup here and give it you when you ask for it."

The vicar seemed to enjoy his tea more than either of his guests though they both tried hard to seem as cheerful as he was. But they were both distressed by his evident physical exhaustion.

"We're tiring you, padre. We ought not to stay," said Sandra

"No. Don't go yet. How is Toby?"

"Quite well and happy. He's gone back to school this term. He would have sent his love if—if he'd known I should be seeing you."

"Yes. A dear little boy. I thought of him when I lifted the brass and saw the paper and later when I was burning it in my study. As I watched it curl up and blacken at the edges I thought Toby won't die this death. I've saved him from that." There was a note of triumph in the failing voice that silenced both his hearers. They exchanged glances over his head but they said nothing. The nurse came in to fetch the tea waggon.

"I'm afraid your visitors'll have to say good-bye now, Mr. Clare. The doctor's just coming up to have a look at you," she said briskly.

Sandra bent over him. "Good night, dear," she whispered. But he clutched at her hand. "No. I want you both to come back when the doctor's finished with me. I have something to ask you. Promise—"

"Very well."

They went out together and met the doctor on the landing. Collier stopped him. "Look here, sir. He wants us to stay. Will it do him any harm?" The doctor looked at him gravely. "Are you a relative?"

"No. A friend."

"Well—you may tire him—but if he likes to have you there—it's only a question of hours in any event." He went in, closing the door after him.

"Were you supposed to get back to the Yard to-night?" asked Sandra.

"Yes. But I'll ring up and tell them I'm detained. It'll be all right. I say"—he leaned over the stair rail looking into the hall below—"the place is like a florist's shop." A nurse was coming up the stairs carrying an immense bunch of red roses.

"Aren't they magnificent?" she said. "Don't talk loudly, please, because there are patients in the other rooms. I thought he might like to have these roses and I'll let him have some of the violets, too, but I can't possibly bring them all up. They keep on coming."

"Good heavens!" said Collier. "Do you mean that these are all for Mr. Clare?"

"That's right. It just shows, doesn't it. The feeling about him is very strong. It's all mixed up with ideas and the loathing most decent people feel for the modern methods of warfare, and all that. I mean, it's like the Peace Ballot, a chance for ordinary people who seldom get a say in things to show what they feel about it."

"You mean he has become a symbol?"

"That's right." She lowered her voice mysteriously. "They were going to try and rescue him if he hadn't been acquitted. So I've heard. I must get water for these roses"—she vanished into the bathroom as the doctor reappeared. "All right," he said. "He's expecting you."

They found him lying as they had left him, his faded blue eyes travelling slowly and contentedly about the room.

"You haven't gone. That's kind. I've met with the most wonderful kindness. In the prison. You can't think. I shall never forget it. I don't deserve it, you know. However good the cause, I sinned, and I should have been punished. The verdict was all wrong." He looked at Collier. "You know that, my boy. Sir James sprung that on me. I had not the least idea when he got up to make his speech that he was going to suggest anything so manifestly absurd. Forget—I know my memory's uncertain over trifles, but I couldn't forget a thing like that." His face was not placid now. "I can live through it all again if I let myself go—walking down the lobby behind him, gripping the handle of the hammer—his body twitched after it had fallen."

Sandra was kneeling by the bedside. She took his hand and held it firmly. "Padre, don't, don't torture yourself. You've punished yourself quite enough. God will forgive you, that poor man will forgive you. Forget the past. Think of the future."

The horror died out of his eyes as he listened to her, He was smiling again. "The future. Dick. He's waiting. Did you see him in the dock? He was there with me all the time. And that reminds me of what I wanted to say. Feel under my pillow, my dear."

She obeyed him. "You wanted to look at these?" She laid a worn little leather case and a leather frame on the counterpane.

"My son's picture and his medals. The V.C. I want you to have them after I'm gone. I'll tell the nurse. You'll take care of them—"

"Yes," she said gently.

"The Inspector brought me the frame. I shouldn't have been allowed to keep the silver frame with the glass. Glass is dangerous. They could trust me with talc. The Inspector's a good fellow. I'm glad you like him, my dear. I'm glad—" He left his sentence unfinished and seemed to be dozing. The clock ticked away the minutes, building the bridge for him between time and eternity.

The two watchers sat silent and motionless. Sandra was thinking of what the old man had said about Toby. Was it true that his, too, was a doomed generation, growing to maturity only to be torn to pieces, stamped to a bloody pulp in the trenches, blasted by screaming shells. Wouldn't God stop it? But God had given men free will.

Collier was going over the whole case in his mind or trying to, but he had been working double tides lately. He was very tired and the warmth of the room and the silence lulled him so that he lost the thread of his thought and joined the dying man who had so strangely become his friend on the borderland of sleep. A white feather, and drawn faces of half grown boys marching, marching, falling, the thin human cries inaudible through the roar of the guns. The grey bird swaying to and fro and sidling towards the bars of his cage. "Go away. I'm busy," and the first slow revolutions of the wheels of the machine that he served, the mighty engine of the law. The grinding wheels. . . . He woke with a start as the nurse came in with a rustling of starched linen skirts, and bent over the bed to take her patient's pulse and listen to the quick and shallow respirations. She beckoned, and Collier and Sandra followed her out of the room.

"One can never be certain," she said, "but I don't think he will regain consciousness. He'll just pass out quite quietly in his sleep. He's worn out. I've seen so many. It wouldn't really matter to him if you went now."

Collier hesitated. He ought to report at the Yard in the morning.

"I'll be getting on then," he said, "though I don't like leaving him."

"I shall stay," said Sandra.

Their eyes met for an instant. Collier glanced at the nurse, hoping that she would go back into the room and leave them alone, but she did not take the hint. He could only grip Sandra's hand rather tightly as he said "Good-bye. You'll let me know how he gets on?"

She looked tired and dispirited, her eyelids red and swollen with crying. At that moment she was positively plain, and he had never been so certain that he loved her. He left her standing there on the landing with the nurse and ran down the stairs.

At that hour there was little traffic on the roads. He reached his lodgings in Denbigh Street in time to get a couple of hours sleep. He was at the Yard by nine o'clock. Superintendent Cardew received him glumly.

"The A.C. was on about you last night, when the news of the verdict came through. He thinks now we shouldn't have brought the case without any corroborative evidence of Clare's guilt. He was blaming you. Hardly fair, of course. The local people and for matter of that, the Public Prosecutor were responsible. But he thinks you were a bit too quick to take Clare's confession at its face value. You've been in the force long enough to know that after most murders the stations are besieged by bat merchants giving themselves up. Next time it happens to you tell whoever it is to hop it."

"Yes, sir."

Cardew leaned back in his chair and regarded the younger man thoughtfully.

"What made you think he really had done it, Collier? You've generally got a flair."

Collier looked past the superintendent at the leafless planes of the embankment and the river beyond, cold and grey under a leaden sky.

"He was guilty," he said flatly.

"Oh. Well, he had the sympathy of the public. I gather there might have been trouble in the town if the verdict had been different."

"Yes. They were prepared for that."

"And he hasn't long to live?"

"Yes. That's true."

The superintendent nodded, dismissing him. "I don't doubt you did your best. Here's the stuff about that coining affair. Take it away and see what you can make of it."

Collier met a constable on his way downstairs.

"There's a trunk call for you from Durchester, Inspector."

"Thanks." He went into his room and picked up his receiver. "Hallo. I am Inspector Collier. Oh, it's you—"

He heard Sandra's voice.

"It's over. He's gone. He spoke again, but he didn't know me. He was trying to tell me all about how his beloved Dick won the V.C. Oh, Hugh, it was heartrending. And then—he looked away from me and his face lit up so wonderfully. He had been hardly audible, but his voice was suddenly quit strong again. He said, 'Ah, there you are, my dear—' He looks so peaceful now. I'm not going to suggest you should come down for the funeral. I don't think he'd want you to—"

"All right. Then I won't. But may I come down after—to see you? I want to ask you something? May I?"

The ensuing pause seemed so long that he could not bear it. He had to break it. "Sandra—they'll cut us off. Be quick—"

"Oh—if—if you're certain—yes."

THE END

KINDRED SPIRITS . . .

Why not join the

DEAN STREET PRESS
FACEBOOK GROUP

for lively bookish chat
and more

Scan the QR code below

Or follow this link
**www.facebook.com/groups/
deanstreetpress**

CPSIA information can be obtained
at www.ICGtesting.com
Printed in the USA
LVHW102131030423
743398LV00017B/162